Born and brought up in Norw
now live in Swindon. She wrote
children were toddlers but the
when she returned to work as a
comprehensive. It was only afte
teacher that she was able to retur
She teaches Creative Writing an _____ ____ writing
workshops as a guest lecturer onboard cruise ships.
Judith's other passion is Tai Chi. She is a qualified instructor
with a particular interest in teaching Tai Chi for health.

For more information, see

www.judithcranswick.co.uk

Also by Judith Cranswick

ALL IN THE MIND
WATCHER IN THE SHADOWS
BLOOD ON THE BULB FIELDS

BLOOD IN THE WINE

To Susan.
Best wishes
Judith Cranswick

Judith Cranswick

Thank you for coming
to my talks and
workshops. Lovely
to meet you on
the Black Watch
Mystery Cruise Nov.'14

Printed and bound by CPI Antony Rowe, Eastbourne

For Alex

Acknowledgements

With grateful thanks to my readers Christine Forskitt,
Joanne Cranswick and Anne Borrowdale, to the many people
who have helped me with the research and to Anu Desai and
Zoi Pearce at Phoenix Holidays.

Prologue

The muddy green Audi was still there. Albrecht had noticed it soon after he'd started work parked less than a hundred yards from the café down the narrow side street leading into the square. If its owner didn't return soon, the traffic warden would beat him to it and he'd find himself with a ticket. Serve him right for driving such a naff vehicle.

Albrecht cleared away the dirty cups and gave the table a disgruntled swipe with the cloth. He wasn't in the best of moods. The café had been busier than usual first thing. Not that he'd benefited much. Many customers had only called in for takeaway coffees and warm crusty rolls on their way to work in the nearby offices and few had bothered to drop anything into the tips box. Perhaps he'd have better luck later with the tourists. The sun was rising rapidly over the high rooftops chasing back the shadows across the square promising a warm day and that always brought them out in force.

Already an older French couple were poring over their Baedeker Guide. Probably planning their day's activities, Albrecht decided. The nearby museum quarter was one of Frankfurt's major attractions. The girls at the far table were talking in German so perhaps they were students rather than tourists. The campus for medical sciences lay just across the river. Two were blondes but it was the pretty auburn-haired one who caught his eye. Now there was a girl he wouldn't mind getting to know better. He slicked back his hair. Perhaps he could wander over and join in their conversation. Better not. Heinrich had already spoken to him about chatting up young female customers and it would be stupid to jeopardize his job over some girl who'd probably give a waiter still in his teens the brush off anyway.

The only other occupant at the outside tables was another foreigner but his dark clothes and morose expression were hardly those of a man on holiday. He showed little interest in the comings and goings in the pretty pedestrianized square with its attractive profusion of flower tubs and colourful shop fronts. Half hidden under the blue and white striped umbrella, his chair was angled more towards the dreary side street lined with characterless grey office blocks and parked cars.

The sound of a car engine attracted Albrecht's attention. He stared enviously at the approaching silver BMW and watched as it pulled up in front of the green Audi. Now there was a car worth having but it would be long time before his meagre finances would allow him to buy his own car, any car, let alone one like that.

Inside the café, Albrecht noticed Heinrich and the other two waiters standing around gossiping with the local regulars finishing their late breakfast. He preferred to stay out in the fresh air. He perched himself on the wide window ledge and looked around.

Two more customers arrived and as Albrecht returned with their order, the solitary man snapped his fingers to attract attention. Albrecht hated it when customers did that.

'More coffee,' he demanded in a harsh, heavily accented voice.

Albrecht took away the dirty cup and went inside. 'About time that old saddo ordered another,' he complained to Heinrich as the café owner put a fresh cup under the espresso machine. 'He's been there for over three quarters of an hour. No paper. Just sits there staring into space.'

'Perhaps he's waiting for someone.'

Albrecht shrugged his shoulders. 'Whatever.'

As he expected, there was no "thank you" when Albrecht laid the cup by the man's elbow. Not even a nod of acknowledgement.

Albrecht returned to his perch on the window ledge and continued his people watching. A short stocky man walked down the side street towards them. Another potential customer? Albrecht stood in readiness but the man took out his car keys, clicked open the door of the Audi and got in.

He heard the engine turn; then everything erupted. A giant ball of orange flame shot into the air; the sudden wave of heat smacked him in the face before the ear-splitting blast flung him back into the window, punching the air out of his lungs. He lay stunned showered by pieces of shattered plate glass.

Hands gripped his upper arms. He opened his eyes and saw Heinrich's worried face close to his, mouthing excitedly.

'What happened?' He ears still rang and he couldn't hear his own voice. Panic-stricken, he struggled to sit up, ignoring the broken glass cutting into his hands.

'Easy, easy.'

A surge of relief swept through him. Heinrich's voice was muffled but at least the deafness had only been temporary. Heinrich helped Albrecht to his feet and righted one of the overturned chairs for him. The initial overpowering smell like a firework display turned to a pungent sickly stench of burning diesel and roasting flesh that made him want to gag.

In the side street, the BMW was now at an odd angle rocked forward by the blast; its once gleaming paintwork now black and scorched. Behind it, nothing could be seen of the Audi but a raging fireball. Would-be rescuers tried to get close but were driven back by the heat. More and more people poured out of the adjacent office blocks and shops.

'Poor devil didn't stand a chance,' Heinrich muttered. He turned back to Albrecht. 'But what about you? You're bleeding.'

Albrecht looked down at the cuts on his hands. 'Just a few scratches. Nothing serious. You go and help the others.'

Hysterical screaming suddenly rent the air. Beyond the toppled tables and chairs, Albrecht saw one of the girls with blood pouring down her face. The other two had also been hit

3

by flying glass but one of the other waiters was seeing to them. The French man had one leg trapped beneath the table and Heinrich went to help lift it off him. The man looked stunned but he didn't seem to be badly hurt.

Albrecht turned to check on the solitary man. He was nowhere to be seen.

The Romantic Rhine

Enjoy one of Super Sun's most popular tours as you sit back in the comfort of our Luxury Class coach to savour the magic of the beautiful Rhine Gorge, famous for its fairytale cliff-top castles, charming medieval villages and picturesque vine-clad scenery. Highlights of the tour include visits to Rudesheim with its cobbled streets lined with traditional half-timbered houses; the old university town of Heidelberg and captivating Koblenz from where we drive along the gentle Moselle to the charming little town of Cochem. No visit to the area, world renowned for its delicious, quality wines, would be complete without a wine tasting in one of the local wine cellars.

Your expert Tour Manager will be on hand throughout your holiday to ensure you have a truly unforgettable experience.

Super Sun Executive Travel
Specialists in luxury Short Breaks and
Continental Tours

Romantic Rhineland *

Tour Ref: RR/G/PC/4

Tour Manager .... Mrs Fiona Mason
Driver .... Mr Winston Taylor
Relief driver (outbound) .....Mr Ted Munro
Relief driver (inbound) ......TBA

Mr	Ernest	Blake	Dapper mid 70s, always wears a hat
Mr	Joseph	Ennis	Rather timid, short and skinny, fair skin
Mrs	Celia	Ennis	Well-built, unassuming like her husband
Miss	Cressida	Flint	Leggy blonde in her 20s! Could be a problem
Mr	Barry	Glover	Early 50s? receding dark hair
Mrs	Elspeth	Glover	Rather serious, easily agitated unlike placid husband
Miss	Holly	Hubbard	20s Cressida's plain friend – spiky hair, wears glasses
Mr	Viktor	Kasar	Short, broad square face, narrow eyes, sallow skin
Mrs	Hilary	Kasar	50s – buxom, platinum blonde, roundish face, - talkative
Mr	Ian	Lambert	Dark hair, grey beard, glasses
Mrs	Rita	Lambert	Mid-late 50s -Thin, pointed chin, long nose. Gossip
Mr	Brendan	Murphy	Thick, grey hair – quiet, a little preoccupied at times
Mrs	Kathleen	Murphy	Very motherly – strong Irish accent like her husband
Mr	Devesh	Najaran	} Good-looking Asian couple. Charming- always polite
Mrs	Anita	Najaran	
Mrs	Gloria	Oldgate	Mid 60s- Plump – fun loving – Flamboyantly dressed
Mr	Sidney	Pettit	Late 70s, tall and thin - Bit vague
Mrs	Daphne	Pettit	Small, efficient. Obviously devoted to husband
Mr	Graham	Spelman	Tall, good-looking, has an eye for the ladies
Mrs	Vivien	Spelman	Smart, expensively dressed
Mr	Len	Webster	} Elderly couple from Eastbourne
Mrs	Edith	Webster	

* with Fiona's added comments

6

Day 1 Sunday

Our feeder coach will bring you from your chosen pickup point to Dover where you will board our luxury Platinum Class coach in time for a lunchtime ferry crossing to Calais.

Our journey takes us through France and into Belgium to the delightful little town of Ypres, which after being largely destroyed in the Great War has been rebuilt to all its pre-1914 glory. The Menin Road Gate bears the names of the fifty five thousand soldiers who have no known grave.

After dinner in a typical Flanders restaurant, we visit the Memorial Gate to see the short ceremony to remember the three hundred thousand allied soldiers killed in the surrounding area before we continue to our overnight hotel.

Super Sun Executive Travel

One

Lights were already beginning to twinkle invitingly in the early evening dusk as Fiona Mason led her travel-weary party across the charming main square of Ypres to the small restaurant. If the fairytale setting and the magnificent mediaeval architecture failed to work its magic then the prospect of food should raise their spirits.

As the last of her passengers shuffled inside, Fiona turned to take a last look at the illuminated Cloth Hall with its massive central tower outlined against the royal blue sky. Apart from the holdup of one of the feeder coaches at the ferry terminal, it hadn't been a particularly stressful journey but it was good to have a moment of calm.

A great bear-like, black man emerged from under one of the hall's enormous arches. She watched him walk towards her.

'Okay, sweetheart?' he asked. 'You ain't worried about that bomb is you?'

'No.' Her soft chuckle brought the smile back to his face. 'Now why would I? It's hardly likely to affect our tour, is it?'

'Too right.'

'Although, it might be best if the more nervous members of the party didn't get to hear about it.'

'Well I ain't telling 'em, sweetheart.'

'If I do have a problem,' she said looking up at him from under her lashes, 'it's that I've never set foot in Germany before so, I'll warn you now, I shall need every bit of help you can give me.'

8

Winston put a protective arm around her and gave an avuncular squeeze. 'You'll do fine, sweetheart.'

Fiona did her best to suppress a giggle. Winston had to be younger than her two boys. Not for the first time, Fiona thanked fate for teaming her up with the unflappable West Indian driver. He'd been a tower of strength on the couple of trips she'd done so far and heaven knows that first one had been a nightmare from start to finish.

'The coach is safely locked up so we'd better go and see how folks is doing.'

Inside the restaurant, there was barely room for the three or four waitresses to squeeze between the tightly packed tables holding aloft the steaming plates. No need to worry that either of her unaccompanied passengers would be left on their own.

'Beef dumplings?'

'Is that what I ordered, Daphne?' A bemused elderly man at the adjacent table asked his wife.

'No, Sidney dear. You said you'd have the pasta.'

To judge from the expressions on several other faces, Sidney Pettit was not the only one with a short memory. How could it be so difficult? They only had a choice of traditional meat dumplings, mussels or a vegetarian dish.

'It never occurred to me to make a note of who asked for what when I took their orders on the coach,' sighed Fiona as she sank down on the chair next to the two drivers. 'I only collected the numbers.'

'If they can't be bothered to remember what they asked for less than two hours ago then tha's their lookout,' Ted said unsympathetically. 'You're their tour guide not their ruddy nursemaid.'

Fiona bristled. Bad enough to have friends and family doubting the wisdom of her taking on a demanding job after thirty years as a homemaker without one of the relief drivers trying to make out she was fretting over some minor hiccup.

Winston chuckled. His enormous hand covered hers giving it a friendly squeeze. 'Our Fiona takes her responsibilities very

9

seriously. Likes to make sure all her passengers are kept happy, don't you, sweetheart? You just sit back for half an hour and enjoy your meal like everyone else.'

Half an hour later, as the waitresses collected the dirty plates, Fiona glanced at her watch. 'Time to remind those who'd like to see the ceremony we need to be leaving soon. It'll be crowded up at the Menin Gate especially as it's the weekend.'

It took several minutes for her to pick her way through the tangle of tables. Winston looked up as she returned.

Fiona sighed. 'Most people are still eating their desserts or claim they're too tired but those still keen to go are happy to make their own way. It's only a couple of minutes down the road and you can see the great archway from outside the restaurant so they can't get lost.'

'You go if you want,' urged Winston. 'It's worth seeing. Quite moving when they play the last post. Ted and I will look after the rest of 'em. They can take their time drinking their coffees then we'll take 'em back to the coach.'

The clock on the Cloth Hall tower struck the hour as Fiona left the restaurant. She could hear the pipes and drums sounding their eerie lament as she hurried the last few yards down the street. Even though the short ceremony was performed every evening, several hundred spectators had crowded around the impressive Memorial Gate and were standing shoulder to shoulder. From her vantage point way at the back, Fiona could just make out the tops of the flags above all the heads although it was impossible to see the presentation of colours let alone spot the bandsmen. Everyone listened in respectful silence to the lone voice calling the roll of the fallen of one of the many regiments involved in the carnage that should have been the war to end all wars.

Once the short ceremony ended and the troops marched off, a great wall of noise erupted from under the arch as conversation began again. Slowly people began to drift away and Fiona eased forward to stare up at the long lists of names carved on every possible surface of the walls of the massive ramparts.

'Impressive isn't it?' She turned to the middle-aged man standing beside her. She recognized the receding hairline and pleasant lived-in face. 'What a dreadful waste of young lives.'

'Exactly.' Fiona smiled and tried to recall the man's name from the passenger list. 'Did you see the ceremony?'

'Heard might be a better description.' He gave a wide grin. 'I could just about see the tops of their heads and the regimental colours but I don't think the girls managed to get much of a view.'

'Me neither, but I was right at the back. Still I'm glad I came.' Fiona looked around. 'So is your wife here too?'

'Elspeth's over there with her sister.' He indicated the two women in their late forties peering up at the writing near the ceiling a short distance away.

Barry and Elspeth Glover that was it! They had come with another couple, the tall attractive man who'd helped carry her case at the port and his rather serious looking wife.

'I didn't realize you were actually related to the Spelmans. I thought the four of you were just friends.'

Though it disappeared quickly, she caught the man's frown and tightened jaw. 'We usually take a short break together this time of year. The original idea was a Rhine cruise but they were all booked up for the dates we wanted so we thought we'd give this a whirl. First time we've tried a coach holiday though.'

'I hope you all enjoy it.'

He looked round to check on the women. 'Perhaps I'd better get back to them before we get separated in the crush. We already seem to have lost Graham.'

Something in the way he said it, coupled with the gleam in his eye, made Fiona wonder if Barry was pleased his brother-in-law had wandered off, but she was probably being fanciful.

On her way back to the coach, Fiona spotted Graham Spelman looking in the window of one the many handmade-chocolate shops further down the street. She was about to catch him and

11

tell him his wife was still with his in-laws at the Menin Gate when he turned away and bent to whisper something to the person beside him. Fiona couldn't see the woman but she heard the low, suggestive laugh. Graham put a protective arm around her and ushered her into the shop.

Obviously, she had made a mistake. Vivien must have left before her after all.

As promised, Winston and Ted had seen to those who'd elected to stay in the restaurant and they were now sitting in the coach contentedly chatting. Daphne Pettit had already inflated her travel pillow and was lying back with her eyes closed.

'Have we got much farther to go?' asked her husband. 'We had to be up at four o'clock this morning to catch the feeder coach.'

Fiona gave the elderly man a reassuring smile. 'Having to change to continental time doesn't help either, does it? But it won't be too much longer now.'

A quick glance established two or three passengers were yet to arrive. Ted was on the pavement outside, finishing his last cigarette, chatting to Winston. Fiona climbed down to join them almost bumping into Graham Spelman.

'Oops! Mustn't get this all over your smart uniform.' His blue eyes twinkled as he held aloft an enormous strawberry ice-cream cone.

He turned to the young girl behind him also holding an ice cream and took her elbow as she climbed the steps. Fiona and the two drivers followed in their wake.

As Fiona knelt up on the front seat, busily counting heads, it was impossible not to hear the whispered exchange between the two youngest members of the party in the seat behind.

'Did he buy you that?' The disapproval was evident not only in Holly Hubbard's words but her whole body language.

'What if he did?'

'For goodness sake, Cressy! He's old enough to be your dad and you can't make eyes at a man with his wife standing there

12

watching.'

Cressida Flint tucked a stray lock of the sleek fair hair behind her ear and grinned at her plain friend. 'They're the safest to play for. And, just for your information, his wife wasn't around at the time.'

There was a sharp intake of breath and Holly's round face was a mixture of shock and disgust.

'Oh don't be so prickly, Holly.' There was a peal of laughter.

'Ha, ha. Very funny.' The girl scowled, wrinkling her freckled nose, and turned to look out of the window. The effect of the disdainful toss of the head was somewhat diminished by the plumper girl's cropped, almost boyish hairstyle. For all its auburn streaks, Holly's mousey coloured hair did nothing to add to her allure anymore than the Harry Potter spectacles. She certainly lacked not only the looks and figure of her friend; she also lacked Cressida's ability to make the most of her assets.

From the moment she had first met the two girls, it had struck Fiona as odd that a couple of twenty year olds should choose to join a group of sedate mostly middle-aged people on a holiday such as this. Surely some Mediterranean beach resort soaking up the sun by day and enjoying the lively nightclub culture by night was more their scene?

Fiona turned round, signalled to Ted he could drive off then settled down in her seat with a twinge of misgiving. She hoped this wasn't going to be one of those situations that blew up into something unpleasant. The Super Sun guidelines for tour managers didn't have a section on how to deal with bored, young women throwing themselves at any man who looked in their direction regardless of irate wives. Now she was overreacting; it was probably no more than a harmless piece of fun.

A peaceful silence settled over her passengers as the coach sped east along the motorway towards the German border. Fiona glanced back and breathed a sigh of relief. The girls were listening to their iPods, and everyone else was watching the DVD or had been lulled by a good meal and the gentle motion of the coach into a doze. Even the two unaccompanied passengers seemed contented enough. Pen in hand, the sprightly Ernest Blake seemed engrossed in his sudoku book and Gloria Oldgate had her head back, eyes closed, snoring softly. She could sit back and relax.

A whole day in the unaccustomed high heels was making her feet ache. No one would notice if she slipped them off. At least tomorrow, she could change back into comfortable flat shoes and everyday clothes and the uniform navy skirt and blazer and bright yellow scarf could be put aside until the journey home. Whoever decided female tour managers must wear tights and a straight skirt on the outward and home-bound journeys should be made to sit on a coach in them for twelve hours at a stretch.

Lulled into a doze herself, Winston had to call her name twice before she jerked to attention.

'Should be there in ten minutes.'

'Great. I'll give the hotel a call and let them know to be ready for us.'

As the coach pulled into the central square of the small town of Muscron, their overnight stop, everyone's interest perked up. Both the church with its elongated spire and the flamboy-ant town hall at the far end, easily the two most impressive buildings, were bathed in illumination.

As soon as all the requisite forms had been completed, several of the more eager photographers were off. One or two of the men even left their wives to carry their hand luggage up to their rooms.

Fiona stood at the reception desk sorting through the essen-tial paperwork when she caught snatches of the raised conver-sation from the two people waiting for the lift.

'How dare you, right under my nose, like that. Apart from making an exhibition of yourself, have you any idea how em-barrassing it is for me?'

'For pity's sake, Vivien! It was only an ice cream. I couldn't ignore the girl.'

14

'I'm warning you,' the venom in the voice was palpable, 'if I see you as much as within ten feet of her again, I'll chop your bloody pecker off myself.'

The sharp hiss of the lift door cut off the rest of the exchange. The unexpected crude threat from such a sedate, well-spoken woman made Fiona turn and stare. She'd met her share of possessive women in the past but Vivien's pent-up outburst was way over the top. Whatever the man had done, did it really justify such a public lambasting?

Day 2 Monday

Leaving our overnight hotel in Belgium, we continue our journey to Germany. After lunch in the beautiful city of Cologne, there will be time to discover some of the highlights of this thriving metropolis at your leisure. Claimed as one the greatest examples of Gothic architecture in the world, the magnificent cathedral whose twin towers dominate the city's skyline is a must. Enjoy the thriving cultural scene and take a stroll around the centre to admire the stylish shops.

We arrive in time for dinner at the 'Rhineland' style 4-star Hotel Pinger on the outskirts of Rudesheim, our base for the next seven nights.

Super Sun Executive Travel

Two

Fiona woke feeling refreshed. The first day of every tour was always tiring and things often ended up a little fraught but, with luck, a good night's sleep would have restored her passenger's good spirits as much as her own.

She stretched out in the comfortable queen-size bed and looked around the spacious room. For a modern city-style hotel, it left nothing to be desired. There was a plasma screen TV on the wall and the en suite even had a spa bath. She'd never used one of those before. Luxury indeed. If all the rooms were as nice as this, there shouldn't be any complaints.

By the time Fiona had reluctantly dragged herself out of the bubbling water and dressed, she went down to breakfast later than she'd planned.

There was quite a crowd waiting by the lift so Fiona opted to take the stairs. Pushing through the door, she discovered this area of the hotel still hadn't been completed. There were gaps in the plaster at the base of the walls still to be concealed beneath skirting. The stone steps indicated a fire escape rather than a customary route for hotel guests.

Fiona was not the only one who'd decided not to wait for the lift. On the flight below, she spotted two of her party. She had no difficulty recognizing the middle-aged, oddly contrasting couple. The man was a short and stocky with flat features and narrow eyes, possibly East European, while his English blousy wife was fair skinned with blonde hair. Fiona wished them good morning. The woman turned to look up then suddenly lost her footing on the last two steps and collapsed with a heavy thump.

She was still in a heap at the foot of the stairs, her husband hovering over her, by the time Fiona reached them. 'Are you alright?'

'M' foot slipped from under me.' She rubbed it tentatively. 'M' own silly fault. Should've looked where I was going.'

Fiona gently examined it. 'Nothing's broken, thank goodness. But it looks a nasty wrench.'

'It'll be okay in a minute.'

'It's Hilary, isn't it?'

'That's right.'

'I Viktor.'

'Viktor doesn't have much English, do you love.'

It took Fiona and Viktor's combined efforts to help the well-built Hilary struggle to her feet. With Fiona on one side and her husband on the other, she hobbled along the corridor. It was fortunate for all three of them the dining room was the first door they came to.

The room was relatively busy but Fiona was far too preoccupied making sure Hilary was comfortably ensconced to check if all was well with the rest of her passengers. She was on her way to the buffet table to fetch Hilary some breakfast, when Sidney Pettit barred her way.

'Have you seen the CNN news this morning?' He was clearly agitated about something.

'Actually no. Is it important, Sidney? I'm a little busy at the moment.'

'There's been a bomb in Germany. Frankfurt!' His reedy voice was almost a wail.

Fiona gave him a reassuring smile. 'It really is nothing for us to worry about. I can assure you it won't affect our holiday at all.' She patted him on the arm and danced quickly round him before he could delay her any further.

On her way back, she caught Sidney's indignant stare and though she could not catch the words he muttered to his wife, Fiona was in no doubt she had some serious fence mending to do with that particular gentleman. Perhaps she should have taken more time to set his mind at rest, but couldn't he see how busy she was?

'Please don't worry about me,' Hilary protested as Fiona put the glass of orange juice and an individual packet of cereal in front of her. 'If I do want anything else Viktor can get it for me. You must have enough to do.'

With her lengthy bath and ministering to Hilary, Fiona barely had time to snatch something to eat for herself before dashing back upstairs to collect her last few bits of hand luggage.

Ted had already driven the coach round to the front of the hotel by the time she arrived back down to the main lobby.

'No reports of any hold-ups on the motorways,' Winston informed her with his customary beaming smile. 'So, if everyone is ready to leave on time, we should have a good run.'

James Fitzwilliam took a deep breath and straightened his tie before knocking.

'Good morning, sir.'

Everyone said Montgomery-Jones was a good man to work for, but James found himself intimidated by the Commander's Old Etonian accent and the present grim expression on the man's face did not make James feel any easier. He was not aware he had made any blunders but five weeks after transferring to the department, he was still finding his feet.

'Stop hovering and come and sit down.' The Commander frowned momentarily but there was no impatience in his voice.

James walked across to the window glancing down at the steady stream of traffic crawling over Vauxhall Bridge. He slid onto the chair in front of the large oak desk and looked into the penetrating grey eyes, waiting for the Commander to speak.

'You have been following this business in Frankfurt. What is the latest news?'

'Forensics established the car was booby trapped though, as yet, the Germans haven't determined if or why the driver was

19

targeted. He was a foreign tourist which is why the BND are involved. They're still trying to identify him. The body was unrecognizable so the only lead is the hire car he was driving and it seems the company paperwork is sketchy. However, they believe he was a Pakistani businessman in Frankfurt for the Aerospace Trade Fair. He arrived on yesterday's flight from Islamabad.' James waited but the Commander's expression remained impassive. Had he missed something? 'Are we involved, sir?'

'I have just had Patterson on the telephone.'

'The CIA?' James's eyes widened in surprise. 'Was he one of theirs?'

'Apparently not.'

'So why the interest? This doesn't smack of terrorist activity. Surely, this is much too small scale? Besides, if it was some sort of protest statement no group has claimed responsibility.'

Montgomery-Jones leaned across the desk, his expression serious, 'According to American sources, the man was staying in an hotel in Wiesbaden which gives them cause for concern.'

'I appreciate, with a couple of their US divisions and the Wiesbaden Army Airfield on the doorstep, the Americans are none too happy, but isn't this hoo-ha a bit OTT?'

'I doubt Patterson would accept that argument for one moment especially as the man's hotel room was found ransacked.' Whether the Commander's sudden pained expression was due to the American's reaction or his own colloquial choice of language, James could not be certain.

'I still don't see why they have contacted us, sir?'

'It would appear his valuables had been left in the hotel safe. Tucked into his papers they found a marketing flier for a British High Tec company based in Maidenhead.' The Commander picked up his pen and pulled a notepad towards him. When he'd finished writing, he tore off the top sheet and handed it over. 'Patterson asked us to investigate.'

James glanced down at the meticulous copperplate. 'Precisiontec. It's not a name I recognize. Do you want me to go and speak to them, sir?'

'Find out all you can about the company to begin with and report back.' James was already halfway to the door. 'And Fitzwilliam, I promised Pattison we would make this a priority.'

'Certainly, sir.'

As Winston had promised, the journey to Cologne proved event free and only when they hit the outskirts of the city did their progress slow to a stop-start crawl. There were sighs of relief all round when Ted eventually drew the coach to a halt below the towering cathedral opposite the main train station. The extra leg room and superior seats of Super Sun's luxury coaches might make travel more comfortable but even the personal headphones with a choice of music and the DVDs didn't make up for the sheer tedium of almost two days of travelling.

Fiona picked up the microphone, put on her best smile, and announced with an enthusiasm she did not feel, 'Ted is going to drop us all off here so we won't have too far to walk to our restaurant. I do urge you all to keep together because, as you can see, the pavement is quite narrow and everywhere is packed with people. Because you could easily lose sight of me, I'd like you to follow Winston and I'll bring up the rear. Once he's parked the coach, Ted will be joining us for lunch, but then we're going to have to say goodbye to him. He'll be joining up with one of the other Super Sun tours on its way back to England.'

Although it was true the great bear-like, black man was much easier to spot than Fiona who barely reached his shoulder, it wasn't the main reason she'd asked the experienced Winston to lead the way. This was Fiona's first Romantic Rhine trip and although she was getting used to leading tours blind, finding the right restaurant in the maze of little streets in this bustling city centre was too great a risk.

It was no mean feat to keep the party together. On more than one occasion, Fiona felt hemmed in by the melee of people towering above her. It was all she could do to elbow her way through, skipping round individuals, squeezing through

21

gaps until she could spot Winston's white triangular flag emblazoned with a bright yellow smiling sun in the distance.

When they reached the restaurant, Fiona almost bumped into the back of Graham Spelman who'd stopped abruptly to pull out his mobile.

'Who are you phoning now?' Vivien snapped.

'Sorry, love. This is business.'

'You're on holiday for goodness sake!'

Vivien ignored her husband's pleading look, gave an exasperated snort, and went inside to join her sister.

The first thing Fiona did when she stepped into the restaurant was to count heads. Apart from Graham, everyone was here. She could relax.

Few people lingered over lunch eager to have as much time as possible to explore the city centre, Fiona and the two drivers were the last to leave. Ted's pickup was not for another couple of hours and, his driving stint done for the day, he had plans for a glass or two of Kölsch in one of the local beer kellers. Winston opted to keep him company, which left Fiona free to explore on her own.

Despite all the hype about the Dom, Germany's largest and most impressive cathedral, Fiona found it dark and oppressive as she approached. Inside, many of the cathedral's star sights lay behind grills. Feeling a trifle cheated, she walked out onto the windy open square wondering how to spend the next hour and a half. Amongst the many tourists wandering around admiring the soaring, filigreed twin spires, she spotted some familiar faces. The Spelmans and the Glovers stood watching a pavement artist working on an enormous portrait. At least Graham had not sneaked off today, dutifully tagging along after the rest of his relations even if his attention appeared to be elsewhere. He stared across the square, a slight frown on face.

To judge by the style, blue background and border, the same artist was probably responsible for the other chalk pictures of well-known composers and Fiona strolled over to look more closely at the portrait of Mozart.

'They're very good, aren't they? I wonder how often they have to renew them.' Fiona wasn't sure if Vivien was talking to her or to her sister and brother-in-law. She smiled and made some noncommittal remark.

As Fiona searched for a few coins to put into the artist's collecting box, a tinny jingle started up. Graham pulled his mobile from the breast pocket of his shirt.

'Sorry, everyone. Must answer this.' Vivien stared at him with pursed lips. 'And then I'll switch it off. I promise,' he pleaded.

He moved off so as not to be overheard. Vivien and Elspeth exchanged looks. When he'd finished his call, his eyes slowly began to scan the crowds. Fiona couldn't help wondering if he'd been speaking with Cressida. Vivien must have thought so to the way she marched over, snatched his mobile and put it in her handbag. Pretending she had not witnessed the incident, Fiona wished them a pleasant afternoon and made her way across the square, down the steps heading south to the Alter Markt and the old quarter of the city.

There were no benches in the area where everyone had congregated to wait for the coach. Clusters of people were perched on or against the wall above the steps down to the narrow pavement. As it was little more than a day since she had met everyone and almost all of that time had been spent travelling, Fiona had not had a chance to talk to all of her twenty-two passengers. She wasn't sure she could pick them all out from the general mass of people standing around taking their ease. As far as she could tell, no one was missing.

'Here it is,' she called as the white coach with its distinctive yellow stripe came round the corner.

She did her best to count them onboard as she stood by the steep steps offering a helping hand to the older members of the party, which Sidney pointedly ignored, and did a double check as she made her way down the aisle to the front.

The last stage of their journey south along the Rhine valley

23

was particularly scenic and Fiona decided there was no need for any additional entertainment. The DVD she had taken out in readiness could wait until later.

They'd been travelling for just under an hour when Viktor tapped Fiona on the shoulder. 'Hilary need bandage for foot.'

Instantly, Fiona felt a pang of guilt. Despite the woman's reassurances she'd noticed Hilary struggling as she'd helped her onto the coach. She'd intended to go back and see her once she'd checked everyone else but, in all the hubbub, it had slipped her mind.

She reached up to the parcel shelf for the first aid kit.

'Here let me,' said a voice in her ear.

Graham, sat in the seat opposite, jumped to his feet.

'Thank you. It is a bit of a stretch for me.'

'Don't worry about putting it back up. I'll see to it while you attend to your patient.' Graham took the box from her, his smile revealing the too perfect teeth that could only be the result of some very expensive orthodontic work.

'Thank you. That's very kind.'

Hilary looked up as Fiona made her way towards her. 'Sorry to be such a nuisance.'

'You're not at all,' Fiona tried to reassure the woman. 'I'm afraid there were no crepe bandages in the box. This is all there was, but it's better than nothing.'

Dark bruises were already developing not just round Hilary's ankle but all down the sides of her foot. She had obviously given it a nasty wrench.

'That'll teach me to go walking around after lunch but it seemed a shame to waste the opportunity. If I'd had any sense, I'd have got it strapped up before we left the hotel.'

Even through the layer of makeup, the woman's skin looked pale. The pain showed in her eyes. Would she be able to cope with the rest of the tour?

What with Hilary's ankle and the mounting friction between the Spelmans threatening to turn into an ugly scene, trying to create a pleasant holiday atmosphere was proving a decided challenge Fiona thought as she made her way back to the front. Not helped by Sidney's peevishness or the current raucous laughter from the girls who had obviously spent much of their free time in Cologne sampling the beer kellers.

Three

Precisiontec was located on a small industrial park to the east of the town just off the M4. Traffic on the motorway had been heavy but there'd been no hold-ups and James Fitzwilliam drove into the car park well ahead of schedule.

The main reception was housed in a modest-looking, brick-fronted building and as he made his way across James glanced at characterless box-like units on the far side of the car park. These were obviously a recent addition but there didn't appear to be a great deal of activity going on inside. The rumours that Precisiontec, flushed with its success, had over-stretched itself and projected new orders had not kept pace with the escalating expansion costs appeared to be borne out. Some serious investment would be necessary in the near future if the company was to achieve its goal to become a significant player in the market.

Philip Cawston was not one of those senior executives who liked to emphasize their importance by keeping people waiting. After a brief call to announce his arrival, James was shown up to the man's office straight away. The casually dressed man, shirt sleeves rolled to his elbows, with overlong hair and untamed beard, who looked up as James entered, was not the conventional managing director he'd expected. Nor was Philip Cawston sitting behind a large impressive desk in some smart executive office but leaning over one of the many design tables studying plans.

Introductions were made, coffee sent for, and James asked without preamble, 'What you said on the phone this morning was all very interesting, but it would help in a case we're investigating if you would tell me a bit more about thermal imaging technology and its potential.'

'Thermography, long wave infra-red imaging, is now the leading non-invasive and non-destructive tool used in an ever-widening range of areas.'

As anticipated, given the opportunity to extol the benefits of his work, Cawston was in his element although James found much of the man's explanation so technical it was pure gobbledygook and several times he had to ask for clarification.

'Isn't that what they use in weapon guidance?' James asked with apparent innocence when the man came to the end of his spiel.

'The same technology has military uses admittedly, but you need a special licence for that. Here at Precisiontec we deal solely with commercial applications. We design, develop and manufacture a whole range of radiometric thermal imaging equipment.'

James detected no evasion or defensiveness in the man's answer. 'I see. But, in layman's terms, what exactly is it you produce?'

'Currently, we have some big orders for non-intrusive people monitoring equipment – tracking the number of customers coming into shops, banks and similar service areas, even large leisure centres, cinemas and nightclubs. Areas where there can be security issues as well as queue length monitoring. We also produce systems to monitor the movement of all types of transport – town centre traffic, car parks and intelligent traffic lights. Plus there's a growing market in health monitoring in hospitals and medical centres.'

'You obviously cater for a wide range of clients. Do you do any business with overseas companies?'

James feigned interest as the man talked with evident pride about the company's growing activity in Europe. 'How about further afield?'

'Not as yet.' Was there a slight narrowing of the eyes? 'We're still quite a young company, although rapidly ex-

27

panding.'

Indeed it was. Too rapidly. Best not to let on what his morning's investigations had revealed about the true state of the business. James smiled and said, 'So I understand.'

'We started up eight years ago. I handle the design side and my partner deals with marketing and product placement.'

'Have you known each other long?'

'We were both engineering students together at Manchester and then some fifteen years later we ended up working for the same outfit. When Mitrex Engineering was taken over and there was a major restructuring, we both took voluntary redundancy and used the capital to help set up the partnership. We'd been talking about the growing market for highly specialized thermal imaging equipment for some time. And, though I say it myself, we've done pretty well. Earned a good reputation in our field,' he concluded with a smug grin.

'So what next?' Having lulled him into a good mood, James decided it was time to get down to business. 'Wasn't there some talk of a contract with an Asian Country?'

The atmosphere suddenly became frosty.

'There was some contact between the Marketing Manager and an Asian representative, but it was no more than an initial discussion. No designs were ever made.'

'Could you give me some idea of what was proposed?'

'I can't help you. I don't know any details. As I've just said, I was never involved. You have to understand a significant percentage of proposals come to nothing, often because the final product would prove too costly to be economically viable for the customer.' There was a distinct truculent edge to Cawston's tone.

'I see. Would it be possible for me to speak to your Marketing Manager?'

'He's on holiday at the moment so I'm afraid you will have to wait until he returns.'

'Do you have a contact number for him?' James smiled but to no avail.

'We don't hand out that kind of information.'

James gave him his best Montgomery-Jones stare. It took all of thirty seconds for Cawston to capitulate.

The main road hugged the riverside all the way up the gorge to the small village of Assmannshausen, to the west of Rudesheim. The coach left the river road, clattered over the railway crossing and turned into the narrow street between towering shops and hotels huddled on either side.

It was early evening and though the sky was still quite bright – a clear cloudless turquoise – and the stars had not yet begun to appear, the streetlights were lit casting a rich orange glow over each of the quaint half-timbered houses. Lights twinkled in the windows and the faces of Fiona's jaded travellers became wreathed in smiles as heads turned eagerly to take in every detail of the magical scene.

How Winston managed to negotiate the sharp right angle bend without clipping the overhanging gables of the houses on either side was a mystery to Fiona, but no doubt it was a skill he'd had to master pretty quickly in this part of Germany with all its hairpin bends and steep gradients.

They turned the corner and the sight of Hotel Pinger sent a warm glow through Fiona and not just because they'd reached their destination at long last. It could have been the set for some Hollywood movie and would not have disgraced a Disney Theme Park. The already narrow road forked into what looked like two pedestrian passages on either side of the truncated triangular-shaped building although the road signs indicated otherwise.

As the coach waited for several cars to come down the steep left hand fork, Fiona had time to admire the hotel in all its glory. The small triangle of land in front formed an outdoor sitting area with a slatted roof held up by huge wooden arches strung with lights. The end wall covered several floors with an ever-decreasing number of windows in its triangular top. Like all the buildings in the village, the cream plaster between the attractive patterns of dark timbers was gaily painted with abstract flowers in subtle shades. To complete the fairytale pic-

29

ture, on either side rose small octagonal towers with attractive tiled domed pinnacles.

Whilst everyone collected their bits and pieces, Fiona hurried into the small side door to check the arrangements.

On her return, she announced, 'If you give your names to the young lady behind the desk she will give you your keys and you can go straight up to your rooms.'

Urging everyone inside, Fiona gave her attention to Hilary leaving Winston to help the other passengers down from the coach. Despite Hilary's insistence her ankle had stopped throbbing, she still needed Fiona's help up short flight of steps inside the hotel and along to the lift whilst Viktor collected the key from reception.

When she returned to the coach for her own hand luggage, Winston was unloading the cases helped by a couple of the hotel porters.

'This won't take long. You get up to your room,' he urged.

Tired after the long journey and her mind still focused on Hilary, Fiona failed to listen to the instructions about the location of her room as she collected the key. How hard could it be to find room 28 on the third floor?

Fiona had failed to appreciate that the building was far from a uniform rectangle with a central corridor and regular sized rooms on either side. The whole village clung to the steep valley side so that the hotel was built on several levels from front to back. Because the ground plan was roughly triangular, no corridor ran straight for more than three rooms before changing direction and at every turn, there were two or three more steps to negotiate. This meant any consecutive numbering of rooms was impossible.

Making her way along a stretch of corridor that formed an enclosed bridge over the road, Fiona arrived in the annex. Checking with the number on the flower painted, wooden key fob, Fiona eventually found her room. The building may have been old but there was nothing ancient about the furnishings. Beautiful lightwood fitted furniture covered the far wall and, even in the rapidly fading light, two large picture windows gave the room a bright, airy feel. There was a small table in one corner with a vase of fresh freesias whose subtle change of colour from yellow hearts to orange tips brought a smile to Fiona's lips. She took a moment to breathe in their distinctive perfume strong enough to overlay the smell of polish.

A collection of colourful leaflets stacked in a large, ornate letter rack caught her eye and dropping her hand luggage on the queen-sized bed she went to investigate. Excellent! There was information on Rudesheim and Boppard and, although they were all in German, the pictures and the town plans would prove useful. As indeed would the ones on the cable car and the musical instrument museum they would be visiting in nearby Rudesheim.

Graham sat on the end of the bed, his head in his hands. What a real bitch of a day! It had started badly with him still in the doghouse over that stupid girl and then gone from bad to an absolute bloody nightmare. All in all, it was a relief Vivien had gone next door to Elspeth ostensibly to compare rooms until they could get on with the unpacking. If she thought she was punishing him, she was deluding herself. Nothing suited him better at this moment than the cold shoulder treatment. He had far more important things to worry about than Vivien's hurt feelings. He needed to think. That phone call had rocked him to the core.

He'd waited all morning for a call from the buyer to arrange a time for their meeting so when his mobile rang outside the cathedral the call was virtually over before he realized it was from someone else entirely.

So who the hell was it from and what did it mean? He wasn't even sure he remembered the words exactly; something about forgetting the deal and he was being watched. It wasn't the words so much as the menace in the harsh, guttural whisper that had sent a cold shiver down his spine. Who else knew about his plans? He'd thought it was just between him and the buyer. A secret deal. He'd been so stunned it had taken some time before he'd thought of checking the call register. The number had an international 998 start code which meant nothing to him. What the hell had he got mixed up in?

Now he didn't know what to do. Should he go to Frankfurt or not? Did he have any choice?

There were noises in the corridor, a knock on the door. The cases had arrived.

Four

The Commander had been at a meeting all afternoon, ever since James had returned from Maidenhead. The only option was to leave a brief report on the boss's desk. It was almost six o'clock by the time James was summoned. So much for his promise to take Laura to the early showing of the latest George Clooney movie followed by a meal out somewhere.

'Cawston claims to know nothing about the deal, sir. I got the impression he wasn't happy about his partner involving the company at all and he was very reluctant for me to contact the man. However, this Marketing Manager is out of the country so I haven't been able to speak to him. I kept ringing his mobile all afternoon but he must have it switched off. I've looked into his background. Big house in the fashionable suburbs, top-of-the-range car, expensive holidays two or three times a year, the works. His wife did come into some money when her father died but most of it's gone and, according to his bank statements, though he still has his head above water he can't keep up his current life-style for much longer. Which gives him a motive for attempting a risky deal.'

'Exactly. What about Cawston?'

'He's living well within his means. Work appears to be his passion. He's well liked at Precisiontec, considered an excellent guiding hand at the top and a good man to work for. Having met him, my instinct is he's above board. If there is any funny business going on in the company, I doubt he's involved.'

The Commander gave a slow smile. 'His partner does look a

33

more likely suspect, but it would be prudent not to cross Cawston off the list too soon. What else have you managed to ascertain about this foreign trip? Do we have any idea of where the man is?'

'On a touring holiday in Germany according to his secretary.' James could not hide the gleeful smirk.

The Commander's right eyebrow lifted slightly, 'Really. That is interesting.'

'She wasn't sure exactly where but she thought he'd gone with a coach company.'

'After what you have just said, that does not sound at all like the man's style.'

'Exactly what I said to her, but apparently it's just a short break although, to be fair, the tour is supposed to be a cut above the norm. Top class hotels and luxury coach. And it's not their main holiday. He and his wife are off on a cruise down the Amazon in the autumn.'

'Very nice too. In which case, we need to establish which coach company he is using.'

'I have already contacted all the likely ones, sir. Super Sun has a tour based near Rudesheim, 50 kilometres west of Frankfurt, with Wiesbaden between the two. Spelman and his wife are definitely booked on it.'

'Good.'

'Would you like me to ring the hotel and ask to speak to him?'

The Commander sat back in his chair looking pensive. 'No,' he said eventually. 'Not just yet. We need to find out exactly what game the man is playing.'

'You mean, place him under observation?'

'Take a look, certainly.' He put his elbows on his desk and steepled his fingers. 'In the mean time, I would like you to obtain a copy of the tour itinerary. With timings, if possible.'

'I have already, sir.' James took two sheets from his folder and handed them over with a self-satisfied smile. 'Plus a copy of the passenger list.'

If James hoped for some form of recognition of his resourcefulness, he was unlucky. The Commander took the printouts without comment. Swallowing his disappointment, it struck James that if he was going to make this temporary promotion stick; he was going to have to pull out all the stops.

The Commander's eyes scanned the list of names and his smile broadened. 'I might have known.'

'Sir?'

'A couple of the names are familiar, that is all.'

'Known terrorists?'

The Commander gave a low chuckle. 'Certainly not. Quite the opposite in fact. Things might well work in our favour, although I have to admit the good lady has proved to be something of a thorn in my side in the past.'

'Sir?'

The Commander sat back in his chair looking thoughtful.

'Patterson is under the impression we are not taking the situation in Germany sufficiently seriously. To reassure him that is not the case, I agreed to send a liaison officer to ensure I am kept fully up to date with developments as they happen. It is too late tonight, but book yourself a flight and get out there first thing tomorrow. As you are going to be in the area, you can also assess the situation vis-à-vis our Mr Spelman.' He must have seen the startled look in James's eyes. 'Do you have a problem with that?'

'You want me to work in the field on my own, sir?'

'I thought that is why you joined the service or would you prefer to remain my glorified secretary?'

'No, sir. I mean, umm.'

'Then see to it.'

'Certainly, sir.' At the door, James turned. 'And thank you, sir.'

'And Fitzwilliam, do try to look like a tourist. In fact, it might be a good idea to take Miss Philips with you.'

James stared back at the Commander feeling like a startled rabbit caught in the headlights. 'Err, yes, sir. Thank you, sir,' he eventually managed to mumble.

He closed the door behind him and took a few deep breaths.

How in heaven's name had the Commander found out about Laura? No one was supposed to know. Office relationships could lead to complications. Perhaps it was just a coincidence the Commander had suggested her, but there were plenty of other researchers to choose from. It was a surprise to learn he even knew her name. But then, as he was fast learning, very little escaped the Commander.

Now they had arrived at their destination, Fiona arranged to hold the customary briefing meeting in the bar before dinner, but first she needed to check with Marthe, the receptionist-cum-waitress, about the meal times and all the other hotel arrangements she would need to pass on to her party.

For such a small establishment – Hotel Pinger boasted a mere 34 rooms – the bar was surprisingly large. Apart from the dining room, it was the only public area. Marthe had set out the welcome drinks on one of the tables arranged around the outside of the central dance floor.

Not surprisingly, one of the first arrivals was the ever-punctual Ernest Blake now sporting a smart, navy blazer and a paisley cravat. The next to put in an appearance was a sulky-looking Holly Hubbard.

'There's wine or orange juice,' Fiona said pointing to the tray. Dare she ask? 'Cressida not with you?'

'I won the toss for first in the bathroom and she's still putting on her slap.'

'We don't normally get people your age on our tours. What made you decide to come on this one?'

'It wasn't really our choice.' The short, dumpy girl gave a doleful sigh. 'Mum and dad booked it for themselves but dad fell over and broke his leg last month. They'd already paid and rather than all the hassle with the insurance company to get the money back, mum suggested I ask a friend and come instead. Cressy wasn't going to turn down the chance of a free holiday, especially when I told her about the wine tasting, so we contacted Super Sun and changed the names. But perhaps this wasn't such a good idea. Neither of us realized everyone

36

else would be so old.'

Sensing this might be yet another cause of friction between the two friends, Fiona tried to reassure the unhappy girl. 'Not to worry, I'm sure the two of you will enjoy it. There's lots to see and some wonderful scenery. And there'll be music and dancing in here after dinner so the place will liven up a bit then.'

'Hmm.' Holly looked unconvinced.

Fiona mentally crossed her fingers and hoped her reassurances were justified. Trying to keep two disillusioned, morose young people entertained for a week could be something of a challenge.

More people were arriving demanding Fiona's attention. It was good to see Hilary's ankle had not stopped her from coming down which was probably all to the good because Viktor's command of English seemed so poor Fiona doubted he would be able to relay all the information to his wife if he had come alone.

Fiona noticed Celia Ennis and her husband join Sidney and Daphne Pettit at the table nearest the door. The little group appeared to be talking quite animatedly. Something was clearly not as it should be. But then, as she was fast learning, it took very little to agitate Sidney Pettit.

'Is everything alright?'

Sidney looked up at Fiona as she hovered above them. 'We're trying to work out how far we are from Frankfurt.'

'It's a good twenty miles or so. You'll need a taxi if want to visit. Tomorrow's a free morning; I could order one for you if you like.'

Sidney's face went purple and his eyes widened in horror. She shouldn't have done it even though the man's obsession was driving her to distraction.

'I told you this morning,' he stuttered. 'There's been some kind of major terrorist incident there.'

'Hardly that! It's true a man was blown up in his car but, dreadful though that is, no one else was hurt.' Her voice exuded a calmness and patience that belied her instinct to tell

37

him she had better things to do than listen to him whinging every five minutes. 'The media love to speculate and often blow things out of all proportion.'

'He might have been a suicide bomber and something went wrong before he reached his target. There could be others out there planning a major offensive just like London.' Sidney was not yet ready to give up on his idea.

'I'm sure it's nothing we need worry about. Frankfurt definitely isn't on our itinerary.' Her smile encompassed all of the small group. 'Now what about that drink? Would you like me to fetch you all a glass?'

'But it's right on our doorstep.' Sidney's voice rose to a wail.

Daphne patted her husband's hand. 'If there was any danger, I'm sure Super Sun would whisk us away immediately.'

'Exactly.' Fiona gave them all her most reassuring smile. 'There really is no cause for alarm and if I hear any more, I'll let you know, I promise.'

The tables were filling up fast and she had to give all her concentration to the briefing meeting. The last person to put in an appearance some five minutes later was Cressida. Her entrance caused a stir and all eyes turned to look at the tall, sylph-like figure. Now dressed in the shortest of skirts – showing off the long legs to maximum advantage – teamed with a top that fitted like a second skin indicating the absence of a bra and cropped high enough to revel several inches of bare midriff plus a diamond navel stud, she strutted on four-inch high sling-backs across the central dance floor to collect her drink.'

'Someone's forgotten to put her skirt on,' said Gloria Oldgate with a wicked gleam in her eye.

It wasn't only the front view that attracted every pair of male eyes. When Cressida turned away, in the small of her back visible in the gap between her top and the hipster skirt, was a striking tattoo of a large colourful butterfly.

'Goodness me,' muttered Ian Lambert, pushing up his glasses to ensure a better view.

'Well, she may have wings but I'd like to bet she's sure no

angel. Still, whatever gets your clock ticking,' Gloria added giving Ian a mischievous grin much to his embarrassment and his wife's pinched look of disapproval.

Time to stop this before things got out of hand. 'If everybody's here now, shall we make a start?'

Five

Nearly everyone wandered along to the dining room straight after the meeting. Fiona waited for those at the corner bar ordering drinks to go with their meal. Only Graham Spelman remained. He sat at the bar showing little signs of wanting to go and eat.

'Aren't you coming?' Fiona asked.

'Just getting a decent drink. Can I get you one? Try this.' He raised his glass. 'The famous Assmannshausen burgundy, pinot noir. Very palatable.'

'Not for me, thanks.' Apart from the odd half-glass of white to be sociable when the boys were home, Fiona rarely indulged. She'd never been much of a drinker and when Bill's medication prohibited alcohol of any kind, it had been no hardship to give it up altogether.

'You can't come to one of the world's leading wine producing areas and not sample the stuff. Let me tempt you to a Riesling. Famous for its fruity and aromatic qualities,' he joked. 'Or do you fancy a glass of bubbly? How about a Sekt? That's another local speciality.'

Despite the hour, she wondered if he was drunk. 'Our diner will be getting cold.'

'Let me pick something for you,' he said, ignoring her comment. 'I've been reading up on my Rieslings. I'm hoping to do a bit of business with one or two local growers while I'm over here so I wanted to try some of the wines as soon as possible. How about an elegant, zesty off-dry Kabinett or a Spätlese. Or there's the exquisite Eiswein made from grapes picked while they're still frozen.'

'So you're in the wine industry, are you?'

'No, not at all. Engineering's my line. There's a possibility my company might be able to come up with something to speed up the process for the growers hereabouts. The classic German wines are top quality but in recent years, they've suffered considerable competition, especially from the New World producers. They tend to use much cheaper methods such as adding sugar and putting in oak chips to ferment the wine rather than aging it naturally in traditional oak barrels as happens here.'

'If the German producers are so strong on their traditional methods, will they be interested in new technology?'

'It won't change the actual wine production. What I'm talking about is sophisticated equipment to provide a quick, easy and much more accurate measurement of all the relevant environmental factors such as temperature and humidity plus things like water analysis and sugar content. It would speed up the testing process considerably and be far less labour intensive. The technology can be used in variety of applications which I'm sure you don't want me to bore you both with.'

'No, it sounds fascinating,' she said trying to sound sincere. At this rate, the meal would be over before she managed to get him to the dining room.

'Tell you what,' he said enthusiastically. 'If you're really interested, I've one of our glossy brochures up in my room. I'll get it for you.'

'Thank you. That is kind but perhaps later. We're missing dinner.'

'I'll pop up now in case I forget. Won't be a jiffy. See you there.'

The tables allocated to the Super Sun party were separated by tall, carved wooden screens at the far end of the room on the raised section reached by three steps.

At the end of their meal – vegetable soup, a choice of chicken casserole or a pork dish followed by chocolate gateau topped with thick cream – people began to drift to the bar. A slight commotion at the far table attracted Fiona's attention.

'Is there a problem?' she asked as she went over.

A flustered Sidney Pettit was searching for something.

'I seem to have lost my spectacles.'

'Are you sure you brought them down with you, dear?' Daphne asked him patiently.

Sidney held up the empty case as proof. 'I took them out to read the menu. Perhaps they dropped onto the floor.'

Looking for the missing reading glasses involved a considerable amount of squirming on the banquettes to peer under the table. It was Ernest Blake, sitting next to him, who eventually found them hidden under Sidney's napkin beside his coffee cup.

Fiona accompanied the Pettits through to the bar where they found several of the other hotel guests were already sitting in small groups facing a low stage. Gloria Oldgate sat with the other elderly couple, Len and Edith Webster, and invited Fiona and her companions to join them at their table.

'It looks as though we're about to have some entertainment,' said Len Webster. 'That will be jolly.'

'As long as it's not this noisy, tuneless stuff young people listen to nowadays.' A long-faced Sidney didn't seem to share his enthusiasm.

They watched a man in black trousers and flamboyant scarlet shirt busily arranging speakers and other sound paraphernalia. After a few minutes, an attractive-looking blonde woman similarly dressed in red blouse and long black skirt joined him.

The reason for such a large bar lounge soon became apparent. Once the music got underway, outsiders came in through the now-open street doors on either side of the stage to join the resident guests. The hotel obviously had a reputation for its evening entertainment.

The musician proved to be both able and versatile, abandoning his keyboard every now and then for an electric guitar and even the odd solo piece on a saxophone. Occasionally, he also joined in the singing. The woman had a good, strong voice and their repertoire of popular easy listening cocktail music went down well with their audience. It was going to be a good evening.

The two girls stood at the bar and Fiona felt a momentary qualm when she saw Cressida climb onto one of the high stools, one toe left provocatively on the floor to expose the maximum amount of thigh, placing herself deliberately in Graham's line of sight. A fact not lost on Vivien.

During the short break in the performance, Graham Spelman rose to his feet. It was only because of a lull in the music Fiona, at the next table, heard him say, 'Just going for a breath of fresh air.'

To judge by the expressions on the faces of his wife and in-laws as they watched him cross the dance floor to one of the outside doors, his sudden departure did not go down too well.

Fiona eyes immediately sought out Cressida who was still at the bar. Should she go over and try to keep the girl talking? If she disappeared too, the consequences might prove explosive.

'Dreadful business isn't it?' commented Daphne sitting next to her.

'Pardon?' Fiona's heart gave a little flip as she turned back sharply to her table companions. Had they all noticed what was going on?

Fiona realized the question had not been addressed to her but to Edith Webster. Evidently, the group were already deep in the middle of some discussion the beginning of which Fiona had missed.

'We asked that nice driver how far away it is. He said not to worry, but you can't help it can you? These terrorists get eve-rywhere.' Surely, Sidney wasn't still on about the car bomb in Frankfurt!

'No point in looking for trouble now is there?' Thank good-ness, Gloria wasn't one to be drawn into the gloom-and-doom brigade. 'Let's drink and be merry. That's my motto.'

'Humph!' Sidney looked affronted.

'Last I heard the police were still keeping an open verdict.

Most likely it'll turn out to be a discarded smouldering cigarette end or something. The faintest whiff of anything to do with Moslems and the media start whispering Al-Qaeda. Spices up the news. Gives 'em a sense a sense of power. It's up to us to ignore it all. We mustn't let it spoil our fun must we?'

Sidney looked quite put out at Gloria's refusal to take the situation with the gravity he clearly thought it deserved. Daphne rushed to her husband's defence. 'Isn't that rather irresponsible? We all need to keep on the alert.'

'Why worry? There's sweet Fanny Adams any of us can do about it, so there's no point in fretting?' Gloria gave one of her irrepressible laughs. 'The only thing that's going to do is cause wrinkles.'

'Sidney's nephew was injured in the London bombings. He was in the tube and lost his foot. Dreadful business. In hospital for months he was. He'll never be able to work again. So naturally, we are concerned. We don't go up to London anymore.'

If Daphne expected Gloria to look abashed, she was disappointed. 'That's playing straight into their hands. Exactly what they want. Let's refuse to give in to 'em. Don't give 'em the satisfaction. Drink up everyone and let's enjoy ourselves. Who's for another?'

Even though their glasses were almost empty, the others turned down Gloria's offer. Fiona had only taken a few sips from her lime and soda so she gave Gloria a broad smile and hoped the woman did not take her refusal as a sign of disapproval. Not that Gloria appeared in the least bothered.

'Okey dokey, if you'll all excuse me, I'm going to get myself a drink and look for a fit young man to take me for a spin around the dance floor.'

'Well, really!' Edith Webster was clearly not impressed.

'Totally irresponsible,' agreed Daphne.

'We mustn't be too harsh.' Blank stares greeted Fiona's plea. 'And she does have a point. She may not express it as we would wish, but it would be a shame to let unsubstantiated rumours upset the holiday.'

Everyone lapsed into silence watching Gloria now busily chatting to two strangers propping up the bar as she waited to be served. From the occasional peals of laughter, she'd obviously found more lively company. Gloria Oldgate was proving to be quite the merry widow and as such, a bit of a mixed blessing.

Fiona bit the inside of her lip to stop herself giggling at the lemon-sucking expression on Edith's face. 'Why can't that woman act her age? Someone should tell her she's too old for high-heeled, strappy sandals and painted toenails.'

Another sudden loud guffaw from the bar produced tuts of disapproval from Daphne.

'And a bit more decorum wouldn't go amiss,' she muttered to her husband.

'What's that, dear?' Sidney looked vacantly around.

Although Gloria Oldgate had clearly blotted her copybook as far as the older members of the party were concerned, Fiona had quite taken to the fun-loving, forthright woman who clearly had no intention of growing old gracefully.

After ten minutes or so, the entertainment duo returned and the volume of noise and bustle on the crowded dance floor made general conversation difficult. After a quick glance round to see no one in her party was on their own or needed any help, Fiona settled back sipping her drink. She still had to check with Winston about the next day's arrangements but that could wait until later. For the moment, she could relax.

She noticed the incomers included a group of young men in their late twenties and early thirties, though whether they were locals or fellow tourists staying in the area Fiona could not tell. One of them was dancing, if that was an appropriate word to describe his provocatively gyrating hips, with Cressida. He seemed more intent on manoeuvring into a position where he could peer down into the ample cleavage barely covered by Cressida's low cut top. Even Holly appeared to be enjoying herself chatting with some of the other lads at the bar. It was a pity Holly didn't laugh more often, Fiona thought. Without the owl-like glasses and with her plump features wreathed in smiles, she had a pretty face.

Fiona had long since given up all thoughts of a stroll round the village. She'd been looking forward to seeing it lit up at night, but she consoled herself they were here for a week. She was still toying with the idea of an early night when she heard a woman's strident voice cut across the general merry tumult.

Everyone at the nearby tables turned to look. Graham Spelman had returned and was hovering by the table. Vivien, her face dark with anger, slammed down her glass on the table, rose to her feet and stormed towards the door.

Day 3 Tuesday

Take time this morning to relax and enjoy your new surroundings in the pretty village of Assmannshausen nestling among the famous Reingau vineyards. Why not stroll through its narrow streets lined with romantic half-timbered houses? Or for those feeling more energetic, there is an optional country walk. A chairlift will take you to the start of a forest trail to the Neiderwald Monument built to mark the unification of Germany at the end of the Franco-German War in 1871. Enjoy the excellent views of the Rhine from the summit before descending by gondola cable car and your return journey to the village by boat.

After lunch, we will drive to the beautiful riverside wine town of Rüdesheim with its 1000 year-old Broemserburg Castle which today houses the Wine Museum. We end our visit with a guided tour of the Siegfried's Mechanical Museum containing one of the world's largest collections of self-playing mechanical musical instruments.

Super Sun Executive Travel

Six

Barry Glover sat on the end of the bed rubbing the towel between his toes. He turned to his wife as she came out of the shower.

'Those two are at it again next door.'

Elspeth pulled a face. 'Not again. I hope it's not going to be like this all holiday. It won't be much fun for any of us with them at each other's throats the whole time.'

'I thought you said you'd spoken to Vivien. Told her to give him some slack.'

'I did. We had a long chat before dinner yesterday and things were better for a bit.' Elspeth went over to the wardrobe, picked out a pair of pale grey slacks plus a pink and white check shirt, and laid them on her side of the bed.

'Well it didn't last. She sniped at him all through coffee and again in the bar. I'm not surprised Graham decided to go for a walk. It was either that or face a stand up row.'

'You know what a bad traveller she is. And she had a headache.' The strident voices from the adjacent room rose to a crescendo. 'I had hoped after a good night's sleep, things would be back on an even keel again.'

A loud crash came from next door followed by a long silence. Elspeth and Barry looked at each other, eyebrows raised.

Barry stood up. 'Some hopes. Sounds as though they've started throwing things.'

'You're not going to leave that wet towel on the bed are you?'

'Now don't you start doing a Vivien on me, pumpkin.' Barry smiled and moved towards her. 'I could take yours back at the same time if you like.'

He gently tugged at the towel she had wrapped around her still slim figure and let it fall to the floor.

'Hey you,' she tried to protest as he pulled her into his arms. 'We're supposed to be meeting the others for breakfast at half past.'

'Plenty of time,' he said softly nibbling at her ear. 'Another ten minutes won't hurt.'

'Not now, Barry.' She pulled away. 'We've both just had a shower.'

'What's that got to do with anything?'

'I don't want to end up all sweaty again.'

'Very romantic.' There was a distinct edge to his voice.

She strode over to the chest of drawers on the far side of the room and took out clean underwear. As she turned to pick up the rest of her things laid on the bed, she saw him still standing staring at her, his face dark and serious.

'What's wrong?'

'You're not still…'

'Of course not!' she interrupted. 'We went through all this ages ago. We agreed, neither of us would ever mention it again.'

'You act differently when he's around. Makes it kind of hard to forget.'

She came over and wrapped her arms around him. 'I do know how lucky I am to have you. What possessed me, I'll never know. We'd both had too much to drink. But it was only the once. A momentary aberration. I've never regretted anything as much as that. I do love you, Barry and only you, but I can't keep on saying sorry. You have to let it go.'

Winston was already in the dining room when Fiona came down to breakfast. He gave her a cheery wave. She collected some fruit juice and cereal from the buffet and went to join him.

'Not many people down yet. I expect they're all having a lie-in,' she said as she slid onto the banquette opposite him. 'Some of them made quite a night of it but it's a free morning. There were only a half dozen takers for the optional excursion but, after last night, I did wonder if the two girls will still be coming.'

Winston gave one of his throaty chuckles. 'Those two certainly know how to party.'

'They were a bit on the rowdy side weren't they but, by all accounts, that's quite normal for young women these days. At least they didn't drink themselves into a stupor or start throwing up all over the place.'

'They weren't the only ones keeping the barman on his toes. Our merry widow and the blonde lady with the foreign husband were still knockin' 'em back long after you went up.'

'Then it's a good job the older members of the party left early. They would definitely not have approved,' she said with mock severity. 'So what are you going to do with yourself this morning? Don't tell me, clean out the coach and wash down the windows.'

The big, round face broke into a wide grin. 'Yep, and then I'm going to take a stroll up the path to the top of the valley.'

'I'd rather walk up there than take the chairlift any day,' Fiona said ruefully. 'Coming down in the cable-car I can just about manage – at least it's all enclosed – but I'm not too good with heights and the thought of going up in the chairlift with my legs dangling into space with only a steel bar between me and a sheer drop for hundreds of feet is making my stomach do somersaults already. I don't suppose you'd consider doing a swap for the morning and take them up for me? I'm more than willing to clean the coach.'

'Good try, sweetheart.' He gave a deep, throaty chuckle as he eased out of the seat. 'Have a good time and I'll see you at lunch.'

Fiona was debating whether to allow herself to be tempted by any of the delicious-looking German breads on offer when she saw Vivien and Elspeth by the buffet table. The expression on Vivien's face and the absence of her husband did not suggest marital harmony had been restored. Fiona sighed. She did not wish to pry but Graham and Barry were supposed to be going on the optional tour. Was Vivien aware Cressida and Holly were also booked on the excursion? That might explain the decidedly dark countenance.

Although Barry came in a few minutes later, Graham had still not arrived by the time Fiona had finished her breakfast. Perhaps she should check if he was still coming on the morning's trip.

'I expect so. He should be down soon and you can ask him.' Not even bothering to look up at Fiona, Vivien's fingers played restlessly with her coffee cup.

Fiona turned to Kathleen Murphy who was sitting next to Elspeth. 'Is your husband having a lie in? Nothing wrong I hope?'

'Oh no,' came the gentle lilt. 'We got to the top of the stairs and Brendan said he'd forgotten his tablets. Though what's keepin' him all this time, the good Lord only knows. I expect he can't remember where he put 'em. Here he comes now!'

Puffing and panting and looking flushed, Brendan hurried up the short flight of steps to the Super Sun tables. 'Sorry, me darlin'. Got completely lost. Turned the wrong way when I cum out the room and ended up over in the annex. Took ages to find someone to show me the way back.'

Vivien got to her feet and moved out to let Brendan squeeze along the bench seat to the far end opposite his wife.

A good time for Fiona to make her exit. 'If you'll excuse me, everyone, I must get on. Have a good morning, all of you.'

'I'm going up now too,' said Vivien.

'But, Viv,' protested Elspeth, 'You've not finished your breakfast.'

'I'm not hungry.'

Vivien turned and quickly headed for the door before her sister could attempt to change her mind. She was already standing by the small lift by the time Fiona reached the corridor.

It was all too evident Vivien did not want company so Fiona decided to head for the main staircase. With all this extra food, a little more exercise was probably not such a bad idea in any case. However, by the time she reached the top of the second flight, she had already begun to wonder at the wisdom of her decision. There were enough stairs in the building without trying to climb three floors non-stop. As luck would have it, no one was about at the top to see her as she waited for her heart to return to normal, draped over the newel post like some marionette after the puppeteer had let go of the strings.

Moments later, above the sound of her own noisy panting, she heard a long keening cry. She peered down the corridor. The noise appeared to be coming from the open door of the first room. The eerie wail rose to a crescendo reverberating in the confined space.

'What on earth...' The scene inside the room made the words die on her lips. Vivien was on her knees at the foot of the bed, her back to Fiona. She was cradling the body in her arms, rocking back and forth, her head thrown back as the animal cries continued.

The strong metallic stench hit the back of Fiona's throat making her want to gag. She swallowed hard forcing herself to take a few hesitant steps closer until she could see them both more clearly. Graham's face was buried in Vivien's blood-soaked bosom but his arms hung limp and lifeless. Steeling herself to keep calm, Fiona put a hand on Vivien's shoulder, but there was no response. The woman seemed impervious to her touch.

'Vivien, there's nothing you can do. Come away.'

It was like talking to a zombie. Vivien could neither see nor hear her. At first, Fiona thought she would never be able to prise the dead man from Vivien's embrace, but eventually her gentle urging seemed to penetrate and the howling subsided. After all the noise, the silence added to the nightmare unreality.

Without warning, collapsing like a rag doll that had suddenly lost all its stuffing, Vivien let go of her husband's body.

It took all Fiona's self-control not to cry out as she caught Graham's falling corpse in her own arms. The unseeing eyes seemed to stare up at her; the lips parted in surprise. She lowered the body gently down onto the floor. There was blood everywhere and now she was as covered in it as Vivien. How could one body possibly produce so much? Then she saw it. The knife stuck to the hilt into the flesh of his stomach in the centre of the vast patch of red at his waist that merged the fabric of shirt and trousers together. She couldn't let him lie there. Not like that. The rumpled bedcover lay at the end of the unmade bed. Fiona reached up and pulled it down over the body, blotting out the horrific spectacle.

Seven

Fiona heard footsteps coming down the corridor.

'What's happened? Oh, my God.' Elspeth stood at the door. 'Vivien what have you done?'

'Help me get her away.'

Together they managed to half carry, half drag, Vivien to Elspeth's room next door. As Elspeth sat on the bed rocking the distraught woman trying to quieten the now pitiful, mewling sobs, Fiona phoned down to reception. Catching sight of herself in the mirror, she realized she would have to change and wash the blood from her face and arms.

Only when she was alone in the quiet of her own room, did the full enormity of what had happened sink in. In all the panic and chaos, someone had needed to handle the immediate situation keeping a calm clear head and remain detached from all the horror. Forcing herself not to break down now, she stripped off her things and stood under the shower letting the tepid water pour over her. It couldn't wash away the dreadful picture but at least it helped to calm her raddled nerves.

What would happen now? Would the police arrest Vivien? Though Elspeth had assumed her sister had been responsible, Fiona had given it no thought till now. Surely, one thing didn't quite add up. Even if the lift had whisked Vivien up to the third floor immediately, Fiona could not have been more than a minute behind her. Surely, there hadn't been time to inflict such appalling injuries. Everything had happened so suddenly. And why hadn't she heard some kind of altercation or, at the very least, a cry of protest from Graham before that chilling animal howl?

Fiona had to admit there was little she could tell the two policemen when they eventually got round to speaking to her, but it surprised her they asked so few questions. All they really wanted to know was if anything in the room had been touched. They oozed a courteous insincerity that made her feel they were simply going through the motions.

She doubted they'd be able to get much sense from Vivien for some time. They'd tried to interview her before the doctor arrived but it quickly became evident the woman was in no fit state for questions.

Despite Fiona's protests, Winston insisted the police doctor see her before he left. Though Fiona had no intention of taking them, he left sleeping tablets for both her and Elspeth though thankfully she had been spared the full horror of Graham's mutilated body.

When she at last she escaped to the privacy of her room, Fiona sank down onto the dressing table stool dropping her head into hands. All the calm, collected control she'd managed to maintain for the last hour had suddenly ebbed away. Someone else could cope. Take over the responsibility.

'Pull yourself together, woman.'

Instead of sitting here feeling sorry for herself, she ought to be checking through her notes for the afternoon's walking tour of Rudesheim. Always assuming it was still going ahead, of course. She gave a deep sigh, sat back and rubbed her eyes.

'Oh, Bill! I don't think I can do this.' Her whisper sounded surprisingly loud in the silent room. 'Don't tell me I'm strong. That I've coped with disasters before. That I've seen worse. So what if I've dealt with accident victims brought into hospital with limbs torn off or with vicious stab wounds from broken bottles after a pub brawl, battered and bruised beyond recognition? That was thirty years ago and back then, it was my job. This is different.'

Now she really was going doolally. Talking to her dead husband in her head was one thing but holding a conversation out loud as though he were actually present was quite another.

True, that's exactly what he would have said. Reminded her of her days as a scrub nurse in his theatre where the sight and smell of blood was part of their daily routine. But then it had been so much easier to remain detached. Today things had taken her by surprise but Graham Spelman was not just another patient. Vivien and Elspeth were more than distraught relatives in need of reassurance. Though she didn't know them well, she was involved with these people. Responsible for them. She wouldn't be able to give a comforting hug before sending them on their way, move on to the next patient and close the door on all of the misery at the end of her shift. They were her responsibility and needing her support until they all went back to England.

This new job was supposed to provide her with an interest, help her get her life back on track after Bill's death. The way things were turning out, it was proving to be anything but. So far, it had only presented her with more dead bodies than a bad night in casualty after the pubs had closed. On her very first assignment on the trip to the Dutch bulb fields, there'd been no less than three murders and even her own life had been threatened. Admittedly, the only body she'd seen, a pale figure smothered by a pillow, was nothing like the horror-movie bloody corpse she'd just witnessed. Back then, she'd had to carry on guiding the rest of her unsuspecting party through the tour as though nothing had happened. Not that she could keep this death a secret. And more to the point, here in Germany there was no Peter Montgomery-Jones to take charge as there had been in Amsterdam.

Chin up. Just concentrate on the job in hand, Bill would have said as he gave her that special, reassuring smile of his. She pushed herself onto her feet and walked over to the bed for her handbag. From its protecting side pocket, she pulled out the small photograph and stared into the brown eyes she

56

knew so well looking back at her from the informal holiday snap. With the tip of her finger, she stroked his cheek. This was how she liked to remember him; tall, strong and so full of the joy of life. That handsome face had become so gaunt and strained as the long years of illness took their toll but the eyes – loving, reassuring – they had never dimmed. Not until the end. Tears began to well behind her eyes impossible to blink away.

'Oh, Bill. My darling, darling Bill. I miss you so very much.'

Fiona washed her face, tidied herself up and stared at her reflection in the mirror. Even after refreshing her makeup, her face looked strained and drawn. She made her way downstairs to see what progress the police were making only to discover they had already left the hotel.

What surprised and disturbed her even more however, was to be told they had taken Vivien with them to the police station for further questioning. Understandably they wanted to talk to her about what had happened and if she knew of anything in Graham's background which might explain why he'd become the victim of such a frenzied violent attack, but was it really necessary to do that at the station? Vivien was already in such a state that not to let her sister go with her when she most needed support seemed unnecessarily cruel. Fiona's indignation gave way to a sudden surge of guilt. Had she been around instead of wallowing in her own self-pity upstairs in her room, she could have protested and insisted, as the person responsible for the welfare of everyone on the tour, she should go with Vivien. Why had no one informed her? She should not have been left to find out by chance from Marthe at reception.

Fiona wondered if the officers intended to return to interview any of the other members of her party. Surely, they would want to question those who had rooms on that short section of corridor if nothing else. And what of the afternoon's excursion? She'd not even been told if she could continue with it. Best to talk it over with Winston.

'No point in us sittin' around here twiddlin' our thumbs all afternoon.' Winston's calm logic helped steady Fiona's nerves. 'We'll be back for dinner. If the police want us, they can find us then. It's not as if we're movin' hotels.'

'Thanks for taking Devesh and Anita Najaran and the girls on the trip for me this morning, Winston. Did they all enjoy their walk up on the top?'

'They had a great time,' he said with a smile. 'So it's off to Rudesheim after lunch then, is it? Your call.'

'Yes. You're right as always. Let's go.'

Winston put an arm around her and gave a quick, reassuring hug. 'You sure you're okay, sweetheart? You're still as pale as a ghost. Why don't you stay here this afternoon? Go have a lie down. I can manage on my own.'

Fiona looked into the concerned, deep-brown eyes and gave him the most beaming smile she could manage. 'I really am alright, Winston. I can cope.'

'Well if you sure, sweetheart. I know just what you need. A tot of good old Jamaican rum. Put some colour in those pretty cheeks of yours.'

Fiona chuckled. 'No thank you, Winston. Even though the thought of some Dutch courage before I face everyone with the news is very tempting. Folk are beginning to drift back to the hotel already and I still haven't worked out exactly what to say. I'd have preferred to tell them on the coach rather than in the public dining room but if I wait till after lunch rumours will spread. Some of them may have heard already.'

'Don't you worry. I'll be there right beside you. We'll fend off the questions together.'

'Winston, you're a brick.'

'Well, we's a team aren't we, sweetheart?'

A stunned silence greeted Fiona's brief announcement. But not for long.

'Was it a heart attack? He didn't look the type.'

'But why were the police here?'

The barrage of questions had begun.

58

She knew the fact Graham had been murdered would come out soon enough, but Fiona was determined they would not hear the full story from her. The longer she could keep them from knowing the grisly details, the easier it would be to maintain some semblance of normality.

'I'm sorry, ladies and gentlemen; I cannot tell you any more than that. Now if you'd like to help yourselves from the buffet and sit down…' Fiona waved a hand towards the tempting spread cold smoked meats, cheeses and salads.

Nearly everyone had filled their plates and were tucking in by the time Elspeth and Barry came down. Elspeth's face was blotchy and her eyes red with crying even though she had tried to conceal the worst with makeup. Thankfully, every one had the good sense not to ask her questions.

Conversation remained hushed over the meal and Fiona couldn't help stealing a glance at Cressida as she walked up the steps from the buffet table. Thank goodness she hadn't made a scene when she heard the news, but then it wasn't as if there'd been anything between her and Graham other than some blatant flirting on her part. The girl appeared to be more subdued than usual, but that was probably true of most of the group.

As the meal progressed, Fiona could see Elspeth ate very little. Fiona went over to speak to her, but apart from making a few meaningless conciliatory noises, there was little she could say to console the woman. It wasn't only the appalling death of her brother-in-law; it didn't help that Vivien had been whisked away by the police.

Eight

The coach was alive with whispered exchanges. No prizes for guessing what they're talking about, Fiona thought ruefully. Elspeth and Barry were almost the last to get on the coach, which meant, at least for the time being, the couple were spared any questions.

When they arrived in Rudesheim, Barry was very protective and, apart from the odd embarrassed, 'So sorry to hear the news,' or words to that effect, everyone respected Elspeth's privacy.

Best not to hang around. Hoisting up her guide pole, Fiona led the group towards the town centre. Passing the Eagle Tower which served as part of the city wall, they arrived in the market square. Fiona pointed out the fourteenth century church of St Jakobus with its unusual onion-type spire on top of the tower. No one seemed much in the mood to listen to long explanations. Best to keep the spiel to a minimum and get straight to the Music Museum.

'Rudesheim is probably the most visited of all the wine towns along the valley and, as you can see, we may have difficulty keeping together as we walk down here. Please try not to become separated. There'll be plenty of time later for you to explore.'

Fiona led her slowly meandering party passed the colourful half-timbered houses, many of which had been turned into interesting tourist shops and bars, until she reached the cable-car terminal.

'When we've finished the tour if any of you would like to

see the spectacular views from the Neiderwald Monument at the summit you can take the cable-car from here.'

'It's really huge, that statue thing up there. Isn't it?' commented Ian Lambert, shielding his eyes against the sun. 'You can just about see it's a woman brandishing a sword.'

'A Valkyrie.'

'You could get some really stunning pictures at the top,' Ian added enthusiastically.

'Well you're not getting me up there so if you want to see it you can go on your own,' Rita informed her husband vehemently much to the amusement of everyone else.

If Fiona hoped to put all thoughts of the morning's horror to the back of her mind, Elspeth's pale, worried countenance proved a constant reminder. The woman was so preoccupied she had noticed little of her surroundings as she walked along in a daze. Sightseeing in the gay little tourist town was so obviously not where she wanted to be, but what was the alternative? Sitting alone brooding in her room at the hotel?

'Right,' said Fiona rather more abruptly than she'd intended. 'Let's move on. Our next stop is Siegfried's Musik Kabinett which is located in a picturesque old house known as the Brömserhof once owned by a local noble.'

Once inside, Fiona was able to relax and take a back seat handing over to their museum guide, an attractive, remarkably thin, leggy girl eccentrically dressed in a man's tail suit complete with top hat. Putting them all in the mood, the guide began by playing the famous Lorelei music on the concert-piano-orchestrian. Even Elspeth smiled when the girl began to do a sinuous Charleston to entertain them as she set the next instrument in motion.

They were led down to the cellars where they gathered in half dark until the lights were switched on to reveal a magnificent collection of gaily-decorated fairground barrel organs. Their guide turned the handle of a huge Turkish affair which completely filled the great arch on the end wall. In the centre was a marvellous almost life-size figure of a turbaned sultan with richly dressed maidens in the niches on either side.

Not everyone was enraptured by the spectacle. Elspeth's gloom had returned and she and Barry were now standing at the back a little apart talking earnestly.

'I can't get a signal in here.' Fiona could hear Elspeth's plaintive wail over the noise of the organ. 'What if Viv tries to ring me?'

'Then she'll leave a message, won't she? Just like you've been doing to her all afternoon.' Barry's patience was wearing thin.

'But...'

'She knows you're here for her. Give her some space, pumpkin,' he said more kindly. 'You've done all you can for the moment.'

The Commander took the news of the man's murder with his usual calm.

'I didn't mange to speak to him, sir. Spelman was dead before our plane even landed. His wife was found with the body covered in blood. The local police appear to have it down as a domestic.'

'Then I take it Spelman's wife has confessed?'

'Not so far. They're still questioning her, but as yet they haven't managed to get anything sensible from her. She's still in shock. But it looks as though that's the end of that particular line of enquiry. There's nothing more to report on the Frankfurt situation, but if there are any developments I'll let you know.'

'Fine, but keep your ear to the ground on the Spelman investigation. It would seem too convenient that the man is murdered two days after his possible contact is blown up in a car bomb less than fifty miles away. I do not like coincidences and there are far too many of them for my liking in all of this. Keep me informed.'

'Certainly, sir.'

Once Fiona had seen to the half dozen people opting for the cable-car ride, she was free to do a little window-shopping herself. Though not something she would normally think of doing, the displays were particularly attractive and far from the usual cheap souvenirs. The goods were geared to the tourist market, but nonetheless they tended to be quality craft products for which the region was famous.

Drawn by the inviting smell of freshly brewed coffee, Fiona discovered a pleasant-looking café with a magnificent array of cakes and pastries – the Germans certainly knew a thing or two about cake making. She decided not too tempt her resolve and took a seat looking out into the busy street with her back to the mouth-watering display as she drank her well-earned cup of tea.

If she'd hoped for some quiet time on her own, Fiona was quickly disillusioned. She had only just sat down when a group of Super Sun people came into the café.

'You don't mind if we join you, do you? It's getting quite busy in here now isn't it?' Rita Lambert sat beside her and her husband looked around for another chair so that the Irish couple, Kathleen and Brendan Murphy, who had come in at the same time, could join them.

'That museum was much more interesting than I expected.' At least Fiona was spared the necessity of having to make conversation. Rita Lambert turned out to be one of those who loved the sound of her own voice. 'That young lady who showed us round was quite a character, wasn't she?'

Rita received nods and polite smiles all round.

'This is nice. I always think one of the best things about holidays is meeting new people, don't you? Not that I've had a chance to talk to everyone in our party yet. I never did speak to that poor man who died this morning. Wasn't that an awful business? So young too, but then you hear of so many people in their fifties who have heart attacks. It's all this stress of modern day living. You never know when these things are going to happen but to tell you the truth, I didn't think he looked a well man. I said as much didn't I, Ian?'

Her poor husband looked somewhat nonplussed but before he could make any comment, Rita was off again. 'We were talking about it to that good-looking Indian couple while we were waiting for the coach. Nice people. And so polite. You wouldn't think she's old enough to have grandchildren would you? That black hair I expect. You wouldn't know they were foreigners to hear them speak either. So well spoken and not a trace of an accent.'

'Really?' Kathleen said more out of politeness than interest.

'Not like Viktor who sits on our table in the hotel. He's from one of those countries that used to be part of Russia. I think he looks a bit Mongolian with those eyes of his – Genghis Kahn without the beard – but apparently, he's from somewhere in the Caucusus wherever that it is. Not been over here long so his English isn't that good. I only catch half of what he says; though, to be fair, he is the other end of the table.'

Ian stifled a hiccupping cough. The angle of the light on his spectacles made it impossible for Fiona to gauge what he was thinking. If intended as warning, it had no effect on his wife. Now she was in full flow, it was going to take a bulldozer to stop the totally un-PC Rita.

'His wife Hilary, the lady who hurt her ankle, now she's as English as they come. Don't you think she looks just like that Judy Finnegan from the television? Same round face, wide mouth and fringe. And she has the same chunky build.'

Brendan Murphy was obviously none the wiser. 'Who?'

'Richard and Judy. That programme that's on every afternoon.'

'I've heard of their Book Club, but we don't watch day-time TV very much.'

Evidently eager to change the subject, Kathleen Murphy asked, 'I see you've already made time for shopping. Have you bought something nice?'

Rita opened the Käthe Wohlfahrt bag and took out a small wooden soldier doll. 'A traditional nutcracker figure. Isn't he gorgeous? Just like the two enormous ones outside on either side of the door. I do love his curly moustache. As soon as I saw him, I had to get him for my grandson. Boys are so much more difficult to buy for than girls don't you think.'

Kathleen gave a weak smile and said softly, 'I wouldn't know.'

'Don't you have any grandchildren?'

There was a definite pause before Brendan said, 'Unfortunately not.'

'Well there's still time I expect. You do have children?'

From her position, Fiona could see Brendan take his wife's hand under the table.

'We were blessed with a daughter but she ...' His voice tailed off.

'The Good Lord took her last year,' finished his wife softly with an anxious look in his direction.

'I'm so sorry. How dreadful for you.' To give the garrulous Rita her due, she put the doll back in its box and slipped it out of sight onto the floor.

It proved difficult to resume the general chitchat after such a revelation and, after a painful five minutes, Rita and Ian bid their farewells and they all stood up to go their separate ways.

'Don't forget your sweater,' Fiona called after Brendan.

Before she could pick it up, Brendan snatched it from the back of the chair, bundled it up and tucked it under his arm.

When he saw her surprise expression, Brendan gave an apologetic smile. 'Be forgetting m' head one day, eejit that I am!'

'I don't know why you didn't leave it on the coach, m' darlin' like I said. That's the second time today. You'd have left it in the church earlier on if I hadn't noticed,' scolded his wife affectionately.

It wasn't only Rita Lambert who had been tempted to start spending the holiday money in earnest. Given the collection of packages most of them were carrying as they returned to the coach, few had resisted the urge to shop. The Käthe Wohlfahrt bags were much in evidence. Once the last stragglers arrived, Fiona climbed aboard to find an excited hubbub as goods were unwrapped and shown to neighbours. Trying to squeeze her way down the crowded aisle to check no one had been left behind proved a slow process.

'Isn't he gorgeous?' Anita Najaran showed Fiona a foot high wooden figure. 'The Nutcracker King, just like in the ballet.'

Daphne and Sidney Pettit had bought a whole crib set and, as well as the large pair of dangly, wooden earrings she was now wearing, Hilary Kasar had a musical carousel complete with horses that went up and down as it turned around.

Fiona enthused suitably and gave Winston the thumbs up to leave. With everyone insisting on showing her their purchases as she passed, it took so long to wend her way back to her seat she barely had time to pull out her notes before the next attraction.

'Over on our right you can see the ruins of Castle Ehrenfels, a thirteenth century customs fortress, and over to the left on the island in the middle of the river, that pretty white tower is Mäuseturm or Mouse Tower, supposedly built by Archbishop Hatto II of Mainz, the local prince, in order to collect taxes from passing shipping.'

Although there was no room to stop on the narrow road, Winston slowed the coach to let the photographers take pictures.

'It has a rather interesting story attached to it. According to legend, the Bishop was a greedy man and even when bad weather ruined the crops, he continued to demand the same amount of tribute from his subjects as in the good years. The starving villagers rebelled and stormed the Bishop's stockpiles of grain, but once inside, Hatto ordered the building to be locked and set on fire. The flames forced all the mice that used to feed on the stockpiles to run to the palace in search of food. Bishop Hatto panicked and fled for the stone tower thinking the mice would not be able to cross the river, but they followed and ate him alive.'

Was Graham's death some kind of just retribution? What a ridiculous thought, Fiona scolded herself. If only she could banish that awful picture from her mind.

Philip Cawston barely glanced at the document he'd been

handed. He was far too preoccupied watching the small army of men that had invaded Precisiontec and were now busily searching through the every filing cabinet, cupboard and desk.

'You've no right to do this,' he protested.

'That warrant,' said the tall, grey-haired man standing beside him, 'clearly states that we have.'

'But this is a perfectly legitimate company. Just what are you trying to accuse us of?'

'As I explained,' the man said without emotion, 'your partner has been murdered. We need to establish if his death was related to his business affairs.'

'But how could there possibly be any connection? Graham was on holiday for goodness sake. It happened in Germany not in here in his office.'

'The young Indian sitting at the computer looked up. 'Excuse me, sir. Can you tell me Mr Spelman's password, please?'

'I've no idea.'

'The man is dead, Mr Cawston.' The Commander's voice continued to show no trace of impatience, but it brooked no dissent. 'There must be a way of accessing his records.'

'Naturally I have access to everything except his personal files, but as I say, there I cannot help you. Company policy is to change passwords every month for security reasons.'

'Not to worry,' said the man at the computer. 'Most people use perfectly predictable passwords. I expect we'll find it soon enough.'

'Is all this really necessary?'

The only reply Philip Cawston received was a polite smile. 'It's not his wife's name. Can you give me the names of his children?'

It took several more suggestions until, some ten minutes later, they hit upon the correct password.

'There are several files in the folder labelled Project Ariadne on his personal drive. It appears to be a series of designs by the look of it. But that title doesn't bear any relationship to the files in the shared project folders.' The Asian looked up expectantly.

When nothing was forthcoming, the Commander asked, 'Can you enlighten us, Mr Cawston?'

Philip shook his head. 'All our projects are given names relating to the design specification plus a number code.'

'Do you recognize the designs?'

Reluctantly, Philip came round to peer over the shoulder of the man seated at the computer. 'Nothing I've ever seen before. Certainly not my design. Must be one of his.'

'I thought Mr Spelman was the Sales and Marketing Director.'

'That's true, but he was an experienced design engineer. He only took on the promotional side of the business full time when Precisiontec started expanding. Besides, he wouldn't be much good at the job if he didn't understand what's involved at every stage. Each project is individually engineered to match the specific needs of the client. Graham needed to know what was possible and what was not. This must be something he was toying with just to keep his hand in.'

The Commander looked him in the eye. Although there was no trace of sarcasm in his voice, the disbelief was all too apparent. 'I appreciate I am no engineer, but those designs look complete to me. It must have taken a considerable amount of time to put these together. That being the case, is it not a surprise to find them on his office PC and not his own laptop?'

'Here he'd have access to all our design software plus it's much easier on large 25 inch screens.'

'I take your point.' The grey man stared at the monitor. 'Presumably, for security reasons, files cannot easily be downloaded from any of your machines?'

'That's true. But because Graham went out to clients, he had the facility to copy certain of the smaller files across onto his laptop.'

'Mr Spelman appears to have taken considerable trouble with these designs. To the uninitiated, they would appear to be workable designs. Can you tell me what they might be?'

Philip stared at the computer screen and clicked the zoom tab. 'At this scale, it's difficult to tell what I'm looking at. I'd need to print them out full-size to even hazard a guess.'

'When my colleague was here two days ago, you mentioned a project Spelman proposed but it was decided to abandon. Could this be it?'

There was a slight pause before Cawston answered. 'Possibly. Graham was keen, but it wasn't our sort of project so it wasn't taken any further. I presume he never got round to deleting the files.'

'Are you saying, as the senior partner, it was your decision not to follow it up?'

'Yes.' Cawston's jaw visibly tightened.

'Why was that?'

Cawston licked his lips. 'At the time we had orders for so many projects we were in no position to take on anything new.'

'So can you enlighten us as to what it was for?'

'I can't remember.'

The Commander stared at him. He did not question the contradiction in Cawston's account but let the silence hang in the air. 'Were you aware he had worked on the design?'

'No. I thought they'd got no further than an initial discussion. As I said, I've never seen these designs before.'

'He may not have shown them to you, but do you think he might have worked on them with anyone else? His brother-in-law, for example?'

'Barry Glover?' Cawston gave a derive snort. 'I doubt it. Barry may work for Precisiontec but he's an accountant. He wouldn't know a transistor from an ink blot.'

'That may be so, but is it possible they discussed it in general terms. The two men obviously spent time together.'

'I wouldn't have said they were that close. Their wives may be sisters, but Graham and Barry didn't exactly have a lot in common. Barry's the quiet type, likes gardening, DIY and fishing. Graham is … was much more of a social animal. Member of the golf club, chairman of the local Rotary, that sort of thing. Don't get me wrong, they were friendly enough as far as I know, the four of them even took short holidays together, but the men didn't exactly live in each other's pockets. Here at work, their paths would rarely cross. Barry works over in the other block. He's never been in this office as far as I know.'

The Commander gave him a shrewd look but, to Cawston's relief, changed the subject. 'The file name means nothing to you?'

Cawston shook his head and looked away. 'No. Not at all.'

'Ariadne.' There was a hint of humour in the grey eyes. 'I take it the man was a classical scholar?'

'Not that I know of.' Philip frowned. 'He was widely read. Went to a minor public school so I suppose he learnt Latin if that's what you're getting at.'

The Commander smiled. 'Actually, Ariadne is a Greek myth. Interesting Spelman chose to name the project after the woman who gave Theseus a ball of string to help find his way out of the labyrinth.'

Cawston stared at him blankly.

'Could these be the designs for a homing device, a guidance system of some kind?'

'I very much doubt it,' Cawston snapped. 'I don't know what you're implying, but all our work is strictly for the commercial market. How many times do I have to tell you, I know nothing about this? Graham never sent these designs to me. You can check my computer if you like.'

'Oh we will, Mr Cawston. We will.'

Nine

Elspeth Glover was first off the coach when they arrived back to the hotel. She barely waited for Winston to bring it to a halt before she was out of her seat and waiting impatiently for the door to open.

'Someone's desperate for a pee!' laughed Gloria from a few rows behind.

More like desperate to know if her sister had returned from the police station, Fiona thought as she helped everyone else down the coach steps.

'How's that ankle today, Hilary? You look as though you're still having a few problems.'

'Much better thanks, Fiona. Overdid it a bit yesterday, so after a teensy bit of retail therapy we went for a sit-down in a cafe.'

She certainly looked in better spirits. Fiona helped her to the door and went back to check the coach for forgotten items, all the more important as the parking area was some distance from the hotel, and stayed chatting to Winston for a few minutes. When she finally made it inside, everyone else had collected their room keys and quite a crowd had gathered by the lift, so she made for the stairs to begin the long climb up to the third floor. Six flights of nine steps. By the end of the week she should at least be fit.

She'd reached the last flight when she heard hurried footsteps coming along the corridor above. Elspeth rounded the corner.

'Fiona! Just the person I was looking for. May I have a

word?'

'Of course. Is something wrong?'

'Not here. Can we go somewhere private?'

Elspeth seemed not to want to talk in front of her husband, which ruled out going back to the Glovers's room, so Fiona suggested the two of them go to hers.

'It's Vivien,' Elspeth informed her without any preamble as soon as the door closed. 'You know the police took her to the station in Mainz and she's still not back. I've checked her room and they haven't seen her at reception. I've not heard a word from her since she left. She's not answering her mobile. I don't know if they've confiscated it or what.'

'Vivien probably switched it off while she was answering their questions and forgot to switch it back on again.'

'But why are they still keeping her? It's not as though she killed Graham.' Not the time to point out she'd been the first to assume her sister was guilty. 'I've just tried ringing the station to ask if she's still being questioned but the people on front desk can't tell me anything useful. Oh they're perfectly polite, but they say when there is any news we'll be informed. Whatever that means.'

'These things take time. I expect you'll hear something soon. I'm not sure what I can do to help.'

'Perhaps the police will listen to you.'

'But if you and Barry can't get any answers, I don't see why they should pay any attention to me.'

'Barry thinks we should just wait but I've got to do something. Can't you insist as the Super Sun representative?'

Like Barry, Fiona doubted her efforts would prove any more successful but she could hardly refuse Elspeth's pleading. As it turned out, the person at the other end of the line had so little English, a sensible conversation proved impossible. All she managed to glean was the equivalent of the not very helpful, 'Mrs Spelman is helping with enquiries.'

'That's what they say when they're about to make an arrest,' moaned Elspeth with a despairing sob in her voice.

'That's not what they said at all.'

'But she couldn't have killed him! He was alive when Vivien and I came down to breakfast and she was with me the whole time. Graham was dead when she came back up. You can confirm it. You were there.'

'Not quite, but very soon after. Which is what I told the police.'

Elspeth suddenly leapt to her feet. 'I'm going down to the station and demand they let me see her.'

'Do you think that's a good idea?'

'Barry and I will get a taxi. And if he won't come with me, I'll go on my own.'

'But...' Fiona watched the figure disappear through the door. 'You'll miss dinner,' she finished to the empty room.

It was a typical British summer's afternoon. Dark clouds were gathering and although the forecasted heavy showers had not yet begun, they could not be not far away. Just in time for the rush-hour exodus.

The light was fading fast. The Commander looked up from his desk and frowned but before he could reach the light switch by the door, the sudden jarring buzz of the phone broke the silence. He turned and picked up the receiver.

'It's Mukherjee, sir. I'm still at the Spelman house. His wife left a spare key with a neighbour to go in and water the houseplants. There was an ancient PC in his study, but when I started it up it didn't have enough memory for any of his work files. There's no sign of a laptop.'

'We have already established from the German police it was not in his hotel room.'

'Could it have been stolen, sir? Do you think that was why he was murdered? For the Ariadne files?'

'There is no evidence to suggest that. His wife is still the main suspect. It is possible for security reasons Spelman chose to hide his laptop away in his own home somewhere?'

'We'll keep looking, sir.'

As the Commander put down the receiver, heavy rain began to strike the windowpane. The downpour had begun. He stared out of the window watching the lights appear throughout the buildings on the far side on the Thames, mesmerized by the growing pinpricks distorted by the descending torrents of water.

Fiona came down the stairs for dinner and saw Winston waiting by the reception desk. He turned and raised an eyebrow. She crossed the corridor and went up the three steps to where they could talk without being overheard by passers-by.

'Any news about the lady the police took away?'

'Not yet, I'm afraid. She was in a state of shock and it may be they haven't been able to question her yet.'

'She's not the only one. How about you, sweetheart?'

'I'm fine, Winston. I think most people are still stunned by it all. Some more than others, although everyone's been rather quiet this afternoon. I dread to think what the response will be when the full story comes out. And it must eventually.'

'Let's cross that bridge when we get there. Till then, it's up to us to keep smilin'.' He gave her an appealing grin, put an arm around her and gave a quick hug. 'Rightyho, sweetheart. Let's not keep the troops waitin'. You'll feel better with some food inside you.'

Barry Glover had evidently failed to persuade his wife of the futility of her mission. The couple were nowhere in sight when the rest of the party gathered for the evening meal and still hadn't put in an appearance by the time the soup was served.

Fiona did not like to leave Mr and Mrs Murphy sitting at the table on their own, especially after the unfortunate incident in the café earlier on, so she decided to join the softly spoken Irish couple.

'I hope you enjoyed your day?' Fiona asked with her brightest smile as she slid along the bench seat next to Kathleen.

'Oh 'twas lovely, me dear.' Kathleen's round face broke into a cherubic smile and the pale blue eyes twinkled with genuine pleasure. 'And weren't all those musical instruments a real marvel.'

Fiona sat back and let the loquacious Kathleen lead the conversation. Brendan seemed considerably more reserved than on the previous evening but perhaps the man was tired after walking around all day. To Fiona's relief, neither of them made any reference to their missing fellow table guests.

Although almost everyone in the main offices had left the building long ago, the Commander was still at his desk. Not that he had his head buried in paperwork. Far from it. He sat back in the chair, long legs stretched beneath the desk and arms loosely folded across his chest, to all intents and purposes staring into space lost in thought. Those who knew him well would appreciate appearances were probably deceptive. Fast, decisive action was often crucial at the beginning of an operation. Success invariably necessitated collecting as much evidence as possible before it disappeared and the culprits covered their tracks. Nonetheless, though he had a reputation for quick thinking and incisiveness, that was not to imply the man was impulsive. He was not one to jump readily to conclusions or to let instinct prejudice the investigation. Analysis of the evidence always took precedence over gut feeling.

He was stirred into action by the sudden insistent ring of the phone. He picked up the receiver.

'We've found it, sir. Eventually. He'd hidden it up in the loft.'

'Does it contain the Ariadne files?'

'Yes, sir. Do you want me to bring it over?'

The Commander glanced up at the clock on the far wall. 'There is no urgency. Make sure it is kept secure overnight and let me have it first thing in the morning.'

'Certainly, sir.'

'And Mukherjee, good work today.'

'Thank you, sir.'

The absence of the Glovers at dinner prompted little interest. Tonight's gossip focused on another couple entirely.

Fiona followed Sidney and Daphne Pettit into the bar-lounge, which was filling up fast. Sitting at one of the few empty tables near the door were Anita and Devesh who looked up and smiled at the elderly couple as they passed. Completely ignoring the Asian couple, Sidney marched past with a briskness Fiona had never seen him display before and he and his wife went to sit further along at a table where extra seats from elsewhere had to be brought for them.

Appalled at such pointed rudeness, Fiona smiled at Anita.

'May I join you both?'

Some ten minutes later, Fiona went to fetch herself a cup of coffee and as she skirted round the central dance floor, she caught the tail end of the conversation at another table.

'There's no smoke without fire. Why else would emigration cart them off at Dover like that? Questioned them for twenty minutes, they did. What worries me is they still haven't caught those Muslim terrorists who blew up that car in Frankfurt.'

On the day of their departure, everyone had been held up at the port waiting for one of the feeder coaches detained at passport control. As everything had been resolved and with so much else to occupy her thoughts at the beginning of the tour, she hadn't asked which couple were involved although, in the light of what she'd just seen and heard, it didn't take much guesswork to determine who they could be. As if she didn't have enough to worry about without rumours linking the Najarans with Muslim terrorists spreading through the party.

By the time Fiona returned to her table, the singer and her accompanist were up on the podium. They cut striking figures dressed in rich royal blue, silk shirts and the same black trousers and skirt as the night before.

Devesh tapped his foot in time with the music. 'Would you think us very rude if we abandoned you for the dance floor, Fiona?'

'Please do.'

The Indian couple were excellent dancers and though they returned when the number ended, it was evident they would dearly have liked to stay on their feet.

Conversation proved difficult and after trying to make themselves heard above the noise for a few more minutes, Fiona pleaded a headache and excused herself. She climbed the stairs to the third floor with a sense of relief. An early night would do her shattered nerves no harm at all.

Having come to the end of a chapter, she put down her book. As she tried to find the bedside light switch, there was a knock at the door. A tearful Elspeth hovered in the doorway.

'I'm sorry. You were in bed.'

'It doesn't matter. Come in.'

Fiona put an arm around Elspeth and guided her to the cane armchair where she sat perched on the edge. Fiona pulled the edges of her dressing gown more tightly around herself and sat on the bed opposite her visitor.

'How did you get on? Did you manage to speak to Vivien?'

Elspeth shook her head and stared down at her hands clenching and unclenching in her lap. 'It was all a waste of time really. She's still there but they won't tell me anything. Barry asked if she'd been given a solicitor but the officer at the desk said as she hadn't been charged she didn't need one.'

'Can they do that?'

'That's exactly what we said.'

'So what next?'

'Barry says there's nothing more we can do tonight. But what can we do?'

'I've no idea how these things work in England let alone Germany. All I can suggest is to get in touch with the British Embassy. There must be someone there who can at least point us in the right direction.'

The prospect of being able to do something positive brought a tentative smile to the woman's face and Fiona sent her on her way at least more reassured than when she'd arrived. Just what help the embassy could provide was quite another matter, Fiona thought ruefully. But that would have to wait until the morning.

4 Wednesday

*Our drive today takes us along the spec-
tacular Rhine Valley with its breathtaking
views. Looming above the dramatic gorge is a
line of massive castles built by medieval rob-
ber barons to extort taxes from passing mer-
chants and traders. From Bingen to Bonn
there were no less than twenty-eight castles
including fifteen customs stations – the greatest concentration of castles to be found anywhere in the world.*

*We will see the famous Lorelei Rock where
the mythical water nymph is said to have
lured passing sailors onto the rocks with her
seductive music.*

*The ferry will take us across the river to the
charming town of St Goar, home to the
world's largest cuckoo clock. We journey
north to the spa town of Boppard said by the
Romans to be the "Pearl of the Rhine" because
of its therapeutic saltwater springs. There will
be time to explore the narrow streets of its
picturesque historic quarter before lunch after
which we take a cruise along the river.*

Super Sun Executive Travel

Ten

After a surprisingly restful night, Fiona woke feeling more optimistic. Once Vivien had recovered sufficiently to talk to the police, this dreadful situation would be resolved.

The departure time for the day's excursion was not until nine o'clock so Fiona was surprised to see a huddle of her passengers gathered in the dining room when she came down just before seven.

She was about to wish them all good morning when she noticed the serious expressions on the faces now turned towards her. Her heart sank. She knew exactly what was coming.

'Fiona did you know that poor man was murdered?' Edith Webster's voice rose to a wail. She could hardly tell them she was doing her damnedest to forget the fact not to mention the whole gory scene that went with it.

In the excited hubbub that followed, Fiona found it difficult to make herself heard. Urging them to lower their voices she ushered them up the small flight of steps to the Super Sun area out of the hearing of other hotel clients.

'I assume the company are making arrangements for us all to go home.' Sidney Pettit glared at her accusingly.

'Do you really think that's necessary?' Fiona wanted to tell the man to pull himself together and stop acting like an hysterical schoolgirl.

'With a murderer on the loose! Isn't it irresponsible to leave us here and put all our lives in jeopardy?'

'Oh I don't think there's any chance of that, dear,' Daphne quickly intervened patting his arm before Fiona had a chance

79

to think of a reply. 'If the police have already arrested his wife, I can't see the rest of us are in any danger.'

This was not the time for Fiona to say no charges had yet been brought against Vivien. In which case, assuming they were still collecting evidence, the police might not allow them leave the area.

'But we can't simply continue as though nothing has happened.' Sidney was not to be so easily mollified.

'By all means, if that's what you want, I'll look up the flight times and arrange for a taxi to take you to the airport.' Fiona gave him a reassuring smile. 'If your travel insurance won't cover the cost when you return home, the company may offer you some compensation given the circumstances.'

'Why can't we use the coach? I'm sure we all want to go back.' He glanced around the small group looking for support only to be met by blank stares and dubious expressions.

'Would we be compensated for the loss of our holiday?' Rita asked.

Fiona frowned. 'The company would be under no obligation if you made the decision to return. I think it would be difficult to argue that tourists in this area are under any threat when no other companies are taking their parties home.'

The muttering began again and several people drifted away to their tables. Despite his wife's capitulation, Sidney was not prepared to loose the high ground so easily.

There was a stubborn set to his jaw as he turned to Fiona and said, 'Well, I still think we should go home.'

'In that case, as soon as I've had my breakfast, I'll ring Frankfurt airport for you.'

'Frankfurt!' Sidney's face was a picture. Fiona had to stop herself from laughing out loud at his wide-eyed look of horror.

'Well yes. You're lucky. Not only is it the nearest, it's one of the biggest in Europe so there're bound to be direct flights to London.' After all the fuss the man had caused, Fiona could not resist making the most of the situation.

'But that's where the bomb went off!' Sidney's voice rose to a screech.

'Not in the airport.'

'But it said on the news they'd set up added security in the airport and they wouldn't do that if they weren't expecting trouble.' The truculence had returned.

Fiona smiled sweetly and bit back the instinct to point out if the danger were that great they would close it down all together. 'Well let me know what you decide. Now if you'll forgive me, I must have a word with Winston about the details for today.'

It was not a lie but it was a convenient excuse. Every morning they would run through the day's itinerary together checking the timings for each of the planned stops, although the vagaries of traffic and weather conditions often meant last minute adjustments.

She slid onto the bench opposite the big West Indian and breathed a sigh of relief.

'Well done, sweetheart!' he said dropping his voice to a whisper and giving her a friendly wink. No matter how grey the skies or close the storm clouds loomed, she could always rely on Winston's sunny smile. 'You handled that like a trouper.'

'You heard all that?'

'Oh yes. Well, we knew it had to come out eventually.'

'True. But I had hoped it wouldn't be quite so soon.'

'I heard them all talking last night. I tried to warn you but they got in first. Did you get a chance to speak to that poor lady's sister and her husband when they got back last night?'

'Only briefly. Not that there was any news. The police are still holding Vivien for questioning though she hasn't been arrested.'

'The story goes she and him had a big bust up about the way he'd been carryin' on with that fair-haired young missy. Not the first time they've had a set-to this holiday about him playing away apparently. Someone overheard the two of them arguing in a café in Cologne when she accused him of gettin' up to his old tricks. Said she'd had enough and, if he didn't behave himself, she'd stick a knife in him. That's what they told the police apparently.'

'My goodness me!' Fiona's eyes widened in horror. 'Do you know who that person was?'

'Not exactly. It was a woman's voice back there.' He pointed a thumb over his shoulder indicating the table behind.

Fiona frowned. So Hilary Kasar, Edith Webster or Rita Lambert must be the culprit. 'How on earth did they find out about Graham being stabbed?'

'Word soon gets round, sweetheart. You can bet the contents of your piggy bank they've been talking about little else since it happened.'

'Her sister is convinced that Vivien is innocent,' Fiona protested.

'She would be, wouldn't she?'

Fiona felt deflated. If even the easy-going Winston, who never had a bad word to say against anyone, thought poor Vivien was guilty then no wonder the German police weren't looking for other suspects. If it were true, a murderous threat, on top of Graham's flirting with Cressida, was all the evidence they would need.

'Besides, sweetheart, as long as they all think his wife did him in, they won't be worried about a murderer on the loose now will they?'

Fiona looked into the deep brown eyes and managed a rueful smile. 'You're right as always.'

'That's my girl.' He patted her hand.

Dear Winston. He always managed to lighten her spirits. Time to change the subject. 'It's a pity it's so overcast this morning. Do you think it will clear up later or are we in for some rain?'

'Your guess is as good as mine, sweetheart. We'll keep our fingers crossed. Now, must be off. Need to give the coach the once-over before we start.'

Winston threw back the last of his coffee and left Fiona to finish her breakfast.

She stared at the half-eaten slice of dark crusty rye bread, but suddenly she had lost her appetite. She knew she would have to speak to Elspeth soon, but she definitely wasn't looking forward to the prospect. Apart from anything else, she was fresh out of platitudes. She poured herself another cup of tea.

Knowing she could put it off no longer, Fiona put her dirty crockery together and got to her feet. Fixing a reassuring smile to her lips, she moved round the partition.

Elspeth looked haggard. She must have aged a good ten years in the last twenty-four hours.

'You are still going to phone the embassy for us, aren't you?' Elspeth had no time for the niceties.

'Shouldn't we wait to see if the police are going to release her first?' Fiona appealed to Barry who appeared far less happy with the idea than his wife.

'But you promised.' Elspeth voice rose to a wail. That was news to Fiona but, given the state Elspeth was in, she could hardly protest.

'If that's what you still want me to do, of course I will,' Fiona said quickly to pacify her.

'They're bound to pay more attention to someone official rather than me or Barry.'

'Look, love.' Barry took his wife's hand. 'I keep telling you not to pin too much on this. 'Even the British Embassy can't go barging in demanding her release.'

'But we can tell them exactly what happened.'

Barry shook his head. 'We don't know what happened, love.'

'Someone else obviously went in after we all came down for breakfast.'

'We heard the row earlier, yes. Everyone in the hotel must have done the way those two were at it, but neither of us actually saw Graham that morning.'

'But we both heard him say he'd be down in a minute when Vivien asked if he was coming.'

There was a pause. 'You did. I was still in our room if you remember.'

'You make it sound as though you think she did it!' Elspeth

glared at him, fury blazing in her eyes.

'That's not what I'm saying, love.'

Fiona wondered if she should leave. Any minute now, one or other of them would pull her into the argument.

'Look, Elspeth. We have to face the fact the evidence against Vivien is pretty damming. The two of them hadn't stopped arguing from the moment we left the ferry. She even threatened him at one point.'

'But she didn't mean it! It's just something you say when you're angry. And God knows he drove her to it. You didn't tell the police what she said did you?'

'Of course not, Elspeth. What do you think I am?'

So it was true. Fiona wondered if she should let them know the police had already been told.

'After that appalling business with his secretary, you'd have thought he'd have known better. I told her she should have chucked him out long ago. She was a fool to believe his empty promises.' Elspeth shook her head violently. 'Why did she ever go back to him?'

'By all means let's talk to the embassy and ask their advice,' Barry's voice was conciliatory but his patience was rapidly running out. 'Whatever you do, pumpkin, don't start making up evidence or Vivien won't be the only one in trouble with the police.'

'It's still a bit early yet but how about I find the numbers to call and meet you in half an hour?' Fiona put a hand on Elspeth's shoulder, nodded to Barry and made her retreat.

It took several phone calls, first to Berlin and Munich and eventually Düsseldorf before Fiona eventually found someone prepared to listen to the full story of what had happened. Although the person she spoke to seemed sympathetic, apart from taking Vivien's details and promising to make enquiries, he had little to offer in the way of concrete help.

'Do you think it's actually worth going to the consulate? Sometimes you need to make a nuisance of yourself before these people pay any attention.' Elspeth desperately clutched at any crazy idea wafting in her direction.

Before Barry could say anything to widen the gulf growing between them, Fiona intervened. 'That really isn't a good idea, and besides Düsseldorf is a long way north. The man I spoke to assured me they would do everything that can be done. That is their job. He promised to get in touch as soon as there was any news. All we can do now is to leave everything in their hands.'

Perhaps she was wrong to put such an optimistic slant on what he'd said, but she had to leave Elspeth with some hope.

'Thank you for everything, Fiona. Elspeth and I really appreciate the trouble you've taken, don't we love?' Barry put an arm around his wife's shoulder.

'No problem but, if you'll both forgive me, I must go now or I'll be late.' Fiona hovered trying to find the appropriate words. It was pointless to tell Elspeth not to worry. 'I'm sure everything will be sorted very soon.'

James was still on the phone when Laura came out of the bathroom.

'Was that the Commander again?'

'No. It was the guy from the embassy I talked to yesterday. He says he's just had an earful from the tour manager complaining Vivien Spelman is still being held for questioning by the local police. She's demanding the embassy people do something about it straight away.'

'So why is he bothering you with it?'

'Because I asked him to keep me informed of any developments, though I must admit I can't see how this is relevant.'

'I thought you said it was Vivien's sister kicking up a fuss.'

'She and her husband turned up at the police station yesterday. I presume she's now persuaded this other woman to help fight her corner.'

'But wasn't it the tour manager who found Vivien with the body?'

'That's why she's convinced Vivien couldn't have done it, because there wasn't enough time according to her. The two women left the dining room together but the tour manager took her time coming up the stairs.'

'How long does it take to stick a knife into a man's ribs?' Laura snorted.

'True, but there was no sound of any struggle and it does take a few minutes to bleed to death. Plus, she claimed the body was cold when she got there.'

'So the wife stabbed him before she left the room. You said yesterday, several people reported hearing the two of them having a good old ding-dong. Things could have got out of hand and, when she realized she'd be arrested for murder, she had to cover her tracks and pretend to find him when she came back. I know the Commander said to keep an open mind but logically, who else could it have been? No one else saw him that morning.'

'Apart from the clothes she was wearing when she was found with the body, there's no blood on the rest of her things. She couldn't have done it without being covered in the stuff and then gone down to breakfast without changing. Apart from the couple of minutes travelling up in the lift, she was never alone after leaving her room with her sister.'

'So the tour manager got the time wrong or she's covering up for some reason.'

James shrugged his shoulders. 'In the mean time, I suppose I'd better let the Commander know. By all accounts, he's met this tour manager before.'

'Surely if she had a hand in Graham Spelman's death she wouldn't be trying to protect the wife? What would she hope to gain by doing that? Unless they were in it together.'

'No. I don't think she's involved. There's no evidence connecting them before the trip. From what he said, the woman's not one of the bad guys. I can't remember his exact words but he smiled when he saw her name and said something about her not being one to stay on the sidelines, whatever that means. Told me not to underestimate her.'

Laura sighed. 'Very little of this whole business makes sense to me. If you and the Commander are right in thinking Graham Spelman was trying to do a deal with Muslim radicals behind his partner's back, who killed the go-between and why? Even if Spelman had a change of heart, it can't have been him. The man was blown up before the coach party left Dover.'

'Someone who didn't want the deal to go ahead presumably.'

'Is that what the Commander thinks?'

James pulled a face. 'If the Commander has any thoughts on the matter, I doubt he'd share them with me. Besides, it's one of his maxims; speculation makes you twist the facts to suit the theory if you're not careful.'

'So what are we supposed to do now? Go over to Assmannshausen to speak to this tour manager? I suppose I can kiss goodbye to seeing the sights of Wiesbaden you promised me?'

'Sorry, love.' James stood up and bent to kiss the top of her head. 'Let's see what the Commander says first. You never know we might get lucky.'

Eleven

Several of the small gaggle of people that had accosted Fiona at breakfast still had glum faces as they climbed onto the coach but the rest appeared to have put yesterday's tragedy behind them and were ready to enjoy themselves despite the weather. Fiona watched Cressida crossing the narrow road to the coach with a touch of apprehension. Perhaps she still hadn't heard the circumstances of Graham's death and Fiona wondered how the girl would take the news. Neither she nor Holly was their normal giggly selves but they both looked more hung-over than distressed. No surprise. Like most young women, those two knew how to enjoy themselves in the evenings much to the disgust of the several of the older members of the party.

Predictably, the last to arrive were Elspeth and Barry. No doubt a deliberate ploy to prevent a barrage of questions or well-meaning but unwelcome sympathy.

Fiona made a quick resolution to do her best to protect the couple as much as she could but, for the next few hours, the rest of her passengers were her main concern. Time to check her notes. At least today, there were no guided walks to worry about. All she had to do was read out the notes she'd prepared back home. Best to keep up the flow she decided. Give them something more pleasant to think about than dwelling on what had happened.

'As you probably already know, the Middle-Rhine Valley is a UNESCO World Heritage site. Now if you look across the river, just below Castle Reichenstein, that pretty white and pink church is Clemens Chapel built in the 13th century and is one of the oldest churches along the Rhine.'

The cameras were out and clicking and an excited chatter started up behind her. Grey, overcast skies had leeched the colour from the landscape, sucking the life from the vibrant emerald slopes to a muddy sage. Following her excellent diagrammatic map, which included small drawings of each of the castles, Fiona identified the first half dozen sombre fortresses on the far bank without difficulty.

'Burg Stahleck was first mentioned in 1135. Originally in the possession of the Cologne Archbishops, Emperor Frederick Barbarossa gave the castle to his brother Konrad. His daughter, Agnes, secretly married her childhood love, Henry of Welfen who was the son of Henry the Lion . . .'

The gathering clouds made the castles seem more menacing than magical and after they'd passed the first half dozen, the only person who seemed much interested in their history was Ernest Blake. He had come well prepared with a guidebook so perhaps it was time to ease up on the detail.

Interest perked up again when they reached the picturesque, pink-and-white Pfalzgrafenstein Fortress resplendent on a rocky island in the middle of the river.

'Built to look like a ship making its way upstream, as you can appreciate this is one of the most beautiful of the Rhine castles. The rocky promontory and swift current make it virtually impregnable so it was never taken and is one of only two fortresses that have remained intact in the valley. You'll have a chance to take some even closer shots this afternoon when we're on our cruise.'

The next castle to dominate the skyline was little more than ruins, but her audience perked up whenever she began recounting one of the local legends. Luckily, this part of the Rhine abounded in fantastic myths.

'There are a series of rocks known as the Seven Maidens just under the surface of this next stretch of river. The rocks mark the spot where certain prudish young women were turned into stone because they resisted the advances of their suitors.'

'Quite right too,' came a cry from the back, which produced whistles and shouts of approval from the men and noisy mock protests from the women.

'It's a story all the ardent young men hereabouts are supposed to tell their lady friends in the hope,' her voice took on a seductive note, 'it will persuade them to succumb to their charms.' Laughter broke out and even Elspeth managed a wan smile.

'Very soon we'll be coming up to the famous Lorelei Rock. There are several versions of this legend but they all involve a beautiful maiden who fell in love with a young knight who left to go to war. In his absence, her legendary beauty attracted many suitors but she remained faithful to her true love and, when he failed to return, threw herself headlong into the river in despair. She was transformed into a siren and, perched on the rock combing her long flaxen tresses, she lured sailors to their deaths with her hypnotic singing. The legend probably arose because so many boats foundered in this dangerous stretch of river. Here the Rhine is forced into its narrowest point as it cuts a 180 degree bend around the resistant granite outcrop of the Lorelei rock increasing the current and making it difficult to navigate.'

Winston brought the coach to a halt in the small parking area at the top of the rock. It was impossible for Fiona to keep an eye on everyone as they moved between the viewing points to peer down into the valley below. The more intrepid even ventured further round beyond the railing to look upstream.

'The views are spectacular from here. Quite breathtaking. Do come and look, Rita,' urged her husband. 'You can see a train disappearing into the tunnel.'

'Umm. I can see from here thank you, darling. And I'd rather you didn't go any further.'

'It's perfectly safe,' Ian assured her.

Rita Lambert wasn't the only one wary of getting too close to the precipitous edge. Even Fiona was relieved when the time came for her to herd everyone back onto the bus.

Watching the antics of more adventurous determined to get a better shot had brought her heart into her mouth. British Health and Safety officers would have a field day out here. It would not take much, just an extra stretch to compose a better picture, for one of them to go hurtling to the bottom. She already had one death on her hands and the last thing she needed was another.

The phone lines between London and Germany had been hot all morning. The frustration was beginning to show. Patience and composure might well be two of the Commander's most notable qualities, but the continual delays were pushing even him to the limit. The tension was palpable. The other occupants of the top floor looked warily at each other, fearing the worst. It might be a rare event but, when the Commander lost his temper, everybody suffered.

A young officer came up from the floor below and made his way purposefully to the chief's door with a memo concerning the next Joint Chiefs of Staff meeting. He looked surprised and then affronted when two of his more experienced colleagues leapt into his path and all but pinned him down. His protests fell on deaf ears. He was sent away, still clutching the relevant sheet of paper, and told to come back later. Much later.

There were no bridges across this stretch of the Rhine and to get to the far bank they had to take the ferry from St Goarshausen. Although the sun still stubbornly refused to put in appearance, the skies had lightened considerably and spirits were high.

'From this side we have a better view of Katz Castle built to outshine its puny neighbour, Maus Castle which you can see further downstream.'

'Cat and Mouse Castles,' Holly piped up with childish enthusiasm, which made everyone laugh.

'Exactly. The next two castles, Liebenstein and Sterrenberg, built by two brothers are also quite close together as you'll see in a minute or two. The fronts of the castles known as the

Warring Brothers actually face each other and are separated by a high wall. The two fell out when they both fell in love with their father's ward. Some say it's simply a myth but others claim it's a true story.'

Fiona was pleased to see the occasional patch of watery blue sky managing to break through the blanket of grey cloud as the twin, white-and-grey towers of St Severus Church came into view and the coach drove into Boppard, another of the Rhineland tourist. At least her passengers would have a chance to explore the town without getting soaked to the skin.

Before they left the coach, Fiona listed some of the highlights they might like visit such as the remains of the Roman military camp, the church, the Carmelite Monastery and the town's museum in the Electoral Castle.

'What about the shops?' Rita's priorities were quickly established.

'The best place to start is probably the Market Square. Just head for the church. And finally, everyone,' her voice rose above the chatter that had broken out, 'please be back here on time so we're not late for lunch.'

Winston opened both doors to allow the party off the coach. Everyone began to drift away until only Hilary and Viktor Kasar remained standing at the edge of the car park.

'How's the ankle now?'

'Well on the mend thanks, Fiona. Viktor's quite keen to look round the fort but I think that might be a bit much for me still. I'm going to find a café and leave him to it.'

'I know Sidney and Daphne were planning to take a sightseeing tour on one of the little tourist trains. You could do the same.'

'Is that like the toy train we saw in Rudesheim?' Her eyes lit up. 'That could be fun. Do you know where it starts?'

'I believe there's a pick up point in the main square. It's not far and you can take your time.'

When the call from the BND eventually came through, the Commander snatched up the phone immediately.

'Sorry to keep you waiting,' said the dispassionate voice in a harsh Teutonic accent. 'It took some time to track down the two officers who conducted the initial search. They confirm what the local police chief told us earlier. The crime scene was thoroughly investigated and nothing untoward was found. No laptop, no computer disks, no documents. As you requested, they confirmed the adjacent room was also searched.'

'I do not question their thoroughness or their integrity, but their priorities were concerned with finding evidence in a murder case. The relevance of seemingly unrelated items might easily have been overlooked given the serious nature of the crime.'

'I take your point, but there is little more I can do.'

The Commander waited and let the silence continue for some time. Eventually his German counterpart sighed. 'You want me to send one of my own men.' It was a statement not a question.

'That would be helpful.'

'The local police are never happy when they feel the Bundesnachrichtendienst breathing down their necks.' The Intelligence Chief gave a sigh. 'You owe me, Commander.'

The Commander gave a slow smile. 'Your cooperation is much appreciated.'

The small restaurant was busy and the tables closely packed together. Lunch was a buffet meal and Fiona stood back waiting for the mêlée to sort itself out. Gloria was sitting with Hilary and Viktor Kasar and another chair had been pulled up for Ernest Blake at the table with the four older members of the party so she need have no worries about anyone sitting on their own.

Smoked meats were not really Fiona's thing so she bypassed the salamis, liverwurst and cold sausages and went to the selection of cheeses and breads which to judge from the enticing aroma had been freshly baked. Although the earlier promise of sun had now disappeared and the skies had clouded over again, some people had opted to take their plates out into the small garden at the back. Once she'd checked all was well inside, Fiona decided to join them. After sitting in the coach all morning, she could do with some fresh air.

Cressida and Holly had abandoned the Super Sun party and teamed up with half a dozen people nearer their own age sprawling on the grass or on benches under the trees the far end of the gardens. Fiona wasn't sure if they were strangers or if the girls had met them in the hotel bar back in Assmannshausen the previous evening. The way Cressida was giggling with the square-jawed, blond young man sitting next to her did not suggest they had only just met. The two were hip to hip but, in justice to them both, there were several people trying to squeeze onto the bench. If the girl had any lingering grief at Graham's passing, the man certainly wasn't in her thoughts at the moment. Fiona watched as several of the boys started to throw a frisbee between them. Holly soon joined them, bouncing about like an untrained puppy. At least the girls appeared happy enough.

Whether it was the vague hint of drizzle or the noisy young people who had driven them back in, there were fewer people at the outside tables than Fiona had expected. The Glovers had tucked themselves away at a corner table. Her first instinct was to join them but, given the circumstances, she doubted they were in the mood for social chitchat. On the other hand, constantly brooding about a situation which they were powerless to alter was hardy a desirable alternative. Barry glanced up and caught her eye. He gave her a smile and beckoned her over. Problem solved.

To be fair to Elspeth, even she made an effort.

'That pink and white boat shaped castle in the river was pretty wasn't it? I think that's my favourite so far.' It was good to know not everything had passed her by. 'And weren't the views from the top of the Lorelei Rock magnificent. Barry took lots of pictures, didn't you, dear?'

They chatted on for a few minutes, but it was not long before Elspeth lapsed back into a lethargic melancholia leaving the other two to keep up the conversation. She picked up her mobile lying on the table in front of her and began fiddling with it nervously. Barry tried to take it from her but she snatched it back.

'Why hasn't she rung?' Her voice was near breaking and any minute Fiona expected her to burst into tears. 'I've left dozens of messages.'

'Then there's nothing more you can do, pumpkin.' Barry tried to be reasonable but his patience was clearly wearing thin. 'If she wants to speak to you, she'll call.'

'What do you mean, if?' Elspeth turned on him. 'You know how close we are. We tell each other everything.'

'You used to.' The sudden coldness in his voice surprised Fiona.

Elspeth stared at him. Her bottom lip quivered. All her anger had turned to what? Defeat? Remorse? Fiona had no way of knowing. Tentatively Elspeth put her hand on her husband's arm. For a few seconds he continued to stare resolutely ahead, a frown still clouding his forehead.

'Barry?' Elspeth's voice was little more than a whisper.

He gave a deep sigh then put his hand over hers in a conciliatory gesture.

It was Elspeth herself who broke the embarrassed silence that followed. 'I'll go and spend a penny before there's a queue.'

They watched her retreating figure before Barry turned to Fiona and said apologetically. 'All this is taking a toll on Elspeth and to be honest I'm at a loss to know what to do or say. She's been on that mobile all morning. When she's not leaving messages and texts for Vivien she's on to the police station. Not that she'll get any joy there.'

'It's all very understandable.'

'She's already in pieces and I'm terrified of what might happen when they actually get round to charging Vivien.'

'Do you think they will?'

'Can you think of any other reason why they haven't released her?'

'You sound as though you believe she did it.'

'She's my sister-in-law. She could never do such a thing.' The words came quickly enough, but Barry didn't sound convinced. He shook his head and wiped a hand over his face.

They lapsed back into silence. Fiona pulled out her mobile. No messages. Marthe had promised to let her know if any news came through to the hotel but clearly, there had been no contact from the police. It wouldn't hurt to ring them directly. Let them realize the rest of Vivien's family and the tour company were not prepared to be kept in the dark like this. It was over twenty-four hours since they'd taken Vivien away and there'd been no information since. It was probably still too early to get back to the embassy but once she'd phoned the police, it wouldn't hurt to check they were also putting on the pressure. Make sure they weren't just making sympathetic noises only to sit back and do nothing.

Twelve

The skies grew dark again as they made their way to the quayside where the cruise boats were lined up.

Is that ours?' asked Celia Ennis as they approached a large white vessel with four decks.

'I expect that one's going some distance. Up to the Moselle perhaps. Ours is further down, the one at the end of the third pier.' Fiona pointed to a boat less than half the size. Even so, it took two or three hundred passengers although the weather seemed to have reduced the waiting queues. It looked as though there would be plenty of room for them all to wander around once they were onboard.

Although the majority of the party decided to struggle up the narrow steps to the upper deck to enjoy the best views, apart from some of the keen photographers, only the younger members opted to go out on the sun deck. Fiona found a window seat and sat down. At least for the next couple of hours, she could sit back and relax.

She watched as Devesh and Anita Najaran came up the far set of steep steeps. There were several clusters of Super Sun folk gathered together, but none of them invited the Indian couple to join them. Fiona frowned. Why the sudden hostility? It couldn't be racial prejudice because even Celia and Joe Ellis seemed to be giving the couple the cold shoulder and they had all seemed very friendly at the start of the holiday. The explanation probably had more to do with the constant television reports about possible terrorist activity. It was a good bet, Fiona thought ruefully, Sidney Pettit was fanning the flames of alarm aided and abetted by his wife and Len and Edith Webster. How anyone could consider the mild, considerate Najarans as Muslim activists was a mystery to Fiona. As far as she knew, they were Indian Hindus and had no connections with Pakistan at all.

The dreary greyness of day did little to enhance their journey and they had been travelling upstream for almost an hour before Fiona ventured outside. The steady breeze, although not particularly strong, was chill enough to encourage her to stay on her feet and take a slow meander round the rails taking in the views from all directions. After a quarter of an hour, she decided she'd had enough and went back in for a coffee.

The small café was down on the lower deck. Several of the Super Sun party were sitting around chatting but it seemed more claustrophobic below so Fiona carried her small tray back up the narrow stairs.

The upper deck was getting more crowded. The persistent light drizzle had brought inside all but the hardiest trippers from the sun deck. Fiona looked up to see Kathleen Murphy coming through the doors. They caught each other's gaze and smiled.

'On your own? Do come and join me. There aren't many seats left up here.'

Kathleen shrugged out of her anorak, shook off the worst of the wet and hung it over the back of her seat.

'It's not nice out there anymore but I couldn't persuade Brendan to come in. He's still busy taking photos, but he's going to get soaked, silly man.' Despite the words, Kathleen sounded more worried about her husband than impatient.

She looked back over her shoulder staring through the glass doors to a lone figure standing by the railing on the port side.

'He's a keen photographer is he?'

'Not particularly. And it isn't as if there's much out there to take at the moment.' Kathleen sighed. 'I don't know what's wrong with him. He's been really out of sorts the last couple of days. I've never known him so quiet, but every time I ask what's wrong, he says it's nothing. He was quite cross with me at lunchtime and that's not like him at all. I do hope he's not coming down with something. You know what these men are like.'

Fiona gave a sympathetic smile. Even she had noticed how subdued the man had been of late. A quiet man who'd been happy to socialize with the rest of the party on the first couple of evenings but now he seemed distracted most of the time and was rapidly turning into something of a loner.

'Perhaps it's all the travelling tired him out. It always takes a great deal more out of you than you expect.'

'In that case, he should have chosen somewhere closer to home like we usually do.' It wasn't like Kathleen to snap. 'Oh, I'm sorry m' dear. You're giving us a great time and despite the rain, it's been a lovely trip. It's just I don't understand why we had to come here of all places. Most years we go over to Kerry or up to Dublin where we've got family. We've made occasional trips to England. Places like the Lake District, the New Forest and the Peaks. Country places, you know. And this is very scenic. We're not really town people. I thought he was pulling m' leg when he suggested this. But then, that's men for you.'

Fiona looked up to see Brendan pushing his way through the glass doors. 'Here he comes now.'

Brendan's smile seemed genuine enough as he sat down next to his wife. Fiona kept up a line of inconsequential chatter for a minute or two and then made her apologies.

'We'll be coming into Boppard quite soon. Forgive me if I leave you two and check everyone is ready.'

Winston had driven the coach up from the car park to wait at the end of their pier. Just as well. The rain was getting heavier and, though everyone had Macs or umbrellas, they would have been soaked after the ten-minute walk to where the coach had been parked.

It was still raining by the time they reached St Goar.

'Not much point making a stop here, is there?' Winston said

quietly to Fiona.

Fiona shook her head. 'Not really. We'll get drenched. It was only going to be a half hour stroll down the main road anyway. We'll give the world's largest cuckoo clock a miss. Still, what they don't know about, they won't grieve over as the saying goes. I don't think anyone will be sorry to get back to the hotel.'

'Rightyho. Perhaps they'll be time for a stop another day.'

Fiona slipped the pleated skirt over her head and put on the matching flower print blouse. She stared at her reflection in the mirror and frowned. They made her look even more middle-aged and frumpy than ever. Why had she ever bought them? The most expensive things in her wardrobe and without the dusky pink, tailored jacket, they did absolutely nothing for her. They'd been a hasty buy. She'd needed something for Adam Junior's christening but Bill had been going through a bad patch at the time and they'd been no time to linger. She hardly ever wore the outfit; it reminded her too much of the bad times, but the skirt and blouse were the only things in her wardrobe which wouldn't crease after so long in the suitcase. Besides, she'd told herself she could mix and match the two with other tops and trousers.

No use mooning about here. She wound the stray lock of hair that insisted on curling the wrong way around the styling brush. The unexpected buzz of the phone brought Fiona back from her reverie. She pushed herself to her feet and crossed the room to the bedside table.

'Fiona Mason.'

'Reception here, madam. I have a gentleman at the desk who would like to speak to you.'

'I'll be down in ten minutes.'

'I will inform him. Thank you, madam.'

So much for that restful hour to herself. Which of her many charges had a problem now? It couldn't be Barry; he would've come straight to her room. Had Sidney lost his spectacles again? Or perhaps Hilary was still having problems with that ankle and Viktor needed Fiona's help. Whoever it was would have to wait until she'd finished taming her hair and making herself presentable.

Marthe looked up and smiled as Fiona approached. 'The gentleman is waiting for you in the bar, madam.'

Turning back to the main corridor, Fiona almost bumped into Rita Lambert.

'So glad I caught you, Fiona. May I have a quick word?'

Fiona cut in quickly, 'I'm really sorry but, actually, I am busy at the moment. Could we talk later? It's not urgent is it?'

Rita's top lip puckered into a thousand tiny creases and daggers flashed in the small, narrowed eyes. 'Well no, but . . .'

'Then straight after dinner. I promise.'

Looking distinctly affronted, Rita stalked off, heading for the stairs.

Much more of this Fiona thought and she would scream. She was already tired and irritable and at this rate, the next person to cross her would end up getting an earful.

There was only one person in the lounge bar when she walked in. He sat in the far corner, a tray of tea on the small table in front of him. At the sound of her heels on the wooden dance floor, he looked up and rose to his feet. Tall, imposing, immaculately dressed in a grey, three-piece suit a few shades darker than the silver hair, with the distinctive watch chain across his waistcoat. The last person in the world she expected to see. The very last.

'Mrs Mason. Thank you for seeing me.' The familiar baritone had lost none of its public-school, cut-glass precision.

She put out a hand to take his as he towered above her. 'Mr Montgomery-Jones. Or should I say, Commander?'

After a half-second pause, he replied. 'Most people call me sir.'

'In your dreams!'

There was no answering smile in the pale grey eyes looking at her intently. Not even a twitch of the lips to match her bubble of laughter. Surely the man hadn't been serious? Embarrassment gave way annoyance. If he thought she'd apologize, he could think again. They didn't come much more formal and proper than Peter Montgomery-Jones, but the man hadn't been quite such a pompous stuffed-shirt on the last occasion they'd met? True, they'd had their ups and downs in the Netherlands, but in the end, they'd worked well together. She'd even helped him solve his case.

He motioned her to a chair. 'I have ordered some tea for us both. May I pour you a cup?' Without waiting for an answer, he proceeded to lift the elegant silver teapot. 'Milk?'

'Please.'

Montgomery-Jones was not a man for social small talk but, whatever his reasons for being there, he did not seem in any hurry to get to the point of his visit.

'This is a surprise,' she said when she could no longer take the silence. 'I hope you're not here to tell me I have another smuggler amongst my party like last time?'

'Not to the best of my knowledge. No.'

'Then I take it you're here because of the death of Graham Spelman.'

His eyes met hers but they were impossible to read. 'You could say that.'

What was that supposed to mean? 'Are you here to investigate his murder?'

'No. That is entirely a matter for German police, although I understand you have been calling into question the way they have been conducting this case.'

Did he have to be quite so patronizing? 'So you've come to tell me to stop making waves.'

'I would not put it quite like that. Though I would ask for your co-operation.'

'Then my protests must be having some impact if you've been sent all this way.'

'I sent myself,' he said pointedly. The first glimmer of emotion he'd shown.

'Oh yes, I'm so sorry. I forgot you're the Big Cheese himself.' She glowered at him as she leant forward to place her cup and saucer back on the table. 'Elspeth Glover is convinced her sister is innocent and I will need some extremely good reasons as to why I should allow such an injustice to occur without protest.'

'This matter is not your concern.'

'I assure you,' she snapped, 'the wellbeing of all my passengers is very much my concern. My prime concern. Both Vivien and Elspeth are members of my party and it is my job to ensure they're properly looked after. You're asking me to condone the detention of an innocent woman.'

'I take it you are in a better position to ascertain that fact than the German police, are you?' There was no hint of sarcasm. In fact, there had been no emotion in his voice at all. His calm only served to make her feel more agitated.

'But she has an alibi. She and her sister were having breakfast together when Graham was stabbed.'

'Be that as it may, the police are of the opinion the murder took place before Mrs Spelman left the room immediately after a noisy altercation had been heard between them. By several witnesses, I might add.'

He was obviously up-to-date on all the details of the case even if he wasn't involved in it. Fiona was determined not to let him browbeat her. 'But Elspeth heard him speak just before Vivien went downstairs.'

'Her sister may assert she heard her brother-in-law's voice but her interpretation of what occurred is likely to be influenced by her desire to support Mrs Spelman.'

'So you're saying Elspeth is lying?' How dare the man make such an accusation? He'd never met the woman.

'Not at all,' he said calmly. 'But she is a prejudiced witness. And there is no one else who can confirm her statement. Mrs Mason, I would urge you and Mrs Glover to leave this matter in the hands of those who know what they are doing and I have to point out your interference can only antagonize the German authorities to no good purpose.'

'If that means trying to prevent an innocent woman from being sacrificed to preserve some diplomatic accord, my stirring is totally justified.'

'The woman must have made a considerable impression for you to be so convinced of her innocence in so short a time.'

Damn the man! She could hardly confess, apart from the odd word of greeting, she'd never had what could be called a proper conversation with Vivien. Nor, should he ask her directly, could she deny she'd witnessed a degree of tension between the married couple.

'I assure you, no one is being sacrificed as you put it. As I understand it, Mrs Spelman has not been charged as yet.'

'But the police aren't even considering any one else. There must be other suspects. Other people who had a motive.'

'Do you have someone in mind?'

'Sarcasm does not become you, Mr Montgomery-Jones.'

'That was not my intention, I assure you.' The impassive features broke into a hint of a smile. Now he was laughing at her. 'Your tea is getting cold.'

If he thought by changing the subject, she'd let the matter go, he was very much mistaken. 'Someone has to protest. The police can't continue to hold Vivien without charging her.'

'She is not locked in a prison cell. The German police have simply confiscated her passport and asked her to remain in the area.' Why did he have to be so calm and reasonable? 'It is Mrs Spelman herself who has no wish to return to this hotel.'

Obviously. The last place Vivien would want to be is back in the room where her husband died.

'Surely, there must be something you can do to help?'

'As I am sure the embassy would have told you already, we have no authority to investigate a crime or to intervene in the due process of law in a foreign country.'

'But you did in Holland.'

'No,' he continued in the same patient tones. 'It may have appeared so to you, Mrs Mason, but I was invited to be present at various police interviews only because I was working very closely with the Dutch forces at the time. It was a joint operation. An international operation. That is not the situation here. I cannot insist the German authorities allow my involvement. I am in their hands as much as you are. This is why I am asking you not to antagonize the German Police because it can only make matters more difficult for the embassy staff.'

Much as she appreciated his logic, she wasn't ready to give in so readily. She sat back, pretending to sip the now rapidly cooling tea. 'I promised Elspeth I would help her fight this.'

It was a moment or two before he broke the silence. 'I appreciate you have only recently met Mr and Mrs Spelman, but is there anything you have discovered about either of them might assist?'

'Such as?'

'Any background information. For example did they mention why they chose this particular holiday?'

'I gather it was a fairly last minute decision. Graham wanted to combine business and pleasure. He talked about possible opportunities in the wine industry.'

Montgomery-Jones looked surprised. 'Really?'

'He hoped to sell some equipment to the local producers.'

'Had he arranged any meetings?'

'I don't think it was anything specific.'

'I see.' Montgomery-Jones's eyes narrowed and he looked thoughtful. After a brief pause, he asked, 'Did he bring a briefcase or a laptop with him?'

'Not that I saw. No one did. At least not as hand luggage.'

'Obviously, I can make no promises, but you can assure Mrs Glover I will endeavour to ensure everything is done that can be for her sister.'

Her cup rattled in the saucer as she put them down on the table a little too forcefully. 'Fob them off, you mean.'

'Not at all.' There was a long silence`. Eventually, he said, 'If you wish, I will speak to her personally.'

'Fine.' Fiona jumped to her feet. 'I expect she and her husband are up in their room.'

Best not to give him a chance to change his mind. She was already halfway to the door when she turned and mumbled a belated, 'Thank you.'

Thirteen

Fiona could scarcely contain her fury as she strode down the corridor to the stairs. She stomped up each step, muttering, 'Pompous, patronizing, arrogant, infuriating, autocratic, self-important, condescending, egotistical, exasperating, pretentious, over-bearing ...' but she'd run out of words long before she'd reached the top of the first flight.

Why on earth had she let the man provoke her? She'd made a complete idiot of herself. It hadn't helped that he'd remained calm and so bloody reasonable in the face of her histrionics. She was a grown woman for heaven's sake and she'd behaved like a spoilt child. It was so out of character. What was it about the man that he managed to reduce her to such a state? Nobody else ever had that effect on her. And on top of everything else, she'd probably ruined whatever remote chance she'd had of enlisting his help with the German authorities.

It wasn't as if she didn't have doubts herself. Despite her earlier insistence that Vivien couldn't have had time to murder her husband, she had no proof that Vivien hadn't stabbed him before she came down to breakfast. After the murder, Fiona had been prepared to accept that as the most likely scenario. It was only the highhanded attitude taken by the local police that had made her leap to Vivien's defence. And now, if she'd had any wavering thoughts on the matter, Montgomery-Jones had clinched it. Someone had to stick up for the woman.

Authority figures always put her on the defensive. Nine years of battling with petty officials in her attempts to obtain the treatments and benefits her terminally ill husband was entitled to had taught her to be wary of bureaucrats who thought they were gods. If she was the only one to support Elspeth in her battle to clear her sister's name then so be it. Battle she would.

As Fiona came down to dinner, she noticed Winston standing by the reception desk. He looked up, smiled and sauntered over.

'Everything okay, sweetheart? You look jiggered.'

Fiona gave a weak grin. 'I am a bit tired, I'll admit. It's been a long day.'

He put an arm around her shoulder and gave a gentle squeeze. 'That posh chap with the plumy voice hasn't been giving you grief again has he? He gets around don't he? First Holland now here.' The arrival of Peter Montgomery-Jones had evidently not gone unnoticed.

'Doesn't he just. If I didn't know better, I'd think I had a stalker.'

'Do you know what he's here for?'

'Not really, but it must have something to do with Graham Spelman's murder. He's been talking to the Glovers but he claims that he's not involved in the enquiry, so what else it could be I've no idea.'

'It's not our problem so let them sort it out and you stop fretting. Dinner time. Let's go and eat.'

Fiona was concerned when Elspeth and Barry didn't come down for dinner with everyone else. Surely, they couldn't still be talking to Montgomery-Jones? She was about to ask Marthe if there was any chance of the kitchen keeping something hot for them when the two appeared.

Fiona's relief turned to surprise when she saw the flash of anger on Elspeth's face when their eyes met. Whatever Montgomery-Jones had said had clearly not pleased Elspeth and there was every indication she held Fiona to blame. Barry's expression on the other hand was one of resignation. For the moment, however, there were other guests who needed her attention.

'Did you have a good day, Hilary?'

'Yes, ta. That tourist train was great. And I managed to find a chemist that stocked one of these proper ankle support things. Much more comfy. Which reminds me,' she rummaged in her capacious handbag and pulled out a small paper bag. 'I meant to give you these on the coach but I forgot. While I was in the there, I bought a bandage to replace the one you gave me and there's also a crepe bandage you can put in the first aid kit for future emergencies.'

'How thoughtful, though you really needn't have bothered. I'll pop them both in the box first thing tomorrow. I'm pleased to hear things are improving. We're going to Heidelberg tomorrow. There's a bit of walking around the castle but you can take it slowly.'

Half an hour later, everyone started to drift to the bar. Except, as Fiona could have predicted, for Elspeth and Barry who remained at their table.

Fiona barely had time to ease onto the padded bench opposite them before Elspeth accused, 'You had no right to tell that man what we told you in confidence.'

'I beg your pardon?'

'How dare you say Vivien threatened him and they were arguing before breakfast? And how else would he have known about Graham's secretary?' Elspeth put her head in her hands and her shoulders began to shake.

Barry tried to put a consoling arm around her but she shook him off.

'And you're no better.' She glared at her husband. 'Why couldn't you have backed me up about hearing Graham's voice?'

They'd obviously been through this conversation several times already because Barry made no attempt to refute the accusation.

Barry did not remain the focus of her wrath for long. Elspeth turned back to Fiona. 'You said you'd help and now look what you've done.'

'Other than saying you believe Vivien is innocent, in the couple of minutes I was with him, I told Mr Montgomery-Jones nothing. I wasn't there when you went down for breakfast and I don't know anything about a secretary.'

'She's right, love. Fiona's not to blame.'

Elspeth's keyed up frustration began to ebb as quickly as it had come.

Fiona leant across the table and took her hand. 'If Mr Montgomery-Jones appears to have all the background information, it's because that's his job and obviously he's already looking into the case. It's a good sign. Believe me, if anyone can help Vivien, he can. He knows exactly who to talk to in order to get results and he exerts a great deal of influence.'

'He did promise to go and see Vivien first thing in the morning,' Elspeth admitted in a small voice. 'He even said he'd try and arrange for us to go over and see her.'

'That can't be bad, can it?'

Fewer outsiders had wandered into the bar than on previous evenings and, despite the arrival of new hotel guests, the decibel level was less than usual.

When the couples at her table opted for an early night, Fiona decided she'd done her stint and could beat a retreat with a clear conscience. Only as she squeezed her way out from behind the table did she noticed a woebegone Barry Glover perched on a high stool at the small bar counter set back in a secluded corner. Sitting alone at a bar in that dejected state could only lead to one outcome. She would have to go over.

'Elspeth gone up already?'

'Oh hi, Fiona. Yes, I thought she'd drop off to sleep more quickly without me there. She'd only want to keep taking it over. Can I get you a drink?'

'Not for me, thanks.'

'We'd only end up arguing. I keep trying to tell her she's got to be realistic about all this and then I get an earful for not supporting her.'

'I hope that doesn't mean you intend to drown your sorrows.' Her light laugh belied her real concern.

He looked at her with a sheepish grin. 'Don't worry, Fiona. You're not going to have a belligerent drunk to contend with. Although thinking about it, it's bloody tempting. Elspeth's driving me crazy at the moment.'

'She's overwrought. It's been a difficult day. A good night's sleep will help her to put things in perspective.'

'I doubt that somehow. Once she gets an idea stuck in her head, she won't listen to reason. No matter what the evidence.'

'You make it sound as though you've changed your mind and Vivien did do it after all.'

Barry sighed and put down his glass. 'I honestly don't know anymore. Viv's got a temper. Just like Elspeth. But all my instincts tell me she could never do something like that. Trouble is who else could have done it?'

Fiona shook her head.

'It could hardly be a chance burglar at that time of the morning with everyone going backwards and forwards to breakfast?' He sighed. 'Things seem to be stacking up against Vivien. With all she had to put up with, no one can say she wasn't provoked. The man was an out-and-out rat. It wasn't just he couldn't keep his dick in his bloody trousers, he was a heartless bastard.'

The pent-up venom in Barry's outburst took Fiona completely by surprise. She was at a loss as to what to say. Barry threw back the last of his whisky, slammed his glass down on the counter and signalled the barman.

'Sure you won't have one?' He didn't even look at Fiona as he spoke.

'Not for me, thanks.' Dare she suggest he call it a night as well?

Barry sat staring at his empty glass, slowly pushing it from one hand to the other. 'He didn't even stop messing about after what happened to poor Bernie even though her death was down to him.'

110

'You don't mean he killed her?' Fiona's eyes widened in disbelieve.

'As good as. After the way he treated her, she took an overdose. Bernie was Graham's secretary. Sweet, innocent convent girl. You know the type. Easy prey for a louse like Graham. She was such a sweet kid. What really stuck in everybody's gullet was the fact he showed not one jot of remorse. Six months ago, if someone had stuck a knife in his guts back home, you'd need to line up half the employees in the company as a possible suspect. Me included.'

He looked up and caught the alarm registered on Fiona's face.

'Sorry, Fiona. I shouldn't be laying all this on you. But I can't pretend I had any respect left for the man. I seriously considered changing jobs and moving to somewhere I wouldn't have to work with or even see him again but I couldn't do that to Elspeth. The girls are very close.'

'Did Vivien know about Bernie? Is that why you think she might have killed him for having an affair?'

His laugh was harsh and bitter. 'Viv was used to his string of mistresses. But when she found out Bernie was pregnant, enough was enough, and she walked out on him. Trouble was Viv was the one with the money. Her father had left her a tidy sum. Most of the capital for the partnership is still in her name. Without Viv, Graham had no house, no company, no job. Nothing. So he ditched Bernie and talked her into having an abortion. Bernie had been brought up a catholic and couldn't live with all the shame and guilt.'

'The poor girl.'

'A neighbour found her three days after she'd washed down a whole packet of pills with a bottle of gin.'

'How dreadful.'

'Yep. And he still managed to get Viv to take him back after all that. Can you credit it? He always could twist her round his little finger. But perhaps this time, he pushed her too far.'

'Do you think him paying attention to Cressida so openly is what drove her to it?'

'That's probably what that friend of yours thinks. He asked all sorts of questions about Graham, about his work and his extra-marital goings-on. Looks as though he's trying to build a case for a crime of passion. Get her a reduced sentence.' He looked down at hands resting on the bar counter. 'Thing is, it doesn't add up. If she did suddenly lose control and lash out, she's the sort who would own up straight away. She wouldn't walk away and try and cover her tracks pretending to talk to him when he was already dead.'

'You would need to be pretty calculated to do that, I'll admit.'

'Oh well, time for bed I suppose.' He put both hands on the edge of the bar and pushed himself up.

'Good night. If there is anything I can do, you know where I am.'

'Thanks, Fiona. 'Night.'

It was almost midnight before Fiona finally crawled into bed. So much for an early night! Another eventful day. The only consolation was worrying about Vivien and Elspeth had prevented her from dwelling on yesterday morning's dreadful blood spattered spectacle.

Making an idiot of herself in front of Peter Montgomery-Jones hadn't helped matters either. Why had she been so insistent on Vivien's innocence? As even Barry had admitted, who else was there? Back home it might have been different. There could be a string of irate husbands, boyfriends or even brothers driven to revenge to line up as suspects. There might even be some ex-lover he'd seduced and then discarded lurking in the background somewhere. The only person in the running for that out here was Cressida, but that idea was as preposterous as it was laughable.

Montgomery-Jones was right. It really wasn't her concern any more. If she were honest with herself, for all her vehement pleading of Vivien's cause, it was his highhanded attitude that had driven her to such an hysterical outburst, not any real conviction of the woman's innocence. That and a desire to support Elspeth, what Winston liked to call her mother hen instinct for all her charges. Her immediate reaction when she'd seen Montgomery-Jones was relief. He would take over and she could leave the sorry business completely in his hands. The less she had to do with the whole affair the sooner the nightmares of walking straight into that appalling gory tableau would start to fade away.

Fiona punched her pillow in an effort to get more comfortable, but somehow sleep would not come. Was Barry right in assuming Peter Montgomery-Jones was amassing evidence for mitigating circumstances? Somehow, that didn't quite ring true. Montgomery-Jones had seemed to want nothing to do with the case when she'd spoken with him. At least to begin with. Or was that simply the impression he meant to give? There again, a domestic murder was not exactly the kind of crime that came within his remit. So why was Montgomery-Jones out here at all? Certainly not solely to tell her to stop meddling in police business. It had been ridiculous to accuse him of that. So what other reason could there be for him to come all the way to Germany and why involve himself in this case at all? She did not doubt he had his own agenda and that was his propriety. He'd made it abundantly clear he would not intervene in the murder enquiry. All of which meant she couldn't be sure she should rely on him to ensure justice was done. It really was up to her to keep pushing.

So what was he after? Though he'd never told her exactly what his job was, she'd come to the conclusion Montgomery-Jones was some kind of intelligence chief but there was nothing of national importance involved in this scenario. And why had he been asking about Graham's work? What possible interest could he have in Graham trying to sell equipment to the wine production industry? There was obviously something she was missing here and it would do no harm for her to find out a bit more about Graham and his business activites if only to satisfy her own curiosity.

Day 5 Thursday

Today we journey to the ancient university town of Heidelberg on the Neckar River. After Louis XIV had destroyed much of the province, the town was rebuilt in the 17th century baroque style. Its picturesque setting amidst mountains, forests and vineyards, has inspired many famous artists and provided the backdrop for Sigmund Romberg's 'The Student Prince.' A local guide will join us for a city tour ending with a visit to the majestic, pink sandstone castle towering over the town. Before we return to our hotel, there will be time for you to explore the historic centre at your own pace or perhaps visit the modern shopping plazas around Bismarckplatz where you will also find excellent cafés, bars and restaurants.

Super Sun Executive Travel

Fourteen

Laura's eyes widened in surprise as she opened the door to the Commander. If James was still in awe of his superior, she was even more so. As a humble research assistant, apart from the odd polite greeting when their paths crossed, she had never spoken to him before. According to James, the two of them passing themselves off as a couple on holiday had been the Commander's suggestion, but his unexpected arrival at their hotel room, made her feel acutely embarrassed. Thank goodness, they were both up and dressed; although she would much rather he hadn't seen the unmade bed and the early morning mess everywhere.

'James is just cleaning his teeth.' She seized up yesterday's jeans and tee shirt strewn over the only armchair so he could sit down. 'May I get you a tea or a coffee?'

'Not for me, thank you.'

Still clutching the bundle of dirty clothes, she pulled open a drawer and thrust them out of sight, then hurried to pick up the discarded trainers out of the Commander's way. James wasn't the tidiest of people. Why was he taking so long?

'We didn't realize you were coming, sir.'

'I did ring, but you must have been at breakfast.'

She felt a rush of blood to her cheeks. James was supposed to leave his mobile on at all times but he'd switched it off first thing saying with a wicked glint in his eye that had made her laugh, 'Don't want to be disturbed now, do we?'

She turned back to the bed and busied herself straightening the covers. A surge of relief swept over her when James emerged from the bathroom.

'Good morning, sir.'

James pulled out the padded stool from under the dressing table and sat down.

'I'll leave you two to discuss matters.' Laura turned towards the door.

'No. My dear girl, do stay. You are part of this operation after all. It is important you appreciate what is going on.' The Commander waited until she'd perched herself on the side of the bed half hidden from his view behind the James before continuing. 'I have had the opportunity to speak to Mrs Mason and to Mr and Mrs Glover.'

'Do you think Glover and Spelman were working together, sir?'

The Commander leant back with sigh. 'Impossible to tell at this stage. It is a possibility. Working on the assumption he may have decided to take over where Spelman left off, we need to see if he makes contact with anyone.'

'But …' Laura bit her lip.

The Commander looked at her. 'You were saying?'

'I'm sorry, sir. I didn't mean to interrupt.'

He gave her an encouraging smile. 'Go on.'

'Wasn't the contact man the one killed in the car bomb on Sunday?'

'If the militants are keen to get their hands on the designs then they will send someone else,' James stated the obvious.

'Of course,' she mumbled. 'I'm sorry.'

'Though all of this is simply guesswork at the moment. We still have no real idea which factions are involved. In the mean time, we need to keep all the options open. I think it would be a sensible idea for you two to move to their hotel in Assmann-shausen to keep an eye on things.' The Commander got to his feet. 'The party will be in Heidelberg for the day so there is nothing you can usefully do until this evening. Why not take the opportunity to do some sightseeing? It would be a shame to come all this way without seeing a little of the area and today is probably the last chance you will get. However, it might be as well to keep your mobile switched on. I have arranged to see Mrs Spelman. If I learn anything of relevance, I will give you a call.'

'Yes, sir. Thank you, sir.'

The Commander took the gold Hunter from his waistcoat pocket and checked the time before turning back to Laura with a smile. 'With luck I shall miss the worst of the traffic. Have a pleasant day both of you.'

James hurried to open the door for him.

Their local guide in Heidelberg turned out to be quite a character. Liesel was a large, outgoing woman of a similar age to Fiona, but with twice the bust and a mass of wild grey hair piled in an untidy bun on the top of her head. Apart from a great sense of humour, her main asset was her excellent command of English, which had only the hint of an accent. Fiona's Super Sun clients would have no difficulty either understanding or, because of the strong clear voice, hearing her.

Fiona took herself to an empty seat at the rear of the coach to allow Liesel to take her place for the drive around the town's major sites. With so little experience of guiding to back her up, Fiona was still a touch apprehensive about her new venture into the world of work. This was an excellent opportunity to see an expert in action. She listened intently as Liesel gave a brief history of the town as they headed towards the centre.

'Long ago, the market square is where the town's executions took place and the witches and heretics were burned. Today, I'm afraid we only have only the Neptune Fountain to show you.'

Their tour began in the university area. As the coach wound through the narrow streets, Liesel pointed out the various buildings. 'This is the oldest university in Germany; founded in 1386 and today has 28,000 students, approximately one-fifth of the town's population.'

Before eyes could glaze over with an excess of statistics, Liesel regaled her audience with stories of the twice-weekly duels between the various student fraternities that took place outside the historic student taverns. As the student lock-up was still in use as late as 1914, her amusing tales of their riotous past were probably only a little exaggerated.

'You could not consider yourself a proper student unless you sported a facial scar inflicted by your opponent. Today such duels are frowned upon of course, but the tradition of hard-drinking contests between the different fraternities still survives.'

Fiona received the text message as the coach climbed up the steep hill to the car park below the enormous castle complex. It was short and to the point. Peter Montgomery-Jones had arranged for a car to collect Elspeth and Barry to take them to see Vivien that evening after the day's excursion.

'You can have a long chat with her over dinner tonight.'

'That's wonderful, Fiona.' It was good to see a smile on Elspeth's face again. 'Do thank him for all his trouble.'

'Of course. I'll text him back straightway,' Fiona said brightly.

Not that she felt comfortable about contacting him. He'd touched a raw nerve, but that was no excuse for her outburst at their last meeting. However, a text wasn't exactly the right place for an apology. Best to keep it short for now. Just acknowledge his message and thank him.

There was the added problem; the art of texting was still something of an anathema to Fiona. Apart from strictly emergency use when she was out, after so many years spent more or less confined to her home caring for Bill she'd never needed to master the use of a mobile phone until starting work for Super Sun. By the time she'd managed to punch in her message, Liesel had bought their entrance tickets and her little party were already halfway along the causeway heading for the main gate.

Several groups plus a steady throng of general tourists was milling around, but it was easy enough for Fiona to spot her party. She had offered Liesel her own guide pole with its sunburst logo, but Liesel had her own means of easy recognition.

A voluminous hat with a larger-than-life colourful parrot stuck on top, which she'd perched on the already towering hairdo. Not easy to miss and it certainly amused everyone. However, that particular trick of the trade was not something Fiona planned to emulate. She had neither the audacity nor the height to adopt such an outlandish means of attracting her clients' attention.

There was much to see within the huge castle complex, whose development spanned from the 13th to the 17th centuries, and Liesel was in her element with her amusing anecdotes and tales of daring-do to enliven her clearly extensive knowledge of the history, architecture and art associated with this jewel of German attractions.

It took some time to persuade the last stragglers to leave the Apothecary Museum with its atmospheric shop full of dusty shelves crammed with dark bottles and strange objects pickled in murky glass jars. Fiona could not help wondering how many of the weird and wonderful ancient remedies her party seemed intent on buying would end up untried, even unopened, in the bin, in all likelihood long before they left Germany.

Hers not to reason why. Her limited experience as a tourist guide had taught her the main preoccupations of many Super Sun patrons were food and shopping. Architecture and scenic beauty were simply the backdrop to photography with the desire to widen horizons and experience unfamiliar cultures and customs coming a very poor fourth. She gave herself a mental slap on the wrist for giving way to such unaccustomed, jaundiced bad temper. It wasn't even fair. It might be true of people like Rita Lambert, Hilary Kasar, Cressida and Holly; but Ernest Blake, the Najarans and even Joe Ennis had shown a genuine interest in what each location had to offer. She ushered Sidney and Daphne Pettit towards the door to join the rest of the party outside gathered around Liesel.

By the time they reached the cellar complex, the light spacious entrance was already thronged with other visitors and it

119

wasn't easy to find sufficient room for everyone to gather round for Liesel's next talk. Standing on the outskirts of the tight cluster, Fiona looked around to check no one had become separated by the crowds. She made eye contact with a short, stocky man on the far side of the room with an unkempt grey beard reaching onto his chest. He was still staring directly at her, his low brow furrowed, with an intensity that unnerved her. She turned back and gave all her attention to Liesel.

'Now we go to see the Heidelberg Tun. It took 130 oak trees for its construction in 1751 and has a capacity of approximately 220,000 litres, just over 58,000 of your gallons. It has only rarely been used as a wine barrel. If you climb the flight of steps by the side, you will find a platform at the top which on special occasions is used as a dance floor. There are many, many people so take care especially as you come down on the far side. I will meet you back here in ten minutes.'

The ten minutes stretched to nearer twenty when some of the more adventurous members of the party decided to go down the steep concrete steps into the dark depths of the large pit under the barrel itself.

'It's really spooky down here.'

Whether Holly's nervousness was genuine or simply for effect, Fiona could not tell, but listening to Cressida's echoing laughter she could not help but agree with Holly's assertion.

Winston pulled into the large drop off area close to the largely pedestrianized centre. This was where they were due to say goodbye to Liesel but, as it was on her way, she was happy to walk with them along the busy main thoroughfare, the famous Haupstrasse, to the place where they were booked to have a light lunch.

When they reached their café, Fiona thanked Liesel profusely and hurried in to check the arrangements. The meal consisted of soup, a large crusty roll with a choice of fillings followed by a cake or pastry. A quick glance at the mouth-watering selection laid out under the glass topped display counter reassured Fiona that even the fussiest eater would be able to find something to enjoy.

Whilst Fiona was busy with the manageress, the rest of the party found themselves places at the small iron-legged tables. Before going round to ensure all was well, Fiona made her way over to Elspeth and Barry's table to leave her bag and jacket on one of the spare chairs before another couple could join them. This might well be the best chance she'd have to slip the odd question about Graham's business casually into the conversation without seeming to make a big issue of the subject.

Although the promised visit to see her sister had done much to rouse Elspeth's jaded spirits, it was soon evident she and Barry were still at loggerheads. The two barely spoke a word to each other. It was left to Fiona to attempt to keep up the flow of trivial banter as they tucked into their meal.

Fiona had almost given up hope of finding an opening for her questions when Barry asked, 'As a tour rep, you must see some interesting places?'

'It's not the same as being on holiday yourself of course, but it certainly beats working in an office. So what about your job, Barry? Didn't you say you were an accountant for a high-tech business?'

Barry nodded. 'It's a relatively new company and expanding rapidly.'

'Were you in at the beginning?'

'I joined about five years ago, eighteen months after the start up. It was still quite small back then; only twenty or so employees but, though it pains me to be the one to say it, credit where it's due, Graham had a brilliant eye for marketing potential and product placement and now the workforce numbers well over 300. Philip Cawston is the technical whiz kid but Graham has … had the vision.'

There was a snort from Elspeth. Despite staring vacantly out of the adjacent floor to ceiling window while idly pushing the remnants of her apple strudel round her plate, she was evidently listening in to the conversation. In a voice laden with sarcasm she said, 'Good of you to admit it.'

121

'Yes well, things haven't been going quite so well lately. There's been what you might call a cooling off between the two of them.'

'Oh?' Fiona prompted when it looked as though Barry was about to lapse into silence. 'So what caused that?'

'Things were never the same after what happened to Bernie, but last month there was a hell of a bust up over some contract Graham was negotiating. Philip knew nothing about it and he hit the ceiling when Graham laid the proposal on his desk. You could hear the two of them shouting at each other all down the corridor. Graham was so livid he walked out of the building and since then the two have hardly spoken a civil word to each other. To be honest, things have been going downhill every since. Graham's been doing bugger all since then and Philip more or less told him to either pull his finger out and get some new contracts on the table or resign. That's why we all had to change our holiday at the last minute.'

'He mentioned something about trying to interest the German wine growers in using some of your equipment,' Fiona said. 'He even gave me one of the company brochures.'

Elspeth flashed a sour look in Fiona's direction before turning away and staring out at the passing tourists. Quite what she'd said or done to deserve it, Fiona couldn't fathom.

Some of the others were making a move.

'Time to shift, pumpkin if we're going to see the sights,' Barry said, doing his best to jolly along his solemn faced wife. 'Shall we go and take a look at this basilica then?'

'It's left out of the door and straight on until you reach the Corn Market at the top of the square. You can't miss it.' Thank goodness for the excellent town plan in the Eyewitness Guide.

With time to herself, Fiona could take a stroll and see what the town had to offer. The main streets were crowded but the character of Heidelberg was markedly different from the half-timbered buildings and narrow streets they had come across in the much smaller Rhine Valley towns of the previous day and there was much to see.

The Jesuit Church overpowered the small hemmed in square. At first glance, Fiona wondered if she'd misread her map until she spotted the three statues of saints in the niches cut into the towering redbrick façade. Inside, the clear windows, white pillars and stark white barrelled-ceiling made it much lighter than the most of the other churches she'd seen so far on the trip. She walked up the central aisle to take a closer look at the enormous painting of the Assumption of the Virgin which filled the wall behind the main altar.

As she moved away from the rails, she spotted Brendan kneeling at a side chapel, deep in prayer. Not wishing to disturb him, she turned and walked down the far aisle.

'Hello there.' Kathleen stood by the holy water stoup at the entrance.

Fiona smiled. 'Very peaceful isn't it?'

'Brendan's just lighting a candle. Every church we go in. It's become something of a ritual since we came out here.' Kathleen gave a sigh. 'I keep telling him it doesn't do to dwell on things. It won't bring her back. You have to move on, but you know what men are.'

'How long is it since your daughter died?'

'Last November. I thought he was getting over it but ...' She shrugged her shoulders helplessly. 'The two of them were very close. Her daddy's darlin' she was. He never wanted her to go to England in the first place, but there just weren't the opportunities for her at home. Then she got this great job. A Personal Assistant to one of the directors. We were so proud of her. I think she was a bit lonely at first, but she enjoyed her job enormously. She worked with some lovely people. At least, that's what she told us.' There was a faint trace of bitterness in her voice.

'You mean it wasn't true?'

'It was at first, but something happened. Though only the good Lord knows what but I could tell she wasn't happy.' Kathleen's sigh was heartfelt. 'Then we got a call to say Bernadette was dead. I was in hospital at the time – having my hip done – so poor Brendan had to cope all on his own. He went over for the inquest and had to bring her body back to Ireland. We couldn't bear the thought of her being buried amongst strangers.'

There was little Fiona could say. Instead, she put a hand on Kathleen's arm and gave it a gentle squeeze.

Time to make her way back. Fiona cut through the side streets to make her return journey alongside the river where she could take a closer look at the imposing historic bridge which spanned the Neckar. Now restricted to pedestrians only, it was a great place from which to see the Old Bridge Gate with its impressive white circular towers on either side. Definitely worth a picture to show the boys. As she came back through the gate, she spotted the man with the grey beard.

Telling herself not to be so foolish, even if it were the same man staring at her in the castle, why shouldn't she see him again? What more natural than their paths should cross a second time? This was a tourist city. There must be hundreds, if not thousands of people intent on seeing the town's same highlights.

She walked quickly over to the large bronze monkey statue to read the information plaque beside it. It took a couple of goes to force herself to take in the words.

Fifteen

The journey back to Assmannshausen was lengthy but un-eventful. After their busy day, most people were happy to doze or sit back and watch the DVD. The collection provided by Super Sun was, to say the least, generally uninspiring so Fiona had brought along a few of her own. She flicked through the pile, pulled out the copy of *Chocolat*, and slipped the disk into the player. Most people enjoyed seeing anything that featured Judi Dench, and with Johnny Depp in the cast, it should appeal to the two younger girls. She'd heard them moaning rather pointedly about how ancient the previous films had been.

They arrived back at the hotel in plenty of time to take a rest before dinner or even a short stroll around the village for the more energetic to stretch their legs after the journey.

As usual, the Kasars waited to let everyone else off first so Hilary could take her time.

'Did you manage without any problems today?'

'Yes thanks, Fiona. No worries. We even had a stroll around the town after lunch, didn't we, Viktor? Then I had a coffee while he went off to take some photographs.'

'That's good.'

Fiona watched them disappear towards the hotel then hopped back onto the coach to collect her own things.

'Talking to Hilary just now reminded me. I still haven't put the bandages she gave me into the First Aid kit. Are you in a rush, Winston? I can do it tomorrow if you want to get off.'

'No problem, sweetheart. You do it now while you think

about it. No hurry.'

Fiona knelt up on the seat and lifted down the box.

'I wonder what this is.' Something silver glinted in the bottom, half-hidden by plasters and assorted paraphernalia. 'I don't remember anything like this in here before.'

Winston twisted round and peered over the top of his seat. 'What is it?'

'I thought it was scalpel or a tool of some sort but actually it's a USB stick?'

'Pardon?'

Fiona laughed. 'A memory stick. For storing photos I expect. Heaven knows how it got in here. Remind me to ask tomorrow if it belongs to any of our party.' She dropped the stick back into the box.

'Actually Winston, now there's no one around, there's something else that's been on my mind ever since we left Heidelberg. While we were in the castle this morning, this man seemed to be watching us. It was rather creepy. Made me feel uncomfortable and then later, coming back to the coach this afternoon, I noticed him again. When he saw me, he darted behind someone but I'm positive it was the same man. It's probably nothing but, after all that's been happening, I don't know if I should report it.'

'If someone was following you, you ought to tell someone.' Winston pondered for a moment. 'Might be worth letting his lordship know.'

'Montgomery-Jones?'

'That's the fella. He's more likely to be interested than the police, don't you think?'

'Umm. I suppose so,' she said reluctantly. 'But we didn't exactly part on the best of terms yesterday.'

'You could always ask him if he thinks you should tell the police.'

'That's not a bad idea. Yes. Thanks for that.' She climbed down the coach steps. 'Bye, Winston. See you later.'

Marthe was about to hand over Fiona's room key when the

phone rang. Fiona waited patiently, flicking through the brochures in the stand on the end of the reception desk trying not to eavesdrop on the call only a few feet away.

'I am afraid not, sir; but, if you would hold the line I have someone here who might be able to help you.' Marthe put her hand over the mouthpiece and turned to Fiona. 'Mrs Mason, I have a gentleman on the line who would like to speak to Mr Spelman. He has rung a couple of times before, but I said Mr Spelman was not available. I did not know whether I should tell him the poor man is dead or not. As Mr Spelman was a member of your party, I wonder if you might speak to him.'

Wonderful! What on earth could she say? 'Hello?'

The voice at the other end repeated his request and demanded to know to whom he was talking. At least, that was what she thought the man asked. It was difficult to understand; the rasping voice was so heavily accented.

'My name is Mason. I'm the tour manager looking after the holiday party Mr Spelman was travelling with. I am sorry to have to tell you Mr Spelman is no longer with us. He died a few days ago. Can I help at all?' Was it really only three days? So much seemed to have happened since then.

The line at the other end went dead.

'How odd. He just rang off without saying anything.'

Fiona pulled a face and handed the phone back to Marthe.

The climb up to the third floor sapped the last of her energy and, when she eventually reached her room, she kicked off her shoes and collapsed wearily onto the bed. Her nerves had been on edge ever since she'd come across that dreadful murder and the last thing she wanted was to be reminded of it.

'For goodness sake, woman! You're letting yourself get spooked by a voice at the other end of a phone, no doubt miles away,' she told herself crossly. But it didn't really help.

Why would anyone be phoning Graham here at the hotel? It could be something to do with his business deal of course but, if it was one of the local wine producers trying to arrange a meeting, why hadn't he spoken to Marthe in German?

Should she inform the police about the call? They didn't seem very interested in anything anyone had said to them before, so they would probably think she was wasting their time. Especially as she and Elspeth had already put their backs up by making a fuss earlier.

Perhaps she should tell Peter Montgomery-Jones. It might be important, though quite how the information would help Vivien's case she wasn't sure. But what was the worst that could happen? He might accuse her of meddling again but at least she would have tried. She was hardly likely to get a tirade of abuse. He was much more likely to be icily polite only to ignore all she said the moment she'd rung off. That she could cope with.

'Oh Bill. What should I do?'

She pulled her mobile out of her bag and clicked through her address book for Montgomery-Jones's number. It was still there from when they were in Holland. She'd never got round to deleting it. She took a deep breath and pressed select. With luck, he'd have his phone switched off and she could leave a voicemail.

'Montgomery-Jones.'

'It's Fiona Mason. Um. It's probably nothing, but I thought I'd let you know...'

He listened without interruption as she gave him a brief description of events.

'The caller gave no indication of why he wanted to speak to Spelman?'

'Not to me. But according to the receptionist, he phoned last night and again earlier today, just before we got back. She said he seemed pretty insistent.'

There was a pause before he said, 'I am coming over. We can talk...'

'I don't want to waste your time,' she interrupted. 'There's little else I can add.'

There was an unexpected chuckle at the other end. 'As I was about to say, I was planning to come to the hotel in any case. The German police have given me permission to take a look at the Spelmans' room.'

'Oh I see.' Not that she did. Did that mean he thought Vivien innocent?

'I should be there for six o'clock. Would that be convenient?'

'Certainly.' She stopped short of saying, Look forward to seeing you. Somehow, Montgomery-Jones was not the sort of man to whom you could make such casual pleasantries.

Fiona looked at her watch. Where had the time gone? The car for the Glovers would be here any minute. She threw her mobile onto the bed, seized the room key and made for the door.

At first, she thought they must have gone already, but then she spotted Elspeth and Barry hovering inside the entrance to the corridor to the dining room. There was nowhere to wait in the narrow passageway that ran from the main door past the end of the central staircase and across to the rear door on the far side of the building. Even the tiny reception area was up a couple of steps on a raised section with room only for three or four people at a time.

Taking a moment to catch her breath, she asked. 'I'll just take a quick look outside and see if the car's arrived, shall I?'

Whether the smart, dark blue Mercedes was an embassy car or a private taxi hired specially for this occasion, Fiona could not tell, but the Glovers would certainly be travelling in style.

'Give Vivien my best wishes,' Fiona said as their chauffeur held open the rear door for Elspeth. She wanted to wish them a good evening, but, in the circumstances, that did not seem quite appropriate.

She stood waving after them until the car had disappeared around the corner at the bottom of the hill.

'Was that two of our people I saw getting into that posh car just now?' Rita Lambert was at her elbow. She and her husband must have been out for a stroll and Fiona hadn't spotted them until the sharp-faced woman had come up behind her.

'Yes. Barry and Elspeth Glover. They're going out for the evening.'

'Aren't they the friends of that man who died?'

'Yes. I believe so.' Fiona turned to Ian. 'Have you two had a nice walk?'

'Very nice, thank you, Fiona. It's such a pretty little village isn't it? I wanted to have a look at all the paintings on the sides of the houses while it was still light.' Ian stood aside to let Fiona through the door.

Fiona started to head for the stairs, but she had only gone a few paces when Rita called after her. 'Actually, Fiona, I'm glad we bumped into you. I wanted to say about that film you showed on the way back this afternoon.'

'Chocolat?'

'That's it. Now far be it from me to complain, but do you really think that sort of thing is suitable for this sort of group?'

'I'm sorry?'

'It's not for myself. I'm as broadminded as the next person, but some of the older people on the coach could well take offence at nude scenes like that. I know it only lasted for a few brief seconds but the couple were having sex. I appreciate one can see far worse on the television almost every night, but at home one always has the option of switching off or changing the channel.'

'I take your point, Mrs Lambert, but I have to say no one else has complained. In fact, as she got off the coach, Mrs Webster told me how much she'd enjoyed the film. I chose it because before Easter one of our neighbourhood churches ran a lent group based on the film. Apparently, the course has been used by a great many churches throughout the country. By groups of all denominations with the bishops' seal of approval.'

Though Fiona had tried to keep her tone gentle and conciliatory, Rita Lambert's eyes widened and her jaw dropped, but before she could reply Fiona turned and hurried away.

Perhaps she shouldn't have said that, Fiona told herself sharply as she took the stairs two at a time. The woman had obviously taken offence and Fiona would no doubt be made to pay the price in the days to come. Oh why did people have to be so difficult over such silly, unimportant matters when there was so much else going on?

130

Sixteen

Fiona was down in the reception area in good time. Peter Montgomery-Jones came through the hotel doors at one minute before the hour. The man was nothing if not punctual. As always, he was meticulously polite but as was no surprise, it was impossible to gauge what the man was thinking.

'I've asked if we could use one of the offices where we won't be disturbed.' She led the way along the short stretch of corridor behind the reception desk and pushed open the first glass-panelled door on the left.

It was a small cramped room with not much more than a few filing cabinets and a table under the window on which sat a computer. They pulled out the two chairs and sat facing one another.

'Before I forget I must thank you for arranging for Elspeth and Barry Glover to spend the evening with her sister.'

'I was happy to assist.'

Fiona stared at her hands in her lap. 'Umm. Mr Montgomery-Jones. I owe you an apology. I was out of order last evening...'

The unexpected chuckle made her look up.

'Mrs Mason. Fiona. Our meeting did not exactly get off to a good start for which, I freely admit, I was at fault. I had forgotten what a sensitive soul you could be. Let us draw a line under yesterday's encounter and move on.' At least he wasn't going to make her eat humble pie. 'With regard to the telephone call, you mentioned the man asking to speak to Spelman had a strong accent.'

'Yes, but I couldn't identify it. It was very guttural, possibly mid or east European. I'm not familiar enough with such things to be able to say with any certainty, I'm afraid.'

'And it was definitely the same person who called earlier in the day?'

'Apparently. But I only spoke to him the once so you'll have to check with the receptionist.'

He gave a dry smile. 'I will.'

Of course he would. That was probably another reason why he'd come all this way.

'I wondered if it could possibly be the man who appeared to be following us this morning. Perhaps he was trying to get hold of Graham Spelman, which is why he was so interested in our party when we were in the castle. At one point, I noticed him studying each of our group but when he saw me watching him, he moved off pretty quickly.'

'I see.'

'Though I was on my own when I saw him again in the town by the Old Bridge Gate.'

He probably thought she was being paranoid.

'And he was not with anyone?'

'Not that I could see. Either in the castle or in town.'

'Can you describe him?'

'Short, stocky, swarthy with a straggly beard. In his 50s or 60s. Very intense, not like a tourist somehow. It was that as much as anything that singled him out. He didn't seem interested in the buildings or the scenery at all. Of course, it might all just be coincidence, although I'm convinced, he didn't want me to know he was there that last time. He jumped out of sight so quickly. If he hadn't I probably would have thought nothing of it.'

'Can you think of any reason why anyone should want to follow you?'

She shook her head. 'Do you think it could be related to Graham's murder?'

'You may have difficulty persuading the local police that it is.'

132

There was a long pause before she plucked up the courage to ask, 'Do you know how the investigation is going?'

'I am afraid I have no more information than yesterday.'

That could mean anything.

'But if Vivien stabbed him, surely her fingerprints would be on the knife? Once the forensic results come through, they'll prove she couldn't have been responsible.'

'As I said, I do not know what stage the local police have reached in their investigation but,' he paused, 'I would not put too much hope in that idea. I doubt there was any evidence to find.'

'I don't understand. Why not?'

'He was stabbed with a letter opener.' She was none the wiser. 'You probably have a similar one in your room.'

'There's a letter rack. A rather ornate brass handled affair.' She tried to picture it. 'I've not really looked at it closely but yes, there's a paperknife slotted into the back of it.'

'With a moulded figure for a handle?'

Realization dawned. 'You mean the chances of getting any kind of print from something so intricate are not good.'

'I would imagine so.' He smiled and said kindly, 'However, if the lack of prints fails to exonerate Mrs Spelman, neither can they be used to incriminate her.'

Fiona wasn't sure if this was much consolation. Not unless it led to the police considering other possible suspects.

'This may not be relevant, but I assume you are aware Graham had a major disagreement with his business partner which threatened to split the company.'

'Are you suggesting this partner was responsible for Spelman's death?'

'No. Not at all. But I got the impression from Barry, who works for the same company, there was something not quite right about some contract Graham was trying to negotiate.'

'Has Mr Glover given you any evidence of malfeasance in his brother-in-law's business affairs?'

'No.' Though he might well have done if I had the remotest idea what the word means, Fiona thought. Why on earth had she started this conversation? She might know Montgomery-Jones would succeed in making her feel ridiculous.

Perhaps it was fortuitous that it was at that moment that Fiona's mobile began to ring.

'So sorry about this. I'll turn it off.' She stared at the tiny screen and her heart gave a momentary jump.

He must have read the concern in her face. 'Problems?'

'It's my son. I wasn't expecting a call. I usually ring him on a Sunday.'

'Then answer it. I will wait outside.' He got to his feet and she heard the door close.

'Adam. This is a surprise,' she said trying to swallow the alarm she felt.

'Hi, Mum. Sorry to bother you mid-week but I phoned Martin last night and he said you're thinking of selling the bungalow.'

'That's not what I said. I just happened to mention your Aunt Miriam had been in touch and she'd been going on about how I should consider moving into something more manageable now I'm on my own. She even hinted I might like to live with her.' Fiona laughed expecting him to find the idea as preposterous as she had done. Her sister-in-law might well be good intentioned but there was only so much of Miriam's organizing Fiona could put up with.

'You're not seriously considering it, are you, Mum?'

'Of course not, darling. You know very well, we'd be at each other's throats in a matter of days. It's bad enough having to go and stay, but with your father gone, apart from you and Martin, I'm the nearest thing she has to a relative so I can't keep ignoring her invitations.'

'I meant about putting the bungalow on the market?' he said impatiently.

'Well she does have a point about me rattling around in the place. I don't exactly need four bedrooms and two bathrooms.'

'But you can't sell it, Mum.' He was indignant. 'Martin and I grew up there.'

'Hardly, darling. You were fourteen when we moved in.'

'Okay, but you need all those rooms for when we come to stay.'

Like once every two or three years, if I'm lucky, she thought, though she could hardly say as much to Adam. 'There are all the practicalities to think of. The upkeep on a place that size is considerable. Heating rooms I don't use etc., not to mention things like rates and council tax. Especially as I'm away for much of the time now I'm working.'

'But you don't need to work, Mother. You're not short of money?'

'No, but I can't sit around all day doing nothing.' It was difficult to keep the irritation from her voice.

'But ...'

'Look, darling. I'm really sorry but I can't talk now,' she said firmly. 'I'm supposed to be in a meeting. We'll have a chat later, okay? Give my love to Kristy and the children.'

She rang off before he could start haranguing her again. Dropping the phone into her lap, she put her elbows on the table and slumped forward. She loved Adam dearly, of course she did, but there were times when she wished he would stop treating her like some geriatric incapable of making decisions for herself.

A hand gripped her shoulder with just enough pressure to stop the tears which for some stupid reason had begun to well up behind her eyes. She hadn't heard Montgomery-Jones come back in. He must have seen her through the glass panel in the door.

'Nothing wrong, I trust?'

'Not at all,' she said, quickly pulling herself together. 'It's been a long day not helped by having an overprotective family telling me what I can and can't do.'

He turned the other chair towards her and sat down. 'Surely that is perfectly understandable? Your sons must be concerned about your involvement in all this unfortunate business especially now there has been a murder.'

'They don't know anything about it.' She managed a wry laugh and shook her head. 'If either of the boys got to hear, they'd have me on the next plane back home in double quick time.'

'Which presumably means you did not tell them about your exploits in The Netherlands either?'

She managed a weak grin.

'I must say you do seem to be making a habit of allowing your passengers to be murdered, Mrs Mason. You will be getting quite a reputation, if you are not careful.' The pale grey eyes twinkled and she could hear the gentle mocking laughter in his voice. 'Surely you have not kept to yourself all those daring tales of uncovering smugglers, finding the whereabouts of their haul, not to mention trying to face down a killer all by yourself?'

'Very much so!' She bit her lip in an effort to hold back the burble of laughter; a feat she didn't quite manage. 'So I'm afraid no one else knows about your gallant last minute rescue seconds before the gun went off.'

'Hmm.' He looked down his nose in mock disapproval. 'It should not have been necessary. You were told not to interfere.'

'So you reminded me at the time, if memory serves me right,' she glanced up at him from under her lashes. 'In no uncertain terms.'

He had the grace to laugh. 'You deserved a good reprimand. I already had three dead bodies on my hands. I objected strongly to the possibility of a fourth.' That was as near to an apology for his ferocious outburst back in Amsterdam as she was going to get. 'So, if it is not the job, what is your son objecting to?'

'It's all so pointless really. Adam's upset because he thinks I'm about to sell the bungalow.'

'Surely that is your choice.'

'True. And the frustrating thing is I've never seriously considered it. Why I didn't just tell him I wasn't going to, I don't know. How could I put it on the market? It's my last link with Bill. We had some good times there in the old days. But ...' She stopped and bit her lip again.

136

'Too many painful associations?'

'Exactly. I think that's really why I took this job. I had to get out of there. I know it's a terrible thing to say, but that bungalow became a prison for me those last few years when Bill was confined to a wheelchair. The only time I could get him out of the place was when I took him up to the hospital for his regular tests. If it hadn't been for my OU course and the choir, I would have gone mad.' She sighed and rubbed her eyes. 'I'm sorry. I shouldn't be subjecting you to my tale of woe. I don't usually wallow in self pity.'

'You are a great deal stronger than you think.' She looked up into the smiling eyes.

She got to her feet. 'Shall we go and find the receptionist for you before everyone starts coming down to dinner?'

There was a momentary pause before he rose to tower over her. The gold watch chain across his waistcoat glinted in the light. He stood very close. Too close. She could smell the expensive cologne of his aftershave. Time to go.

Seventeen

It took only a couple of minutes for Montgomery-Jones to establish with Marthe all the telephone calls for Graham Spelman had come from the same man and he'd refused to leave a name or contact number.

'Did you gain any impression of the caller's nationality?' Montgomery-Jones asked.

'I could not tell for certain. Turkish perhaps? We had some guests from Istanbul last week and he sounded much like them.'

'That is very helpful. Thank you, fräulein. Did Mr Spelman leave anything in the hotel safe?'

'Only Mrs Spelman's jewellery.'

'No papers?'

'No, sir.'

'The police have given me permission to take a look round Mr and Mrs Spelman's room. I assume the hotel has been informed?'

'Yes, sir.' Marthe picked up the key with a frown. 'Will this take long? I do not like to leave the desk at this time as guests are returning for dinner.'

'I'll show Mr Montgomery-Jones the way,' said Fiona. 'If that's alright with you both?'

'Of course.'

As they were heading up the last half flight of stairs, Montgomery-Jones asked, 'Did Spelman ever mention any foreign contracts he was interested in other than the ones with the wine industry?'

'Certainly not in Turkey if that's what you mean?'

He smiled. 'Or anywhere else in East Europe or Asia perhaps.'

'No. Although Barry mentioned that the contract that caused such a problem with his partner was with an Asian country.'

They had reached the Spelmans' room. Montgomery-Jones unlocked the door and ushered her in before he asked, 'What more do you know about the deal?'

'That's it. He didn't mention which one and I don't think he knows what it was for.'

For the next ten minutes, Fiona sat silently in the armchair watching Montgomery-Jones make a systematic search of the room. In the bedside drawer, he came across an A4 manila folder and sat on the edge of the bed scanning its contents. Replacing the dozen or so sheets, he flicked back the folder cover. Whatever he had hoped to find wasn't there. All the time he'd been searching, Fiona's mind had been in overdrive. He would never answer her questions, but that didn't stop her wondering.

'Even if the mystery caller is the same man following us around in Heidelberg, he can't be the murderer. He would hardly be asking to speak to someone he had already stabbed to death a couple of days before.' Although he had his back to her, Fiona could see the sudden tension in his shoulders. 'It doesn't help clear Vivien Spelman.'

He pushed in the drawer with slight thump and turned towards her. His face grim. 'Mrs Mason.' The warning was unmistakable.

She gave a weak grin. 'Sorry. Just thinking out loud.'

'Surely you have enough to occupy yourself already seeing to the needs of all your other clients?'

'Indeed.'

'Now we understand one another, Mrs Mason, shall we go?'

They walked down the stairs in silence. They were almost at the main door when Fiona suddenly felt his hand in the small of her back. Without breaking step, he leant down and said in a low voice, 'Strictly no detective work on your part, Mrs

139

Mason. I want your promise.'

With round innocent eyes, she looked up him. 'Would I?'

'Promise,' he repeated.

'Of course.'

'However, should your mystery stalker turn up again or anything else suspicious happen, I would be interested in knowing.'

With a slight shake of the head and the merest hint of a smile, Montgomery-Jones was off. She stood in the doorway watching him walk back to where he had parked his car.

Fiona still had a smile on her face as she turned to see Gloria Oldgate, standing at the foot of the stairs staring at her intently.

'Now who's a lucky girl?'

'I beg your pardon?'

'That gorgeous fella of yours. He can stir my porridge any time.' Gloria shook a scolding finger at her. 'You've been keeping him quiet.'

'He is very definitely not my fella.'

'I saw you coming downstairs together. So what have you two been up to? As if I didn't know.'

'Gloria! What on earth are you suggesting?'

'Then why have you got that grin from ear to ear? I saw him whispering sweet nothings in your ear just now. You can't fool me, kiddo. I saw you with him yesterday. You two definitely have a thing going. I've a nose for these things.'

'You're imagining it, Gloria. Besides he's probably got an adoring wife waiting for him at home.'

'Well he's certainly got the hots for you and don't tell me you don't fancy him. It's written all over your face.'

'I can assure you there is absolutely nothing going on between me and Mr Montgomery-Jones.' Seeing Gloria's startled look at the vehemence in her voice, Fiona attempted to soften the rebuke with a smile. 'He wouldn't look at me twice, believe me.'

'How's that then?'

'For a start I don't have a hyphen in my surname. Plus I don't have the right accent.' Gloria raised an eyebrow. 'He's the sort you have to stop yourself curtseying to whenever he speaks. Our worlds are galaxies apart. I'm right at the far end of his social scale'

'Bit of a snob, is he?'

'No! I'm not saying that at all. It's just sometimes he has this knack of making me feel totally inept and I end up saying something inane and feeling foolish.'

'Oh, so it's like that is it? To be honest he did look as though he had a poker stuck up his backside.' Gloria gave a mischievous grin and looped an arm through Fiona's before steering her towards the dining room. 'You know, I've got a little trick on how to handle these snooty types. Every time he tries to put you down, all you have to do is to picture him in ladies' underwear. Do you think he's a black lace or red silk man? Or if he really is that straight-arsed perhaps, bloomers and a vest.'

'Gloria! You're incorrigible.' Fiona laughed so much, her stomach hurt. 'Actually, I don't need to go that far! Trying to picture him without a tie will be quite enough to cut him down to size for me, thank you very much.' Fiona wiped away the tears of laughter rolling down her cheeks. 'You'll get me into trouble! Are you ready for something to eat?'

'You betcha.'

Still giggling like a pair of schoolgirls, the two of them entered the dining room where people were already gathering.

Gloria wasn't the only one to have spotted Fiona talking with Peter Montgomery-Jones. Winston caught her at the bar later that evening.

'Did you tell him about your stalker?'

Fiona nodded. 'For all the good it will do.'

'You don't think he took it seriously?'

'He did say to phone him straight away if the man turned up again.'

'That's alright then.' Winston still looked uncharacteristically serious. It was a rare event indeed to see the big West

141

Indian without his ever-ready smile.

'There's something else, isn't there?'

He gave a sheepish grin. 'I suppose you didn't see the television news before dinner?'

'No.' The long silence made her even more apprehensive. 'What's happened now?'

'It seems two men were taken in for questioning at Frankfurt airport this morning. They arrived on an overnight flight from Tehran.'

'Suspected terrorists?'

'They didn't say in so many words but …' He shrugged his massive shoulders.

'That won't please the older members of the party.'

'I don't think they're the only ones getting their knitting in a tangle. They was all talking about it over dinner, especially that lady with the penetrating voice. Making a big thing of it, she was. Getting the others all het-up too.'

'Our friend Rita is proving to be a real stirrer.' Fiona gave a deep sigh.

'That's why I thought I'd better warn you.'

'Thanks, Winston. I suppose I ought to see if I can calm them down.'

The evening's entertainment had already begun by the time Laura and James entered the lounge bar.

'Mind if we join you two?'

The bored blonde girl looked up and mumbled something that could be taken for assent.

'Hi, I'm Laura and this is James.'

The other, round-faced girl answered, 'Holly and Cressida.'

'Not many people our age here, is there?' Laura glanced around. 'We've just arrived. Have you been staying here long?'

'Only a few days. We're on a coach trip.'

'With that way ancient lot over there.' Cressida added cocking her head to the tables along the back wall of the room.

'That bad, hey?' James flashed the girl a sympathetic smile.

'Definitely! Like *so* not into having a good time. Yawn, yawn. Go all frosty faced the moment we try and have a bit of fun.'

'Come on, Cressy. That's not fair. Most of them are okay. And Fiona's not like that at all.'

'Yeah, well. That's her job.' Cressida wasn't prepared to give in easily. 'The rest of the wrinklies are a real the pain in the arse.'

'So who's Fiona?' Laura asked.

'She's our tour manager. That's her, sitting at the end table.'

Laura turned to follow Holly's glance. So this was the woman the Commander kept going on about. She couldn't say she was particularly impressed with the sharp-faced woman talking animatedly and obviously laying down the law. 'The one with dyed black hair?'

'God no!' Cressida gave an unpleasant laugh. 'That's the wicked witch of Chelmsford.'

'Well she's certainly got the pointy chin and beaky nose for it.' Best to try and build up the camaraderie if she was going to get anything out them, Laura decided.

'Rita Lambert,' Holly explained. 'Fiona's the pretty one in the cream shirt she's having a go at. If it was me, I'd tell that poisonous old crow to sling her hook but Fiona's like really good with her. Never loses her temper with any of them.'

'Saint bleeding Fiona!' Cressida raised her half-full glass and threw back the contents in a single gulp.

'Ignore Cressy; she's so in a mood 'cause Edith and Len blanked her all through dinner. Actually, some of them aren't that bad. Take Ernest, he's really interesting to talk to. He sits opposite at dinner and he's got some great stories. He's dead ancient, but he doesn't go on about the war or anything. He obviously knows a lot about this area. The history and the buildings and whatnot. Probably more than Fiona to be honest.'

'So which one is he?'

'Oh he never comes in here after dinner. Too noisy for him, he says. He's a bit deaf and he can't hear what people are saying over the music so he takes himself off each evening for a walk round the village.'

'I see.' Laura and James exchanged glances.

A burst of laughter came from the far side of the room.

'Is she one of yours?' James indicated the plump, gaudily dressed woman busy pulling a much younger attractive looking Asian man onto the dance floor. 'She certainly knows how to enjoy herself.'

They watched as the two performed a passable jive, which what it lacked in technique and finesse, made up for in sheer energy and enthusiasm. When the music came to an end, they were clapped and cheered by their audience to which the woman responded with a theatrical curtsey.

'That's Gloria. She's always good for a laugh.' Even Cressida smiled.

'You have to hand it to her,' said James. 'I only hope I have half that much go when I get to her age.'

The keyboard player struck up *The Girl from Ipanema* and Cressida rose to her feet pulling James onto the floor. 'How about us two showing this lot how to do a proper salsa?'

Laura watched with a pang of jealousy as the two gyrated in perfect harmony on the dance floor. She hadn't realized James was such a good dancer. The one time he'd taken her to a nightclub back home, the place was so packed there'd not been room to do much more than jig up and down. He must have realized what a poor sense of rhythm she had and hadn't wanted to show her up a second time. She turned her attention back to Holly.

'So the others are friendly too are they?'

'Yes. Well, they were, but we've been given the cold shoulder treatment lately,' Holly admitted reluctantly. 'They blamed Cressida for what happened.'

'What was that then?'

Holly frowned. 'Didn't you hear about the murder?'

'Get away!' Laura's yelp produced immediate shushing noises from Holly. 'You're kidding me. I knew one of the guests had died, but murder. I thought he had a heart attack'

'That's what they told everyone, but like you don't have police wandering all over the place asking questions when someone just dies, do you? And then Daphne and her husband saw the chap's wife being driven away in a police car when she was arrested.'

'No! Really?'

'Yeah! That's what they're all saying. The two of them had an argument and she stabbed him. There was blood all over the place apparently.'

'So what did that have to do with Cressy?'

'Promise you won't say anything to her, but this chap, Graham, really fancied himself, you know what I mean, and he tried it on with Cressy. She was so not interested, he was way old for goodness sake, but she decided to teach him a lesson so she pretended she fancied him and played up like, sort of stalked him.'

'No!'

'Obviously she never intended it to go that far. She wasn't to know the wife would get jealous and end up sticking a knife in him. Of course all the oldies have branded Cressida a cheap slut and but for her it would never have happened.'

The number finished and James and Cressida returned so the conversation had to come to an end. Fascinating though she'd found the gossip, Laura had doubts the Commander would consider she'd discovered anything of use.

As she lay in the darkness, it wasn't thoughts of mysterious strangers, the murder, Vivien, Elspeth or any of her party that kept Fiona from sleep. Why had she blurted out all that stuff about Bill and needing to get away to Montgomery-Jones of all people? What must he think of her? Every time she met him, she ended up making a fool of herself. Even now she felt a great knot of embarrassment squirming in the pit of her stomach.

It didn't help that he was such a strikingly handsome man. She could still recall the subtle aroma of his cologne as they stood inches apart in that tiny office. Despite her protests to

Gloria, in her heart of hearts she couldn't deny he was the most attractive man she'd met in a very long time.

But that was as far as it went she told herself firmly. Just because he'd been pleasant and understanding this afternoon didn't mean that he wasn't essentially pompous and patronizing.

What did it matter what he thought of her anyway?

She turned over, punched the pillow and tried to push all thoughts from her mind. There was another busy day tomorrow and indulging in adolescent fantasies was no substitute for a good night's sleep.

Day 6 Friday

Our first stop is the historic town Koblenz at the confluence of the Rhine and Moselle rivers where there will be time to explore at your leisure. Next, we drive alongside the magical Moselle, up one of Europe's most hauntingly beautiful river valleys as it meanders between the uplands of Eiffel and Hunsruck. Turreted castles look down from wooded outcrops, bell towers crown the hilltops, and thin graceful spires stand against the sky. The best known of all Germany's wine-producing areas, viticulture has been practised here since Roman times. We end our day's excursion in the charming wine centre of Cochem dominated by the ancient and mighty Reinsburg Castle, dramatically perched on the hillside above the town.

Super Sun Executive Travel

Eighteen

Thursday morning dawned bright and sunny. Fiona wound up the shutters in her room and glanced out at the steep valley side. Looking up into the bright blue of the near cloudless sky above, she felt considerably more relaxed than she had done last night.

Concentrate on the good things. Now Elspeth had spoken to Vivien, she should be suitably reassured, so one problem solved. Hilary's ankle was definitely on the mend which meant another thing to cross off her worry list. Spending their evenings dancing and talking with other guests more their own age, both Cressida and Holly appeared to be enjoying themselves, which just left Rita Lambert. It might be as well to show the woman special attention to make up for the snub she'd given her before dinner last night. Perhaps she could sweet-talk her into a more contented frame of mind and stop her stirring up trouble.

She pottered around the room in no hurry to get down to breakfast where, all too soon if they proved true to form, she would be pestered by a series of petty problems from her Super Sun clients. Pulling her clipboard from the voluminous tote bag that had become a part of her uniform, she perched on the narrow windowsill, her feet propped on the bed, to catch the warmth of the sun on her back. She unclipped the top sheet with the previous day's details and tried to throw it onto the bed. Inevitably, it fluttered to the floor.

'Damn.' It could stay there.

Only three more days to go and they would be heading home again. The week was racing past. Still, today should be a relatively easy one. A bit of background spiel on the journey which she could read from her notes and couple of short introductory talks in Koblenz and Cochem before they disappeared to explore the towns for themselves for a couple of hours. She familiarized herself with the details she'd painstakingly put together back home and checked the location of the major sites on her town plans. For the moment, that appeared to be all. Everything in order.

Breakfast. She eased herself gingerly off the sill rubbing the circulation back into her numbed buttocks and hobbled across to pick up her shoulder bag from the small table.

'Damn!' A sudden thought struck her. She'd told Adam she would ring him back and it had slipped her mind completely once she'd become caught up in everything that had followed. No use ringing now. It was the middle of the night in Canada and Adam would not thank her for waking him. Lunchtime. She mustn't forget.

Checking the day's timings with Winston each morning was never a lengthy affair and, with only a couple of stops on the itinerary, their business was soon completed.

'So, unless the weather suddenly takes a turn for the worse, we can give everyone a couple hours or so after lunch to explore Cochem before we head back.'

'Sounds good to me, sweetheart.'

'Let's hope we're in for an easy day.' Fiona returned her file back to her bag. 'Thanks, Winston.'

Making her way over to the breakfast bar, Fiona noticed Elspeth and Barry were already sitting at their usual table chatting with Kathleen Murphy. She would have to make time to speak to them later when she could get them on there own. It was a relief to see Elspeth smiling again. The evening with Vivien must have gone well.

As everyone gathered outside the hotel for the coach, Cressida and Holly were among the last to emerge causing raised eyebrows from a few of the older members of the party.

'What are they wearing?' Trust Daphne Pettit to take the girls' attire as a personal affront.

Deliberately pretending to misunderstand, Fiona said, 'They might not be very practical with all those straps and buckles but I understand gladiator sandals are all the fashion for younger women.'

'I was referring to their shorts. When they turn round, you can see their buttocks!'

Ian Lambert was doing his best to hide a smirk, Anita had her hand over her mouth and Devesh had turned away, his shoulders shaking gently.

'Well,' Fiona replied, just about managing to keep a straight face, 'if I had legs as long and shapely as Cressida's, I think I'd want to show them off too. Right everyone, here comes the coach. We all need to stand back a little.'

As they all started to board, Kathleen came over to Fiona looking very apologetic.

'Brendan's not feeling too good this morning. He's decided to give today's trip a miss, if that's alright?'

'What a shame. Would he like me to fetch a doctor or anything?'

'Oh no, dear. Sure now, he'll be fine. He's going to have a lie down for a bit and later, if he feels up to it, he'll take a stroll into the village and get himself a spot of lunch. I wanted to stay with him but you know what these men are like. Hate any fuss. Says he's best on his own and he'll be right as rain by this evening.'

'I'm sure he will.'

Fiona had noticed Brendan had been looking pale the last few days. Perhaps a day's rest would put him back to rights.

At least, the glorious day appeared to be working its magic on the rest of the Super Sun party. They all seemed in good spirits as the coach snaked northwards along the Rhine to Koblenz. Although the first part of their route was the same one they had travelled only two days ago, the many castles and little villages looked so much more attractive in the bright sunshine than in the drear grey of Tuesday's mist and rain.

They reached Koblenz by midmorning and drew up alongside several other coaches in front of the flat triangle of land at the confluence of the Moselle and the Rhine known as the German Corner. A sizeable section of the extensive parking area had been commandeered by a newly arrived travelling fairground. The place was bustling with noisy activity as the small army of men set up the various stalls and fun rides.

'Even I can't exactly miss the statue, Winston, but will you point me in the right direction for the bits of the Berlin Wall,' Fiona whispered as everyone collected their things together.

'It should be over there just about where they're putting up those struts for the big dipper.' Winston inclined his head in the general direction.

'Thanks, Winston. You're a life-saver. How would I manage without you?'

Holding aloft her signature guide pole, Fiona led her little band through the frenzy, towards the extensive spur. The colossal equestrian statue of Kaiser Wilhelm I stood on the largest plinth Fiona had ever seen. She waited at the furthest point above the meeting waters for her ambling party to congregate around her and then began her spiel. It took less than ten minutes to explain the town's strategic location, its origins in Roman times and to suggest a few of its more picturesque buildings which they might like to go and see.

'Along here,' she said pointing to the road by the Moselle riverside, 'you'll come to a very attractive Renaissance white building, the Alte Burg, which I mentioned, and in that direction,' she indicated with her left arm, 'facing onto the Rhine, you'll find the schloss, or palace, built by the last of the Trier's electors. You certainly can't miss it because all those columns and arches seem to go on forever. Very impressive.' There were a few nods and shared smiles. 'Now I'll walk back with you to St Castor's Basilica. That's the striking Romanesque church with those high twin towers with "Bishop's Mitre" tops you may have noticed as we drove in. From there, I can point you in the right direction for the shopping areas if you fancy a coffee before you take a look round. Nowhere is far from one or other of the rivers so you can't get lost.'

'You said something about bits of the Berlin Wall being round here somewhere. Is it far?' asked Sidney. Neither he nor his wife was much of a walker as they were both in their late seventies.

'Just the other side of the statue. We're going right past it on our way back. Follow me, everyone.'

Despite Winston's help, finding the wall sections was not

easy, partly because Fiona had no real idea of what to look for. She had expected something a little more impressive than the three upright concrete slabs which with no commemorative information plague, could have been taken for abandoned builders' rubble.

Freed at last from her duties, Fiona planned a roughly circular walk alongside the Moselle, cutting across the town to come back past the Rhine. As she walked through St Florin's square, she spotted Elspeth and Barry going into a café. If she didn't take the opportunity to find out how Vivien was coping, she'd end up with a guilty conscience.

'Viv's putting a brave face on everything but it's obvious she's still in shock,' Elspeth told her. 'She doesn't remember much except for finding him lying there covered in blood when she went in. Not that the police believe her. They questioned her for hours and they obviously think she's guilty.'

'Oh dear.' At least Fiona was saved from asking if Vivien had confessed.

'What she really wants to do is go home of course, but, even though it's obvious she couldn't have done it, the police insist she stay in the area until they've completed their investigation. They've taken away her passport.'

'But she's not in custody?'

'No, no. She's in a hotel not far from the station.'

'It must be very difficult for her, all on her own with no one to talk to,' Fiona said sympathetically.

'Exactly. I said I'd go and stay with her until everything's sorted out, but she insisted I mustn't spoil my holiday.' Elspeth gave a derisive snort. 'As if we can carry on like nothing's happened.'

The woman seemed close to tears. Fiona looked at Barry expecting him to say something or at least make some sort of conciliatory gesture, but he sat there like a statue, his eyes hooded and his jaw set. Fiona suspected it was not concern over his sister-in-law that accounted for the grim expression. The tension between husband and wife was palpable.

'She's still too upset about Graham to care much about her own predicament. The doctor has her so doped up on tranquillizers she's hardly making any sense. In the state she's in, she might confess to anything. Thank goodness, that chap of yours has arranged a solicitor for her. And he's insisting the police can only question Vivien with her solicitor present.'

No doubt it was as good a way as any for Peter Montgomery-Jones to find out what lines of enquiry the police were pursuing and what evidence they had, Fiona thought and immediately felt guilty. Despite her protestations to Gloria the day before, Peter Montgomery-Jones was not always a pompous, patronizing autocrat. He could be genuinely sensitive to other people's problems and, as she knew from her own experience, prepared to put himself out on their behalf. The trouble was you never knew which of the two you were going to have to deal with.

'Well that's something anyway. So what does this solicitor think? Do the police have a genuine case?'

'Vivien didn't say.' Elspeth shrugged her shoulders. 'She kept going on about Graham. She was worried about his funeral but your Mr Montgomery-Jones told her he'd arrange for the body to be taken back to England as soon as the German authorities release it. I don't know if it's all these drugs she's on, but she seems to think the man can perform miracles. Convinced he can sort out this whole mess. I've no idea what he's told her, I just pray to goodness he's not giving her false hope.'

'I'm sure he's being absolutely honest with her.'

'Whatever.' Elspeth did not sound convinced. 'Anyway, she's really grateful to you for contacting him. She said to tell you specially.'

'It was nothing to do with me. He would have done exactly the same even if I hadn't spoken to him.' She could hardly take the credit. Montgomery-Jones had involved himself. It was none of her persuasion.

'Well Vivien seems to have a lot of faith in him. He had a long chat with her apparently. Wanted to know all about

153

Graham. Not that she could tell him anything about the contracts he was working on. What good raking up all that will do to help Vivien's case now, heaven only knows.'

'We must be positive.' Fiona felt helpless. Trotting out platitudes was all she could do. 'With Mr Montgomery-Jones and the solicitor in her corner, there's every hope. We must leave it in their hands. Why don't you both try to put it all to the back of your minds and take a stroll around this lovely city?' There wasn't much more she could say so left them to it.

Peter Montgomery-Jones shook Vivien's hand and lowered himself into a deep box-shaped armchair designed more for striking effect than comfort. Apart from the two of them, the Steigenberger Hotel lounge was empty.

'I apologize for having to trouble you for a second time, Mrs Spelman. I appreciate your husband never discussed his business affairs with you, but I wondered if, now you have had time to think, you recall anything more about the proposed contract that caused such friction with his partner.'

'I'm afraid not. As I said, he didn't mention any details. I've no idea what the equipment was supposed to be for.'

'Nor the name of the country where the company was based?'

Vivien shook her head. 'Just that it was in Asia.'

'Did he ever mention Turkey?'

'No. Not that I can remember?'

The arrival of the red waistcoated waiter with their tray of tea interrupted their conversation.

Once the tea was poured, they both settled back again and Montgomery-Jones resumed his questions. 'Had your husband arranged to meet anyone while he was over here?'

Vivien frowned. 'Not that I know of. He talked about putting out feelers to one or two of the wine growers but he didn't have time to fix up anything. I know he planned to pop over to Frankfurt for the Aerospace Trade Fair but he certainly never mentioned a meeting.'

'I take it his visit was for business and not pleasure?'

'So he said.' Her jaw visibly tightened. 'We had words about it. This trip to Germany was supposed to be a holiday but he said the company was short of contracts and as Marketing Manager it was up to him to make the most of any opportunities that came his way.'

'I see. And as far as you know, it was not related to the Asian contract?'

'I can't see how. Not after all the fuss it caused with Philip. He was still annoyed at having to drop the whole thing after all the work he'd done setting it up. He probably wanted to forget the whole thing. It's one of the reasons we brought forward our holiday. He needed to get away. Get out of the office and calm down again.'

'Very understandable. So it was his decision to come to a wine producing area where he could mix business and pleasure.'

'I can't remember. All four of us talked about where we could go over dinner one evening. We came up with one or two ideas and then someone, Elspeth I think, suggested a river cruise. Someone mentioned the Rhine and we looked up availability on the internet, but everything was fully booked for this week and then this luxury Super Sun thing came up. We couldn't find anything else so Graham booked it online there and then. It wasn't until later that he talked about making contact with wine growers.'

'Did he receive any phone calls while he was over here?'

'He made quite a few,' she answered accenting the verb. 'I made a bit of a fuss about it actually, but I don't remember anyone calling him. I tell a lie; there was one in Cologne. To be honest, I thought it was probably that rather flighty piece, Cressida or whatever her name is. She'd been flirting with him ever since we left Dover and making a bit of a nuisance of herself. After that call, he was quite edgy, kept looking around all the time, but I thought he must be worried she'd suddenly appear and I'd make a scene. I didn't want to say anything in front of Elspeth and Barry but when we got back on the coach I asked him about it. He denied the call was from that girl, even pretended it was a wrong number and he'd no idea who it was from. Is it important? I mean, I don't see how any of this helps my case.'

She leant forward to pick up a biscuit from the plate but it was evident from the abstract way she nibbled at its edge the action had been nothing more than a compulsion to do something with her hands to allay her agitation.

'We must explore every possibility.'

'You think Graham's murder was something to do with that contract?'

'I am simply attempting to build up a detailed picture of events prior to your husband's death.'

After a few more conciliatory questions about her wellbeing, Montgomery-Jones wished her well and took his leave.

Nineteen

Barry and Elspeth sat in the front seats above Fiona and inevitably there were times when snatches of their conversation filtered through.

Although she tried not to listen, Fiona soon realized the tension between them had not eased. It wasn't the actual words as much as the tone of voice, the sharp retorts and the odd hissed replies that indicated all was not well. Fiona could only hazard a guess at the cause of the friction. However, it did strike her as strange, whereas immediately after Graham's death it was Elspeth constantly finding fault with her husband, now it was Barry who appeared increasing sharp with her. Perhaps her obsession with Vivien had pushed him too far.

Not her problem, Fiona told herself as she took her notes out of her bag and picked up the microphone.

'The Moselle is one of the Rhine's longest tributaries and, especially as the sun is shining and it's a lovely day, you'll be able to appreciate this is one of the most beautiful parts of Germany. You may have noticed already how much more slowly the water is flowing than in the Rhine and even the landscape seems more gentle and tranquil. By this stage of the trip you will recognize the vineyards. The best wine is produced on the slatey soils of the steep, south-facing slopes – and try saying that after a glass or two of Moselle!'

They reached the bustling little tourist town of Cochem in time for a late lunch. Due to an unforeseen last minute problem, the restaurant booked for them had closed its kitchen only the week before and Super Sun Head Office had been forced to find an alternative venue at short notice. Fiona refused to let the idea of using an untested establishment increase her stress levels. In the context of the events of the previous few days, this was only a minor hiccup.

The restaurant lay outside the town on the road to the next village. It had the advantage they would be able to reach it directly by coach. Guiding her passengers through unknown town streets to their various eating venues always proved a nerve-wracking experience for Fiona. The major tourist sights were relatively easy to find as they were frequently signposted or at least well marked on town maps allowing her to commit the route to memory before leaving the coach.

The low squat building looked decidedly unprepossessing as they drew into the parking area, which was little more than a flat area of land alongside the narrow road. Fiona's misgivings quickly dissipated when the pretty, young waitress led them round to the rear of the building into the garden. Two long tables were laid out under canvas gazebos with splendid views of the surrounding vineyards and Cochem Castle up on the distant skyline.

Everyone began to take their places although Fiona couldn't help noticing several people, not just Sidney and Daphne, hurrying to the far table after Devesh and Anita had sat down at the nearest one. The constant references to Muslim terrorists on the news reports were driving an ever-increasing number of the party to avoid the Asian couple. Instead of waiting until everyone was settled, as a point of principal, Fiona made her way to the empty space next to Devesh. The stragglers, Hilary and Rita with their respective husbands, were forced to take the other nearby seats.

Throughout their meal, Fiona tried to steer the conversation away from anything remotely controversial, at the same time making valiant efforts to include Devesh and Anita. It was hard going and after half an hour, she felt quite drained.

'It really is a lovely view, isn't it?' Fiona's comment was met with polite murmurs of agreement.

To fill the lull, Devesh replied, 'There are a great many advantages to living in a big city, but it is nice to get out into the countryside and enjoy the peace and quiet and the fresh air.'

'So whereabouts are you two from?' Rita jumped in quickly. If she thought she'd been diplomatic, she'd failed miserably.

'We're from Sutton Coldfield.'

'I meant originally.'

He must have known her game but without a touch of rancour, Devesh answered in his typically polite way, 'I was born in Coventry and my parents moved to Walsall when I was a teenager. Anita has always lived there.'

'So you have British passports?' Rita was like a dog with a bone.

'Oh yes.'

A snort of laughter came from Anita and everyone turned to stare at her. 'Sorry. Talking about passports reminded me about the fiasco at Dover. We got hauled over the coals because Devesh's writing is so difficult to read someone in the Super Sun office mistook a seven for a one on the holiday application form so my passport number didn't match the one on the official list. It's funny looking back on it now but for a while it looked as though we weren't going to be allowed to come at all. Which would've been a great shame because it's been a marvellous holiday, don't you all agree?'

Fiona smiled. Hopefully, Rita would spread that piece of gossip round the whole party although it was probably wishful thinking that the Asian couple would be now be warmly accepted back into the collective fold overnight.

'Do you ever go back to your home country?' Rita was not quite ready to let the two off the hook.

Fiona gave a quick intake of breath but, before she could cut in, Anita answered calmly, 'I still have relatives in Mumbai. My parents took me out there to see my Grandmother when I was about twelve.' Like her husband, she was all smiles, and gave no indication of the resentment she must feel at such blatant prejudice. 'Devesh has never been to India, have you, darling?'

Devesh shook his head. 'My mother came over from Calcutta as a child back in the fifties. She still talks about it a great deal but my brothers and I lead a very British life-style. But I'd like to visit one day. Just to see the place.'

Before Rita could interrogate the couple any further, Fiona turned to Hilary. 'And what about you? Are you a city girl?'

Hilary gave a deep chuckle and the dangling ornaments on the enormous hooped earrings bounced against her neck. 'I'm a Londoner me. Born and bred in Battersea. Wouldn't live anywhere else. When I was in rep, we'd spend six months at a time touring the whole country but I was always glad to get back to Wandsworth.'

'You were an actress?' Rita was impressed.

'Still am. Although, apart from the occasional voice over for adverts, I'm resting at the moment.'

Fiona relaxed again as the discussion focused on Hilary and some of the productions she'd been in. After a few minutes, this inevitably led to questions about what each of the others did for a living. It transpired both Ian and Devesh worked in banks. Ian for HSBC and Devesh, although he claimed it was only small branch, was a Barclays' manager. Rita had been a homemaker for the last thirty-five years with occasional part-time jobs and Anita was an infant teacher.

'So what about you, Fiona? Have you always been a tour manager?'

The question she always dreaded. It would hardly promote their confidence in her abilities if she were to admit she could count on one hand the number of her previous tours.

'Actually no. I trained as a nurse in Birmingham Accident Hospital which is where I met my husband.'

'Was he a doctor?'

'An anaesthetist. I was his theatre nurse.'

Attempting to deflect interest in her affairs, she turned to Viktor who had been left out of the general conversation. Not that the man ever said much.

'And you, Viktor. What do you do?' Fiona asked.

160

He stared at her for a moment before he answered, 'I porter. Covent Garden.'

'It's only temporary until his English improves and he can look for something more suited to his abilities, isn't it, love? He had a good job back home, high powered, but it's not easy to find employment when you can't speak the lingo too well.'

The use of slang obviously confused Viktor even more and, taking a packet of cigarettes from his pocket, he rose to his feet. 'I go smoke.'

'But the waitresses are bringing ice cream,' his wife protested.

'Not for me.'

With that, he was gone.

'I hope I didn't upset him.'

'Not to worry,' Hilary reassured a crestfallen Fiona. 'He can seem a bit abrupt at times. He doesn't mean to be rude, but he doesn't know how to express himself.'

Devesh, with his usual tact, broke the embarrassed silence. 'You have the advantage, Fiona, of working in beautiful places. I'm not saying Birmingham doesn't have some magnificent buildings but we never seem to have time to go and appreciate them.'

'Can't say Chelmsford's got that much to offer,' contributed Ian.

'What about the cathedral?' Rita sounded affronted at her husband's dismissal of her home town. 'And there's Hyland House just outside the city.'

'Which we've never visited.'

'I'm sure Chelmsford must seem quite grand compared to those dismal old Soviet cities that poor Viktor's come from,' Rita snapped back.

'They're not all like that,' Hilary protested. 'Viktor says for a while he worked in Samarkand; one of the most beautiful cities on earth as well as being one of the oldest. It's full of these gorgeous buildings, tombs and mosques and whatnot.'

'I thought that was just an imaginary place,' Rita chipped in.

Devesh shook his head. 'It was founded by Alexander the

Great and the Persian emperor Timur made it his capital.'

'Never heard of him.' Rita shrugged her shoulders dismissively.

'The mighty Tamerlane,' said Devesh so quietly that Anita and Fiona were probably the only ones who heard him.

'So where did you and Viktor meet?' asked the ever-curious Rita changing the subject.

Hilary gave an embarrassed laugh. 'On the internet.'

'Really?' Rita looked shocked but curiosity soon took over. 'Have you been married long?'

'Only a couple of months. This is sort of our honeymoon.'

It occurred to Fiona, given Viktor's English was not up to more than a couple of sentences and Hilary obviously didn't speak a word of her husband's language – whatever that might be – communication must prove tricky at times.

Rita clearly revelled in this sort of gossip and looked set to start a whole barrage of questions. To forestall her Hilary leant across the table to Anita.

'I really like your bangle.'

'Thank you.'

'Love jewellery me. As you can probably tell.' Hilary had rings on almost every finger, and sported enough bracelets and necklaces to fill a supermarket's jewellery counter. 'Is it solid gold?'

'Oh no. It's iron in the centre. Just like this one.' Anita pointed to the dull metal band above the ornate gold one. 'It's the equivalent of a Hindu wedding ring.'

'But you have two,' accused Rita.

'My mother gave me this.' She indicated the plain metal band. 'And my mother-in-law the gold covered one.'

'And was yours an arranged marriage?'

Did Rita never stop prying? Fiona wondered.

'Oh yes.' Anita smiled. 'But we did know each other before.'

'Hindu weddings are very grand affairs so I've heard. Don't they go on for days?' Fiona decided it would do no harm to emphasize the couple were not Muslims.

Anita's pleasant tinkling laugh made them all smile. 'Ours

certainly cost a fortune. My father said it was a blessing he only had one daughter.'

'But he gave you an English name,' Rita accused.

'It's a traditional Hindu name,' Devesh said with a laugh. 'It means full of grace.'

'The same as Ann in English. That means graceful one as well,' Hilary informed them all.

Others began to drift back to the coach. Time to move.

It was less than a ten-minute drive to Cochem. Fiona barely had time to talk about the town's highlights – the reconstructed castle, its sober baroque Rathaus or town hall and St Martin's Church with its unusual Rococo tower shaped like a soldier's helmet.

'It's quite a small place so you won't have far to walk to see everything. Although if you decide to go up to the castle, I should warn you, the path is relatively steep and it's a lot further than it looks. So, everyone have a pleasant afternoon and please remember to be back on time.'

Winston opened both doors and everyone made their way off the coach. He stood at the side door leaving Fiona to help the last few people down the steep steps at the front of the coach.

She said goodbye to Edith and Len Webster and stood watching the couple amble towards the town centre enjoying the warmth of midday sun on her face and arms. A moment or two of peace and calm at last. Perhaps after a stroll through the crowded centre of the village, she would take the path up to the castle. The views from the top must be magnificent. It would be a shame not to make the most of this lovely day, especially after Wednesday's rain and yesterday's cloudy skies.

Even so, best to take a cardigan. The fluffy white clouds and blue skies might not threaten rain but it would be as well to be prepared. The madly flapping flags on the castle pinnacles suggested a strong breeze up at the top and after all that effort, she did not want to be driven back down by a chill wind.

As she went to hop back on the coach, she heard voices from

inside. Not everyone had left after all.

'For goodness sake, woman!'

The words were now clearly audible. Best not to intrude.

'But she's my sister. Of course I'm worried about her.'

Perhaps she should creep away. Apart from anything else, it would be embarrassing to be caught listening in to what was obviously a private conversation. But her bag was still tucked into the little cubbyhole under the dashboard. Without her purse, she wouldn't even be able to buy herself a cup of coffee.

'Please, darling.' Elspeth was close to tears.

'The histrionics are wearing a bit thin. This isn't because you're concerned about Vivien. It's guilt, pure and simple. If you really cared about her, it would never have happened.'

'How can you say that? She means everything to me.'

'So much you slept with her husband!'

Fiona hurried out of sight round the front of the coach as Barry stormed down the coach steps and strode off towards the town without a backward glance.

'If the man was speaking Turkish could he be Hezbollah?'

Montgomery-Jones looked thoughtful. 'That makes the assumption the phone call came from the same group as Spelman's contact.'

'You think it's a red herring?' James found it difficult to keep the frustration out of his voice. Why couldn't the man just come out with what he was thinking?

'No. I do not. It is certainly significant. However, it provides us with more questions than answers.'

'So far, we've got nothing from all the Pakistani leads but where do we start with this? What interest would Hezbollah have in Frankfurt? There's no Israeli presence to interest them.'

'Exactly.' Montgomery-Jones took out his mobile. 'I think our American friends may know more than they have been prepared to share. Time to ruffle some feathers, I think.'

It wasn't until much later the implication of the overheard fracas between Barry and Elspeth began to dawn on Fiona. Perhaps she was reading too much into all of this. It certainly explained the tension between the couple; but did it make Barry a suspect for Graham's murder? That Monday morning, Elspeth and Vivien had come down together. How much longer was it before Barry made an appearance? Time enough for Barry to have nipped into the room, stab Graham and join the women for breakfast? True the murderer would probably be covered in blood and would have had to go back and change. She hadn't seen Barry before breakfast so she didn't know if he wore the same clothes as first thing. Elspeth hadn't remarked on it, but she had other things to worry about by then and probably wouldn't have noticed.

But if Barry had murderous feelings towards his brother-in-law, why wait until they were on holiday? If it was a sudden act of passion and not a premeditated attack, did that rule out Barry? How long had he known about his wife's indiscretion? If he'd only just found out, it might explain why he went in to have it out with Graham and things got out of hand.

Now she'd let her mind run away with her. She had no proof, no evidence to go on, nothing but her own over-active imagination.

Vivien's clothes had been sent for forensic investigation, but what about anyone else's? The police had taken away the things she and Elspeth had been wearing when they discovered Vivien with Graham's body, but only those. No one had asked to see the contents of the rest of Fiona's wardrobe so presumably no one else's room had been searched either.

So what should she do? Fiona had no qualms about not telling the police, but should she tell Peter Montgomery-Jones? It was one thing to keep him informed of possible information that might help Vivien's cause but quite another to repeat something so private and personal without strong justification. She would have to give the matter some thought.

Twenty

They were approaching Assmannshausen but before Winston could turn off the main valley road into the village, a police car came racing towards them, its blue light flashing. Even though it was still some distance away, Winston slowed the coach almost to a standstill. The car approached rapidly then turned sharply across their path.

'Hope the railway barriers aren't down or there's gonna be a nasty accident,' said Winston as they followed in its wake at a considerably more leisurely speed.

The coach clattered noisily over the railway line and turned into the village before negotiating the final ninety-degree corner.

'It's stopped outside our hotel!' Fiona stared at the now stationary police car and let her stomach settle after its momentary flip. Had there been further developments? It was highly unlikely to be anything connected to Graham's murder. Even if Vivien had been arrested, there would no reason for the police to come back here.

The coach pulled into the space by the church that constituted the nearest thing to a lay-by in the village. Before everyone piled off the coach, Fiona warned them all to be patient. It was odds on Marthe was busy seeing to the police and the reception desk would be unmanned. They might have to wait before collecting their keys.

'I'll go and check. You might as well sit here in comfort for a minute or two rather than stand around in the corridor.'

As she had predicted, there was no one behind the reception

desk. Tentatively, she took a few steps along the passage behind to where the hotel offices were located.

'Hello! Anyone around?'

There was no answer. Perhaps she should try the bar or perhaps, at this time in the afternoon, the kitchens might be a better bet.

Eventually one of the girls from the kitchen came to see to reception until Marthe's return.

'Do you know what all the fuss is about?' Fiona asked the girl. The others would be bound to ask when she went back to the coach and, after Monday's trauma, they would be anxious. Who could blame them?

The girl's English was by not as good as the receptionist's and, after a bit of rewording of her question and a liberal interpretation of the girl's reply, Fiona learnt one of the guest bedrooms had been broken into. At least that was what she assumed was meant by, 'Door chopped down.'

'Oh dear! I hope nothing valuable was stolen.'

'Room empty.'

'I expect most people are still out at the moment. Can you tell me if the room belongs to one of the Super Sun party?' That was all she needed. One more thing to sort out.

The girl nodded. 'Man who died.'

'Really? Room 21?

'Ja, ja. Ein und zwanzig.' The girl nodded again, excitedly 'By stairs. At top.'

Fiona felt a surge of panic but said calmly, 'I'll go and tell my people they can come in now, shall I?'

Fiona helped the last person down the steep coach steps and a thought struck her. She pulled her mobile from her bag.

'Montgomery-Jones.'

'It's Fiona Mason. We've just got back to the hotel and you may already know this, but the police are here. It looks as though the Spelman's room has been broken into.'

After a second's pause, a calm, matter-of-fact voice replied, 'I did not. Thank you. I will be over straight away.'

Marthe usually had the keys lined up on the desk as soon as the coach drew up and the girl took a long time sorting them out. So long that Winston had parked the coach and returned to the hotel before everyone had the correct key. Fiona stayed talking with him until the last of their passengers had been sorted. As there was nowhere for them to stand without blocking up the corridor, the two of them wandered back outside.

'Things still not good between those two, I see,' Winston said quietly as he leaned his great bulk against the whitewashed wall.

'Elspeth and Barry? No.' Fiona sighed.

'Not your problem, sweetheart.' He gave her shoulder a gentle squeeze.

'I think I know why. I overheard them talking and I've been trying to decide whether or not I should pass it on to Mr Montgomery-Jones. The trouble is it's personal and I wasn't supposed to hear, but it could well be relevant to the murder investigation.'

'Then perhaps you should. What he chooses to do about it is up to him.'

'You're right of course, but it still feels very underhand somehow.'

Winston put an arm around her shoulder. 'You don't owe these people anything, sweetheart. You're here to show them the sights not bear their burdens.'

Marthe had returned when they went back in and the girl, eager to return to her usual duties, wasted no time scurrying back to the kitchen.

'I am sorry I was not here to see to you all. The police wanted to speak to me,' said Marthe as she handed Winston his key.

'No problem. That young lady sorted us all out. She said the Spelmans' room, No. 21, had been broken into. Is that true?' A bit late to check now, Fiona thought ruefully. If she'd made a mistake and brought Montgomery-Jones out on a wild goose chase, he would not be pleased, to say the least.

Marthe nodded. 'It must have been this afternoon. The door was not damaged at two o'clock when the maid finished. The police are talking to her now.'

'Have they any idea who broke in, or why?'

'Perhaps someone came in from outside. Who can say? Nothing like this has ever happened before.'

Before Marthe could hand over Fiona's key the phone went and it was a minute or two before Marthe could give Fiona her attention again.

'I am sorry to keep you waiting.'

'No worries.' Fiona gave her a reassuring smile.

'No 28 appears to be missing. It is not on the hook.' Marthe began searching under the counter. In all the confusion, the keys had obviously become muddled up. Eventually they found the key in the drop-off box.

'How strange. I'm sure I handed it to you when I left this morning.' Fiona frowned.

'I remember,' Marthe agreed.

'These things happen and there's no harm done.'

Other guests were returning so Marthe was fully occupied seeing to their needs. Fiona slipped her key into her pocket then looked at her watch. She wondered if she should wait downstairs for Peter Montgomery-Jones. As she had no idea where he was staying or how long the journey would take, she might as well go up to her room. Marthe could ring her when he arrived.

In the event, it wasn't necessary. Montgomery-Jones walked in the door before she reached the stairs. She repeated the few facts she'd just learnt from Marthe as they walked up to the third floor.

'At least it couldn't have been one of my people. We were all in the Moselle valley in the afternoon. But if it was an opportunist burglar, why go all the way to the top floor? Do you think he was after the same thing you were searching for yesterday?'

'Fiona!' There was a definite warning in his voice even if he

169

had used her Christian name.

'You can't blame me for leaping to that conclusion.' She gave him her best wide-eyed, innocent look. 'It's not as if I asked you what it was.'

The imperious glare she received in response, indicated he was not about to succumb to her wheedling and he sounded almost threatening as he said, 'If I were you, Mrs Mason, I would think it politic at this point to drop the subject altogether.'

It was impossible to swallow the rebellious surge that rose to her lips. 'Mr Montgomery-Jones, I do not respond well to being intimidated.'

'Would I dare?' He looked down at her with a definite glint in his eye. Now he was making fun of her.

She felt her whole body stiffen. What was it about this infuriating man he could get under her skin so easily? Much of the time she could not fathom what the man was thinking or feeling. She took a deep breath and slowly counted to ten before letting out a long, soft sigh. From past experience, she knew she could never win any argument with him. Best to play him at his own game. 'For the vast majority of us mere mortals, anyone who uses the subjunctive in ordinary conversation is intimidating.'

He gave an explosive laugh, shook his head and raised his eyes heavenwards in mock despair. 'You are incorrigible, Mrs Mason. Incorrigible.'

Fiona gave him a weak smile. After walking up two and a half floors, five flights each of a dozen steps, Fiona was not about to waste more precious breath giving him a response.

A policeman leant against the wall alongside No. 21 idly inspecting his fingernails. He stood to attention as they turned the corner but relaxed again when he realized neither of them were one of his superior officers.

As Fiona stood trying to recover her breath, Montgomery-Jones continued to walk slowly towards him and asked something in what sounded to Fiona like a perfect German accent. He took out what she assumed must be some kind of

170

identity or warrant card and, once he'd shown it to the officer, turned and pushed open the door and looked inside. After another brief exchange, the policeman pointed back along the corridor.

Montgomery-Jones returned to her side and said sotto voce, 'We need to talk.'

'There's a quiet area round the corner.'

As they passed Room 21, Fiona saw the lock had been badly splintered and she could just make out piles of clothing tipped onto the floor from the pulled out drawers through the narrow crack.

They turned the corner and took two steps down into a large oddly shaped landing area, much like a separate room, off to one side of the corridor. It contained a collection of ancient curios, including a large wooden rocking horse and a treadle sewing machine. Montgomery-Jones motioned her to the settee set beneath the small high window. It wasn't exactly private but they would hear any approaching footsteps on the creaky wooden floor.

'He's certainly made a mess in there,' she said as she sat down. 'He must have made quite a racket when he smashed the lock. I'm surprised it didn't attract someone's attention.'

'Presumably there was no one around at the time.'

'I know you told me to drop the subject but, if the person who broke in was the same one who murdered Graham, it couldn't have been Vivien, could it?'

'True,' he said, 'but there is nothing to suggest that the perpetrators are the same individual.'

'Okay. Assuming our burglar wanted something in Graham Spelman's room, how did he know which one to break into?'

'Exactly.' He looked at her intently. 'Have there been any more enquiries about Spelman?'

'Other than the phone calls you know about, not to my knowledge. I can ask if you want me to.'

He shook his head. 'We have no idea if the burglar was working on his own.'

'You think he has a partner?' What was he implying? 'One

171

of my people.'

'It is highly unlikely I will admit, but there is always that possibility.'

'Up till now, I haven't noticed any of them behaving suspiciously, but I can listen out and let you know what happens.'

'Knowing you, Mrs Mason, even if I say no, you will anyway. Please do be very careful.'

She gave him a sheepish grin.

'You have not seen your watcher again, I take it?' He asked after a pause.

'Not today. You think he might be our burglar?'

'I have no idea.' He gave a deep sigh, leant back stretching out his long legs and closed his eyes. 'Absolutely no idea, whatsoever.'

'Not admitting defeat are you, Mr Montgomery-Jones?' She could hardly keep the bubble of laughter from her voice.

Still with his eyes closed, he smiled and said, 'Certainly not, Mrs Mason. Such negativity is not in my nature. Though I am willing to confess a precise strategy for proceeding does elude me for the moment.'

They sat in silence for a while longer until a sudden thought struck Fiona. 'I'm sure it's not relevant at all, which is why it didn't occur to me earlier, but on the day we got here, Graham talked about his job. When I showed a polite interest, he gave me a company brochure.'

'Really? What a singularly peculiar thing to do.' He sat up and looked at her.

'In retrospect, it does seem a bit odd, I'll admit. At the time I really didn't pay it much attention.'

'Have you read it?'

'I had a flick through. It's just straightforward promotional stuff. Lots of pictures.'

'Nothing else?'

'No, just the brochure in a plain A4 envelope.'

'Did anyone see him give it to you?'

'Everyone. He handed it over at the start of dinner. He was the last one down. I doubt it will be of any help, but I can fetch it for you if you'd like.'

'Yes. Please.'

Fiona got to her feet. It felt good to do something positive even though this would hardly solve the case.

Her hurried footsteps sounded surprisingly loud in the silence of the annex. She put her key into the door but at first, it did not seem to want to turn. She took it out and tried again, rattling it in the lock.

'How odd!'

She turned the knob and the door swung open. The door hadn't been locked in the first place. Sometimes the key did jam and it needed to be jiggled until it worked properly. Perhaps, with all the kerfuffle this afternoon, the maid had forgotten to lock the door after the room had been cleaned.

Something didn't feel right. One of the drawers wasn't quite closed. Only a tiny amount but from this angle she could see it clearly. She pulled it out to see her treasured lamb's wool cardigan lay crumpled. Something she would never let happen.

A distinct chill rippled down her spine.

Twenty-One

'Sorry I've been so long.'

'Was there a problem?'

'You could say that,' she said with some rancour. 'Someone's been in my room.'

Montgomery-Jones stared at her, deep furrows creasing his brow. 'Are you positive?'

'Oh yes. There's no doubt about it.'

'Broken into!' He was on his feet.

'No, no,' she said quickly. 'They used a key, but the mechanism sticks sometimes and they failed to lock the door properly when they left. The room wasn't ransacked but I realized my things were not quite as I'd left them. My notes for the various tours I'd left on the table are muddled and out of order.'

'Perhaps the maid dropped them when she was dusting.'

'Possibly, but she would never go into the drawers. All the forms I need to fill in at the end of holiday were in a plain envelope, just like the brochure, in the bedside drawer but someone had obviously looked at them then put them back in upside down bending back the corner of the top sheet in the process.'

'Did they take anything?'

'The only things of any value I brought were a locket and some earrings that belonged to my grandmother and they're still there. But why on earth would anyone want to go through my things? It doesn't make sense.'

Montgomery-Jones shrugged his shoulders and began

looking through the brochure page by page.

After what seemed an interminable wait, she said, 'Perhaps he was looking for the same thing you were searching for.'

He gave her one of his imperious looks. She grinned back undaunted. She hadn't really expected an answer.

When he reached the last page he said, 'There is nothing here. Straightforward advertising material.'

'Presumably as the Spelmans' room was broken-in and whoever went into mine used a key, it's unlikely to have been the same person, but I wonder if the two could be connected.' When he didn't answer, she went on, 'I suppose as nothing was taken, it would be a waste of resources fingerprinting my room?'

'Very true.'

They lapsed into silence, each lost in thought.

Eventually Fiona plucked up the courage to ask, 'We return to England in a couple of days, do you think Vivien will be allowed to come with us?'

'Although she has not been charged, I would imagine, unless there are unforeseen developments, the police will insist she stay until the matter is sorted.'

'At the risk of you shouting at me again, do you honestly think Vivien Spelman is responsible for the murder of her husband?'

He turned and looked at her with a mock-imperious stare. 'I never shout at you.'

She would let that one go. It was probably only a ruse to avoid answering her question.

'Well, do you?'

He shook his head. 'On the basis of whoever stabbed Spellman would have been covered in his blood, it is difficult to conceive how anyone else could have walked through the corridors in such a state and remain undetected and no discarded bloody clothing was found anywhere in the hotel.'

Fiona sighed. It was an idea that had struck her some time ago. At that time in the morning all the hotel guests would have been to-ing and fro-ing to breakfast.

175

'However, if we are to assume Mrs Spelman did not stab her husband in the heat of an argument, we are faced with a chilling prospect. Spellman's killer was almost certainly staying in this hotel. With the exception of the two doors on either side of reception plus the staff entrance by the kitchen, all the hotel entrances remain locked until after checkout time at ten o'clock. The under manager was at the desk throughout breakfast. It is true he could not see either door from that position but an outsider would have to come along the corridor to the stairs or the lift and been spotted.'

'So if it was someone staying here, it could be one of my party.'

'There is that possibility. Though it is difficult to conceive a motive.'

Reluctantly, Fiona said, 'This may not be relevant but, I think I ought to tell you something. It's about Barry.'

He did not seem at all surprised when she told him what she'd overheard earlier in the afternoon.

'You knew already, didn't you?'

His lips twitched in a wry smile. 'Mr Glover has already admitted he knew about the affair. He said it gave him as much motive as his sister-in-law.'

'So I can stop feeling guilty for telling you.'

Montgomery-Jones laughed and rolled his eyes heavenwards. 'Mrs Mason! Anyone one else would be fearful of their own safety, especially immediately after their room had been searched, but all that appears to concern you is your loyalty to a group of people you have known for less than a week.'

'This is all to do with Graham,' she said crossly. 'Not me. Although I can't say I relish the thought of anyone going through my things, I fail to see why I could be in any danger. Do the police know about Barry? They don't seem to be treating him as a suspect.'

'They may well be. I am not privy to the details of the German police investigation. However, Mr Glover's room was searched after the body was found. There was no blood on any of his clothing and he did not leave the hotel before the police arrived.'

'I see,' she said doubtfully.

He sensed her concern and said, 'If I considered you or your party were in any immediate danger, I assure you I would take action, nevertheless, Mrs Mason, I do urge you to take care. If you notice anything out of the ordinary or have any concerns whatsoever, please do not hesitate to contact me.'

'I will. Thank you.'

'I need to speak with the officers in charge of this last investigation before I leave, but it might be a good idea if you came with me to inform them of your intruder.'

As she anticipated, the senior police officer lost interest in Fiona's story once she admitted nothing had been taken. He and his plain-clothes colleague, the one making all the notes, probably thought she'd let her imagination run away with her. At least in front of Montgomery-Jones, they stopped short of accusing her of wasting their time. It was a relief to leave allowing the men to discuss the trashing of the Spellmans' room.

Outside the door, Fiona looked at her watch. Despite all the comings and goings, there was still time for a short stroll through the village before dinner. A breath of fresh air was just what she needed. It had the added advantage, none of her clients could badger her and she desperately wanted to think things through without any interruptions. She could stroll down to the riverfront and perhaps treat herself to a creamy hot chocolate in one of the wine bar cafés and watch the world go by. After all she'd been through, she was entitled to a bit of calorific self-indulgent pampering.

With all the kerfuffle when they arrived back at the hotel, it would have been easy enough for any of the party to pick up her key. Unlike Marthe who was now adept at remembering everyone's room number, the girl from the kitchen had simply dumped the whole pile on the counter and let everyone pick up their own. It must have been a good ten to fifteen minutes from the time the keys were given out until she had gone to collect hers. She had phoned Peter Montgomery-Jones and spent some time talking with Winston. Plenty of time for someone to have taken her key, searched the room and dropped it back at reception while she was still outside.

Could it be the same person as Graham's killer? The police and Peter Montgomery-Jones maintained it had to be someone already in the hotel. But what did they hope to find in her room? Had the murderer dropped something in Graham's room and been worried she might have picked it up? Hardly. But then nothing made sense. One thing she was certain of; Graham's death and this mysterious contract Montgomery-Jones was so desperate to get to the bottom of were inextricably linked.

There were few shops in the village but she paused at one window crammed with interesting little knick-knacks. Still preoccupied with her thoughts, trying to find some logical explanation, she didn't hear the man come up behind her. Only when she felt a sharp tug on the strap of her shoulder bag did she realized what was happening. Before she could retaliate, a violent shove knocked her sideways gazing her cheek against the roughcast wall.

Twenty-Two

Laura finished the last page of her novel and snapped it shut. Had she realized she'd be spending so much time sitting around in their hotel room while James was off doing whatever official business he was up to, she would have brought more books to read. Oh well, much as she loved Sophie Kinsella, there was only so much shopping chic lit one could take in one sitting anyway. Besides, it was almost time for dinner. Always assuming James returned soon.

She moved to the dressing table and was squinting into the mirror to apply a final coat of mascara when she heard the door open.

'So what did the Commander have to say? Do they know who broke into Spelman's room?'

'Not a clue, apparently. German intelligence are as foxed as we are. One of their senior BND men was here apparently. Seems he was present at the interview with Fiona Mason.'

'What did she have to do with it? I though it happened when the coach lot were all out for the day.'

'It did but someone's been through her room searching through her stuff.'

'Couldn't it have been the BND? You said the Commander told them exactly what to look for when they searched every room in the hotel on Tuesday afternoon and came up with zilch.'

'True but it wasn't them. They're professionals. They would never leave any sign of having been there.'

'So was it the same person who broke into the Spelmans'

room?'

'Heaven only knows. This whole thing keeps getting more and more complicated. As the Commander keeps reminding me, finding those designs remain our top priority.'

'So what next?'

James bent down and kissed the top of her head. 'Dinner, I think.'

Fiona did not look forward to facing everyone downstairs. The news would be all round the group by now. She'd passed Celia and Joe Ennis on her way back to the hotel. They'd rushed over when they saw her clutching a bloody handkerchief to her face. No way could she creep up the stairs or sidle into the lift unnoticed. Until she'd been told the full story, Marthe held onto her key and then promptly insisted the local police should be informed despite Fiona's protests she didn't want to make a fuss over such a minor incident.

There was a gentle rap at her door. Perhaps if she ignored it they would go away. She felt much too fragile to face visitors. The last thing she wanted right now was some sympathetic busybody come to see how she was.

The knock came again. Louder this time. Clearly they weren't prepared to take the hint.

'Fiona.'

Her head jerked upwards. The soft baritone was unmistakable. How on earth had he found out? She listened. No footsteps. He wasn't going to go away. Admitting defeat, she pushed herself up wearily from the stool and went to open the door.

'Come in.'

She turned quickly and returned to her place by the dressing table but not before she caught the worried frown on his face. If he said how sorry or concerned he was, she'd burst into tears.

'I told you to call me as soon as anything happened.' The words may have been harsh but his tone of voice certainly wasn't.

They brought a smile to her lips even though she could still feel the tears behind her eyes. 'I would have done, eventually. How did you get to hear so soon?'

'I was about to leave when Marthe called me over. Were you able to identify your attacker?'

'I was too busy trying to break my fall to notice much. By the time I turned to look, the little toe rag had already made good his escape.'

'So it was a youth?'

Even though her nerves were torn to shreds - or perhaps because of it - she felt a childish giggle bubble up inside. Montgomery-Jones was ever the detective. Why had she anticipated anything else? Shaking her head she said, 'I've no idea. I presume so. Aren't they usually responsible for opportune bag snatching? It was my own stupid fault. I always tell my people to put straps right across their chests and not just over a shoulder but this little village seemed so safe.'

'Did he get away with much?'

'Only enough loose change for a drink, my sunglasses and a handkerchief.'

'Nothing of any value?'

'Depends how you look at it?' With all the venom she could muster, she spat, 'That little toe rag took Bill's photo.'

She turned away, blinking back the tears. In two steps, Montgomery-Jones crossed the room, took her by the shoulders and gently eased her round to face him.

'Shsssh, shsssh.'

'It was only a holiday snap,' her voice came in hiccupping sobs muffled into his shirt as he enveloped her in a tight embrace. 'But it was the only decent one I had before he got ill.'

The strong arms held her close until she'd pulled herself together and tried to step back. Still holding on to her upper arms, he bent down until she could see warm speckles of blue in the grey eyes staring into hers. 'You do not need a picture to remind you of what he looked like. You have stared at that photograph everyday since he died. You know every line on his face; it is indelibly printed on your brain. That picture will be with you until the day you die. No one can take that from you.'

She bit her lip, the tears began to flow again and, as she tried to brush them away with the back of her hand, he held out a freshly laundered handkerchief. As she took it from him, she managed a weak smile. 'How could you possibly know that?'

His lips parted in a slow smile. 'Because, Mrs Mason, I know you.'

Arriving late to dinner meant Fiona was spared the embarrassment of being surrounded by her party and bombarded with questions as to how she was feeling and what had happened – although not necessarily in that order.

There were plenty of nods and smiles, even the odd beckoning wave, but Fiona slid into her place on the end of the banquette smiling at the waitress who hurried over with her plate.

'Are you alright my dear? You look very pale.' Sidney, at the next table, had peered round the low wooden partition. 'It's a dreadful world we're living in these days when defenceless older people are attacked in broad daylight even in a peaceful spot like this. None of us is safe. I hope you've reported it to the police.'

'Do let the poor girl eat her meal while it's still hot.'

Clearly affronted at Gloria's interruption of his diatribe, Sidney retreated looking none too pleased.

'It's very good,' Gloria said to Fiona, 'Sausages cooked in a beer and mustard sauce with caramelized onions. Delicious.'

Dear Gloria. Never one to wring the drama out of a situation.

When the time came to move into the bar, Fiona was tempted to retreat straight to her room but she knew it would only provoke more comment and she would have to face them all sometime. Best to make light of it all and pretend it hadn't affected her. At least in the bar, the music and noise would keep the conversations brief.

Nonetheless, she wasn't prepared to sit it out to the bitter end. He head was throbbing and, apart from anything else, she felt incredibly tired. She took one look at the stairs and decided she couldn't face the long climb.

Coming out of the lift she saw Elspeth walking towards her.

'Fiona. I'm so pleased I've caught you. I was about to come and find you.'

'Is there a problem?'

'Oh no.' Elspeth managed a wan smile. 'It's just I wanted you to know, I've decided to go and keep Vivien company. Her room is a twin so there won't be a problem with accommodation in her hotel. She really shouldn't be on her own at a time like this.'

'I see.'

'She took some persuading at first, but Barry and I have talked it over and we both think it's for the best.'

That was one way of putting it, Fiona thought. From what she'd observed, the two of them hadn't been able to speak to the other without snapping or sulking for most of the day. That was the problem with holidays. When tempers became frayed, there was no escape from each other to give time to cool down.

'So have you decided when you're leaving?'

'Viv has still has to clear it with the hotel but I'm going to get a taxi over there tomorrow morning. Barry offered to see I got over there, but it would be a shame for him to miss tomorrow's trip especially as he was so looking forward to the wine tasting.'

From the little Fiona knew of Barry, that didn't seem likely. Unlike his late brother-in-law who'd been a real aficionado, Fiona had never seen him with a wineglass in his hand. Beer yes, even whisky, but Barry didn't strike her as a wine lover.

Elspeth hurried away and Fiona continued to her room. Perhaps it was for the best, assuming she could keep Barry from drinking himself under the table without Elspeth.

Day 7 Saturday

This morning we visit Mainz, the state capital and chief city of the Rhineland, with its 2000 year heritage. Broad, roomy squares, half-timbered houses and magnificent baroque buildings reminiscent of the times of the Electors, give the Old Town its charming character.

After a short walking tour of the city centre, we will visit the Gutenberg museum to see a reconstruction of the master's workshop and its priceless Gutenberg Bible.

During your free time after lunch, why not look at the Cathedral's superb Rococo oak stalls, the acclaimed post-war windows by Marc Chagall in the Church of St. Stephan, or take a stroll along the Kirschgarten to admire the historic half-timbered houses? There are also many interesting shops waiting to be discovered.

No excursion to this beautiful area of Germany would be complete without a visit to a wine cellar where you will have an opportunity to learn more about the noble grape and enjoy a wine tasting.

Super Sun Executive Travel

Twenty-Three

Marthe looked up from her newspaper as Fiona mounted the steps to the reception desk to hand in her room key. Fiona couldn't help noticing the word Frankfurt in the headline on the open page. Her heart sank. It was probably nothing to do with the dreadful events of last week but Sidney Pettit's obsession with terrorism showed no sign of abating and it was beginning to infect everybody else's calm.

'Is something happening in Frankfurt?' Fiona asked, trying to sound casual.

'The authorities have identified the man who was killed in the car bomb on Sunday.' Marthe glanced down at the article. 'His name was Iskander Usmanov.'

'That sounds Russian. I thought he was supposed to have come from Pakistan.'

'It says here, he came from Uzbekistan.'

He could come from Timbuktu for all I care, Fiona thought, as long as Sidney doesn't get to hear about it. She was probably worrying about nothing. There'd been no comment on CNN or the BBC World News to cause alarm. Although she generally made it a policy not to watch the television news while she was away, this trip was an exception. Not that she had any fears for their safety, but the last thing she needed was Sidney having any cause to spread doom and gloom.

As the coach headed east towards Mainz, Fiona felt a little knot of concern in the pit of her stomach. Across the river from Mainz lay the town of Wiesbaden. Would Sidney or any others in his determinedly-anxious coterie notice the road signs? How might they react when they realized they were on the outskirts of the town where the car bomb victim had been staying? With luck, none of them would remember the name of the town, but best to keep their minds on something else. Time for her spiel.

'The two thousand year old city of Mainz was founded by the Romans at the confluence of the Rhine and the Main. The city became an important centre in the eighth century when the English monk, St Boniface, known as the "German Apostle," became its first archbishop and established it as the main centre of Christendom north of the Alps.' She continued at length about the rise of subsequent archbishops as powerful arch chancellors of the Empire and the founding of the Rhenish League of Cities.

So far so good. In her mirror, Fiona glanced at Sidney and Daphne. They were sitting on the right hand side of the bus looking out over the river. Fiona shuffled her notes and lifted the microphone once more.

'Today of course, Mainz is an important centre in the German wine economy and hosts one of the largest wine festivals in the country at the end of August.'

Much to Fiona's relief they crossed the bridge and entered the city. How she had managed to keep talking for so long she wasn't sure. Half of them must have nodded off after all that information although now they all seemed happy and smiling.

No one had mentioned Wiesbaden.

The coach dropped them off by the main square, close to all the major attractions. Fiona gave Barry an encouraging smile as everyone clambered down from the coach but there was no opportunity to speak with him. He seemed happy enough without Elspeth and had lost the morose look he'd had for most of the previous day. She was relieved to see him fall into step with Ernest Blake, the only other single man in the party.

Apart from a quick word on her way out from breakfast,

neither had she had the chance to enquire after Brendan. He still looked pale and subdued but at least he was fit enough to join today's outing.

A sudden thought struck her. When she'd told Montgomery-Jones the whole party were out at the time Graham's room was ransacked she had forgotten about Brendan. Not that it could be relevant. The Irishman was in his late sixties and not particularly powerfully built and much too gentle a person to go shouldering his way into someone else's room. What possible reason could he have? It had to be someone from outside the hotel.

For now, there were more important things to think about. They had arrived in Gutenbergplatz and Fiona led them over to the memorial dedicated to Mainz's most famous historical figure.

'Johannes Gutenberg, the inventor of printing, was born, lived and died here in the fifteenth century. His moveable type allowed the first mass production of books.' They all craned their necks to look up at the life size bronze statue on top of its tall plinth. 'As you can see, the bas reliefs on each side of the pedestal show various scenes of book printing but you will learn far more about that in the Gutenberg Museum which is where we're now going if you'd like to follow me.'

Laura looked at her watch for what must have been the fifth time in as many minutes. She'd already had three cups of coffee and, even if she could have drunk it, the waitress would start to question what she was up to if she ordered another.

James hurried through the door of the café.

'Sorry, sorry, sorry,' he said, not looking in the least apologetic. 'Things were a bit hectic when I got there.'

'You could have rung me.'

'The Commander went ballistic this morning,' he said ignoring her tart, tight-lipped comment. 'He's been saying for days that the Americans have been holding out on us. I know he's got a reputation but I've never seen him like that before. I hope to heaven I'm never on the receiving end.'

All the cutting comments and petty retributions Laura had been dreaming up for the last half hour disappeared.

'Because Spelman's contact was posing as a Pakistani businessman, we've been investigating known Lashkar and other Pakistani extremists plus all the major groups that have known training facilities over there. Bloody tall order! But, there was a report in the local paper this morning that he was an Uzbek. Naturally, the boss was on the line to Koehler straight away demanding to know why we hadn't been told, but it seems it was news to the BND as well. All hell was let loose. The upshot was that the CIA have known for days that the dead man had connections to a militant Islamic group in Uzbekistan and one of their people let it slip to his German girl friend who happens to have a brother who's a journalist.'

Laura giggled. 'So British and American relations are somewhat strained, I take it.'

'Let's just say I think it will take more than sending the loose-tongued idiot on the first plane back to the US before the Commander will be having tea with the CIA again.' James pushed back his chair and nodded at her empty cup. 'I'm parched. Time for quick coffee before we set off. Would you like another?'

'Not for me, thanks.'

The afternoon's itinerary allowed some time for those who wanted to do a little exploring on their own which meant few people tarried over lunch. Ernest, who never wasted an opportunity to see as much as possible, was the first on his feet already clutching his now well-thumbed guidebook. Fiona watched as he said something to Barry, presumably an invitation to join him, but the younger man shook his head and remained sitting. Devesh and Anita followed soon after. Was it because they wanted to spend as much time as possible sightseeing or, as Fiona feared, to avoid the strained atmosphere that their presence appeared to generate amongst an increasing number in the party?

Once the others at her table had left, there was no reason for

Fiona to stay any longer. Only the two oldest couples remained and they seemed happy enough sitting and chatting watching the world go by through the large picture windows.

As she walked out into the busy square, she caught sight of Barry ahead of her. She felt a wave of misgiving when she saw him disappear into a bar, but she could hardly go in and drag him back out. What was it Ted had said to her back in Ypres on their first evening about her being their tour manager not their nursemaid? She walked quickly passed the bar entrance forcing herself not to glance in.

It seemed vaguely sinful not to make the most of the opportunity to do some exploring herself, but the accumulated tension of the week's events not least a muzzy head after yesterday's attack had left Fiona feeling drained. Besides, ever since they'd got off the coach, an idea had been playing at the back of her mind. Something that Montgomery-Jones had said yesterday she knew was significant, but she couldn't quite put her finger on it. Perhaps instead she would find a quiet corner, if such things could be said to exist in this busy tourist city. So soon after lunch the cafés were still crowded, but none of her maps indicated a park nearby. Perhaps if she walked towards the river she might find a peaceful spot to sit.

Fiona was obviously not the only one with the same idea. Half an hour later, as she watched a boat pull up alongside one of the small jetties, she heard her name being called. She turned to see Kathleen and Brendan sitting on a bench set back under the trees at the top of a grassy bank. She smiled and waved back, in two minds whether to stroll on or go and speak to them. Even at that distance, Fiona could see the expectant look on their faces.

'Having a breather are you?' she said as she slid onto the bench beside Kathleen.

'We thought we'd take some time out. Isn't that what the Americans call it?'

'My fault, I'm afraid,' said Brendan with a sheepish grin.

'It's good to see you up and about again. And you've got some colour back in your cheeks.'

They chatted for a few more minutes and as Fiona rose to continue her walk Brendan asked, 'That poor lady, Vivien. Is that her name? Do you know how she is? I overheard Barry saying his wife had gone to be with her. Will they both be coming back with us on Monday?'

'I really don't know. It may take a few more days before Vivien is ready to return to Maidenhead.'

'Maidenhead?' Kathleen said with surprise, a smile lighting up her face. 'Our Bernadette used to work there. She lived in Slough actually but...' She stopped suddenly and cast a quick glance at her husband who'd suddenly slumped forward staring down at his feet.

'Me and me big mouth. I'm so sorry, me darlin'.' She put an arm around his shoulders.

Fiona felt her presence was an intrusion on the man's grief, but on the other hand she could hardly walk away. But what could she say? Trying to change the subject with some banal comment about the view or the weather would be crass. They could not sit here for much longer. If they were to be back in time for the coach, they would all have to leave soon.

Brendan took out his handkerchief and blew his nose loudly.

Kathleen glanced at her watch. 'Best be makin' a move, me darlin'. Otherwise we'll be left behind.'

Fiona jumped to her feet. 'No need to hurry. Take your time. I'll see you both at the coach.'

There was a good chance she might need to extricate Barry from the bar on her way back and it would be best if she had no other witnesses.

It was a relatively short journey back. The distance between Mainz and Rudesheim was only twenty miles or so. As the coach sped along by the riverside, Fiona stared out at the road ahead, her mind working overtime. Was she jumping to conclusions? Could it be anything more than a series of coincidences? She needed to give all this a great deal more thought before deciding what she should do. If anything.

If only she could talk it over with Bill, but then if he were still alive, she would still be back in Guildford playing the humdrum role of a middle-aged, suburban housewife. No more time for musings, they'd arrived in Rudesheim and were approaching their stop.

The small road that led up to the wine cellar was not only steep, it was too narrow for the coach to turn round at the top; however, it was only a short walk. There was no need for her guide pole as no one could get lost, but, nonetheless, the party soon became strung out as the more energetic members strode ahead. Glancing back every now and again to check how the older folk were managing, Fiona tried to restrain not only Cressida and Holly but Ernest Blake who, despite his age, showed no sign of tiring.

Opposite the brick building that carried a simple plaque announcing "Anton Fischer Eingang Wineprobe," was a low wall which made a suitable perch for the first arrivals. It looked as though they might have to wait several minutes for Rita as well as Sidney and Daphne, not that Fiona needed worry about the stragglers with Ian to bring up the rear.

Fiona decided to take a breather herself and, making for a space alongside the wall, found herself next to Barry.

'I take it Elspeth got off alright this morning?' she asked brightly.

'Yes thanks. The taxi was on time and the driver had enough English so no problems.' He still looked a little flushed and, though Fiona detected a faint smell of whisky on his breath, his speech wasn't slurred.

'That's good. Did she say how Vivien was bearing up?'

'She hasn't called me yet. Too busy gossiping I expect. You know how sisters are. I'll ring her later when we get back to the hotel.'

'Actually, Barry, there's something I wanted to ask. I know this is going to sound a strange question but, Graham's secretary, can you tell me her surname?'

Barry's eyes widened and he shook his head. 'To be honest, I really can't remember. We all referred to her as Bernie. I must have heard it at some stage.'

'You said she was a catholic. Was she Irish by any chance?'

'As Irish as they come.' He smiled. 'She had this lovely, soft, lilting voice. And it was an Irish name. Let me think.' He screwed up his face in concentration. 'Maguire, O'Malley, McCarthy. Something like that. Murray. Yeah, I'm sure that's it. Murray.'

'Or Murphy?'

He looked pensive, moving his head from side to side as though weighing up the idea. 'Murray or Murphy. Why? Is it important?'

Before she could answer, Barry's mobile began to burble. The relief she felt at not having to think up some even remotely plausibly explanation quickly turned to concern when she saw the deep frown on his face. Had something happened to Elspeth? Fiona gave a sharp intake of breath; had the German police decided to charge Vivien?

'But I don't understand what you're talking about. What business deal?' After a pause he said, 'Look mate, I think you must have the wrong number.' With that he snapped off his phone and put it back in his pocket.

He turned back to Fiona. 'I expected it to be Elspeth, but it was some nutter. His accent was so strong I could hardly make out what he said.'

'What did he want?'

'Said he's ready to go ahead with some deal or other and wanted to fix a meeting. Didn't make sense to me.'

The stragglers had now arrived so there wasn't much time. Fiona said quickly, 'I think we ought to tell Mr Montgomery-Jones about this.'

'Why? It's just a misdial. Can't have been for me as no one else over here knows my mobile number except Elspeth and Vivien.'

'Don't you remember? You gave it to Marthe at reception earlier in the week in case there were any developments while you were out on a trip. Perhaps someone from the hotel passed it on.'

Barry frowned then nodded his head. 'Possible, I suppose.'

The general shuffling became more marked. People were getting restless if not impatient. She couldn't keep them waiting around any longer; they would have to go in. Perhaps there'd be a moment or two during the introductory talk for her to nip back outside and contact Montgomery-Jones.

Twenty-Four

'Barry is dismissing it as wrong number, but after the calls for Graham earlier in the week, I thought you ought to know.'

'May I speak with Mr Glover?'

'He's inside the wine cellar at the moment for the tour and the wine tasting. Do you need me to fetch him out now?'

After a pause Montgomery-Jones said, 'On reflection it might be more satisfactory to speak directly with Mr Glover. At what time do you expect to return to your hotel?'

'The tour's only just started and it's due to last about an hour. Plus ten minutes or so to drive back.'

'Perhaps you would be kind enough to tell him to expect me.'

'Of course. Thank you.' Quite what she'd thanked him for she wasn't sure, but it seemed appropriate somehow. Why did she let that formal manner of his reduce her to an inarticulate, babbler? Heaven knows what the man must think. It was going to be bad enough having to face him after that embarrassing scene in her room the previous evening without making things worse.

The talk was almost over when Fiona got back and she only caught the tail end. Soon they were ready for their tour of the cellars.

Whatever Fiona had been expecting it certainly wasn't this. Instead of going straight into a cavern, they were strung out in a crocodile through narrow, ill-lit, chilly passageways. The eerie atmosphere communicated itself to everyone and their subdued whispers added to the sense of mystery and re-pressed excitement.

Even the wine hall was little more than a long, brick arched tunnel and the lighting levels were still at a minimum making it almost impossible to see the how far the store extended. The only illumination came from candles perched precariously on the rounded top of each of the huge wine casks running down both sides of the long room. Behind each old-fashioned brass candlestick stood a bottle of wine presumably from the barrel below.

The place reeked of stale, wine soaked wood and a sour taste hit the back of Fiona's throat with every breath. To her surprise, the hardened drinkers seemed to enjoy taking in great lungfuls of the heady air. There was no accounting for taste.

Fiona peered around the group trying to find Barry but, crowded together in such a cramped space in the semi-dark-ness, it was impossible to locate him. Still there was no ur-gency. She could wait until the tasting session.

Even that proved to be more difficult than she'd imagined. They were ushered into yet another long narrow room with no natural light, to sit either side of the central line of trestle ta-bles.

'Now I will leave you in the hands of Deiter, our Vintner-Master,' their guide informed them. 'Enjoy your wine tasting everyone.'

It took some time for the party to settle themselves in the half dark. It was fine for the men with long legs who could step over the benches with no difficulty but the shorter mem-bers of the party, of which Fiona was one, either had make an undignified attempt to clamber over or find one of the narrow gaps to squeeze through. Barry must have been near the front of the group as he was almost at the far end of table. Certainly not within communicating distance.

A line of breadbaskets containing small, bite-sized pieces of crusty bread lay down the centre of the table and in front of each place stood a large balloon glass.

'We'll all be tiddly if they keep filling these up,' Gloria said with relish. 'And we're going to need much bigger chunks of bread to soak it all up if we don't want to roll back to the hotel.'

Even though she'd been speaking to Anita Najaran sitting next to her, Sidney stared at her from across the table. He stretched his scrawny neck, his prominent Adam's apple bobbing up and down, and said in a loud imperious voice, 'I think you'll find the glasses are for spitting out the wine you've just sampled and the bread is for cleaning the palette between times.'

'What a waste!' Gloria laughed gleefully then winked at Sidney. 'I didn't take you for a hardened drinker, Sidney. What a dark horse you're turning out to be.'

Before he had time to recover his equilibrium, Gloria turned back to Anita and Devesh and began chatting. One of the remaining few not to ostracize the Indian couple.

'Good afternoon, everyone.' The babble of chatter died away and faces turned to the smiling Deiter waiting for them at the head of the table. He was an impressive figure of a man; broad shouldered, big-chested and sporting a magnificent, ginger handlebar moustache. 'This winery has been involved in wine production for three generations. Outside, you will have seen our vineyards where we grow the king of white wine grapes, the Riesling. It is late ripening but only has a moderate yield, which makes it difficult to grow. The mineral content of our slatey soils is what gives Riesling its unique flavour and bouquet. Some are fruity, with a hint of peach or apricot, some more tart with a citrus aroma while others have a distinct floral taste.'

The majority of his audience were listening attentively, but a degree of restless shuffling halfway down the table indicated one or two couldn't wait to get to the actual tasting.

'In the past Riesling was more popular and expensive than the finest red Bordeaux wines and today it is experiencing a marked revival amongst connoisseurs.' The big man wagged

196

his finger at them. 'There are many imitations, so if you want a good Riesling, choose a Rhine variety. A good wine keeps well and is worth its cost. Rieslings should be served cool but not straight from the refrigerator.'

He beamed at them. 'This afternoon we have five wines for you to try. We will start with a Qualitätswein which you will discover has a light, fruity taste.'

At the counter behind him, two men had started to pour the wine into small flat-bottomed glasses each with the vineyard crest painted on the side, which they were told they could keep as a souvenir at the end of the tasting. The vintner-master recruited the help of Ernest and Viktor who sat either side at the head of the table to help hand out the glasses. The beehive hum of excited chatter reverberated in the low ceilinged room.

Fiona took a cautious sip of the thimble-full of liquid in her glass. 'It's really rather pleasant, isn't it?'

Gloria smacked her lips and answered, 'Just the ticket.'

'Would you like a top up, madam?' The waiter gave her a knowing look.

'Is the Pope a catholic?' With obvious relish Gloria threw back the contents of the tiny glass and, eyes shinning, added, 'So, what next?'

'Now let us to try a Kabinett. The name comes from the cabinet, or side room, where the best wines were stored and so it came to mean a high quality or reserve wine. They are light to medium bodied, well-balanced in acidity, and dry to semi-dry. This makes them excellent wines to team up with lighter dishes.'

By the end of her third sample, Fiona felt decidedly light-headed. Ridiculous, she told herself. Simply an illusion. She could have drunk no more than half a normal glass.

In the hubbub of the echoing room on top of her unaccustomed state of wooziness, it was a moment or two before she realized Kathleen was talking to her.

'Sorry to disturb you, Fiona m' dear. It's Brendan. He's not

197

feeling too good. A bit faint. I'm going to take him up outside for a breath of fresh air.'

'It is a bit warm in here, isn't it? I'll come with you.'

'No no, m' dear. There's no need for that at all.'

'I insist.' Fiona clambered over the bench to join her. Not an easy feat hemmed in by Daphne Pettit on one side and Ian Lambert on the other. 'To be honest, I'm feeling quite flushed myself.'

A sudden squawk of laughter came from the far end of the table. It seemed as though the girls, aided and abetted by Hilary Kasar, were using the opportunity for extra top-ups to full advantage. Fiona decided she was much too fragile to cope with them right now. Besides, Brendan was her main concern for the moment.

The gentle breeze felt pleasantly cool on what Fiona feared must be her over-reddened checks. By contrast, Brendan looked decided pale and his eyes were dull and sunken.

'Let's see if we can find you somewhere to sit,' she said brightly.

At the side of the building was the dispatch area opposite a parking space for half a dozen cars. Set at about three feet from the ground, presumably for ease of loading directly onto the delivery trucks, was an archway. In front of the two barn-type doors that lay a few feet back into the recess, a single empty crate had been left near the edge. Fiona lifted it down.

'Not the most comfortable of seats I'm afraid, but better than nothing.'

One of the enormous doors was slightly ajar. There were probably more crates just inside but even if she'd been physically capable of climbing up onto the platform, she could hardly trespass.

'Don't you worry. The two of us will manage just fine,' Kathleen assured her.

'Let me see if I can find you a glass of water.'

'No need, m' dear. I've a bottle in m' bag. I'll see to Brendan. You get back now and enjoy the rest the festivities or you'll be having us feeling guilty for spoiling your fun.'

The wine tasting was almost over by the time Fiona she arrived back in the hall.

'You've missed some smashing samples, Fiona. Here let's get you one of these.' Gloria signalled the waiter to come and fill Fiona's glass.

'I thought the previous one was good but this,' she raised her glass holding it out across the table to be filled up again, 'This is really something else. Spit Lazy; now isn't that just the perfect name for a wine?' Her infectious laugh had several people smiling.

'Spätlese,' corrected Sidney pedantically. 'It literally translates as "late harvest," because it's made with over-ripe grapes to produce extra sweetness and flavour.'

'Well, I may not know how to pronounce it,' Gloria gave one of her fruity laughs, 'but I certainly know how to drink it.'

Fiona bit her lip to stop herself giggling. In the battle of the putdowns, Sidney was never going to win.

What with the game being played out around her, plus the increased level of noise and laughter in the room now Dieter had finished his explanations, it took several moments before Fiona realized something was wrong.

Twenty-Five

Some sort of rumpus was happening further down the table. With so many people crowded into so confined a space, Fiona found it impossible to make out the problem. And the semi-dark didn't help. She saw one of the women rush to the door, her hands clapped to her mouth. Moments later, a man followed clutching his stomach, presumably also heading for the toilets. Someone else was bent double over the table.

Well-meaning people had gone out to check up on those taken ill adding to the confusion and it was some time before the situation had calmed down. Len Webster and Holly eventually returned now feeling better if a little fragile which, Fiona was reliably informed, left only Edith. She was the worst affected and had been violently sick but Hilary remained with her.

What had caused the upset was still a mystery. All three sufferers had been sitting together near the head of the table, but the wine they had tasted had come from the same bottles the rest of them had sampled. Cressida, plus Joe and Celia Ennis on the far side of the table, had shared the same breadbasket, but they hadn't suffered any ill effects. Although it might be argued the wine had not agreed with Edith and Len's more sensitive elderly stomachs, this didn't explain why Holly had succumbed. She was young, fit and well used to prolonged bouts of hard drinking as was all too evident in the bar each evening.

Jugs of water and large glasses appeared for anyone who wanted it. Dieter took Len and Holly to one side and, not wishing to overcrowd them, Fiona decided not to interfere and to wait and see if they could come up with any explanation. More from want of doing something to feel useful, Fiona poured out a glass of water and went to check up on Edith.

Following the signs for the toilets along the twisty corridor, she discovered Edith had stopped vomiting and was now sitting in the outer washing area on the only chair.

'I thought I'd bring you some water but I see you already have some.'

'Everyone's been so kind. How are the others?'

'They're both much better. Not feeling nauseous anymore. But how about you? Are you sure you don't want us to fetch a doctor?'

'No, no, no. It's all over now. I'm sorry to cause such a fuss. I'll be along in a minute or two. I expect you all want to be getting back to the hotel.'

'No hurry. Take your time. We're in no rush.'

When she returned to the hall, the rest of the party were either milling about or gathered in little groups talking animatedly. Holly now sat with Cressida, and Len was off somewhere with Dieter. At least nobody else appeared to be suffering any ill effects. Fiona decided it was time to bring some order to the chaos.

'Please would you all come and sit back down for a moment.'

Her calls proved none too effective at first, but after a few hefty bangs on the table, she established some sort of order.

'Just to let you all know, Edith is also feeling much better now, so crisis over everyone. When she comes back we'll all be leaving.'

'What about Barry?' Ernest Blake peered up and down the table. 'He was sitting next to me but he doesn't appear to be here.'

'He wasn't taken ill as well, was he?' Fiona asked. Surely, someone would have mentioned it earlier?

Before she could ask if anyone had seen him, Devesh said, 'Viktor's not here either.'

201

'Probably both in the gents,' suggested Ian. 'They'll be along in a jiffy.'

The minutes dragged on.

Devesh was at Fiona's elbow. 'Would you like me to go and check?'

'Please, Devesh. That would be helpful.'

While he went to investigate, Ernest volunteered to go back outside to see if the two had gone for a breath of fresh air.

Devesh was the first to return. Unaccompanied.

'They could have taken a wrong turn when they came out of the toilet and wandered back into the cellar complex,' he suggested.

It didn't sound a very plausible explanation to Fiona. 'Wouldn't they have retraced their steps once they realized?'

'Perhaps they started talking and ended up in the wrong corridor then couldn't find their way back. It's a bit of a maze back there.'

By this time, Ernest had re-joined them and caught the gist of their conversation. 'They aren't outside either. Why don't Devesh and I go and make a search of the passages with one of the staff?'

Neither of them said it, but they must be thinking, as she certainly was, the two missing men could have succumbed to stomach cramps like the others somewhere. They might even have collapsed. Now she was letting her imagination run away with her.

Fiona banged on the table again and asked if anyone had noticed Barry or Viktor leave the room. There was a general shaking of heads. Apart from all the confusion earlier, and with only the candles and a few low wattage bulbs over the serving table for light, it was only to be expected. Perhaps Hilary would know where her husband had gone. Fiona hurried off to the toilets.

Much to her surprise, Hilary did not appear to be particularly bothered. After an initial frown, all she said was, 'I expect he's wandered off somewhere to get away from the hullaba-loo. He gets confused when everyone starts talking nineteen to the dozen and he can't understand. Either that or he's gone for a smoke. He'll be back in a jiff. Not to worry.'

'I'll let you know when he returns.' If his wife wasn't worried there was no reason why she should be, Fiona told herself.

At the end of the short passageway, before turning back towards the tasting hall, she hesitated and peered in the opposite direction which led back into the rest of the cellar complex. There were so many side passages they could be anywhere. Was she imagining it or could she hear voices?

They became gradually louder and she could see the flickering light of a torch. She hurried to the next bend. Ernest led the way talking over his shoulder. She knew it must be him because she recognized his voice.

'Ernest?'

'Hello there, Fiona.' The light flashed in her eyes but everything was pitch black behind the torch despite the dim overhead bulbs at intermittent intervals.

'Have you found them?'

They were much closer now and Fiona could just make out the two dark figures.

'Viktor's here but we haven't found Barry yet. The others are still looking.'

'What on earth happened?'

They were now back in the section of corridor between the hall and the toilets, which was much better lit, and Fiona could see Viktor's apologetic smile.

'Sorry to give you worry. I lost.'

'Very sensibly when he realized he'd taken a wrong turning and couldn't find the way back, he decided to wait rather than wander even further into the depths. He knew we'd come looking for him. He heard us shouting.' Ernest was all smiles.

Fiona turned back to Viktor. 'But weren't you with Barry?'

'I on my own.'

'You two go back to the tasting hall and I'll let Hilary know you're safe and sound?'

Fiona met the two women on their way out of the toilets. At

least this time Hilary looked genuinely pleased to hear the good news. Perhaps she'd been hiding her real concern earlier for Edith's benefit.

Eventually, the search party returned. Without Barry. Devesh looked apologetic as he came over to tell Fiona, but it was hardly his fault. What next?

Why hadn't she thought of it before? The most likely explanation was Barry had decided to go back to the coach. Kathleen and Brendan were sitting round by the side of the building so may not have spotted him. There was no reception in the cellars; she would have to go outside to use her mobile and check with Winston.

In the event, she didn't have to ring the driver. As she went out of the main door, she saw Winston and Kathleen sitting on the wall opposite with Brendon who had moved his crate into the sun.

'I waited for twenty minutes in the coach and then I thought I'd better come and see what was happening. They tell me two of our party are missing.'

'Viktor's been found but there's still no sign of Barry. He obviously didn't go down to the coach then?'

Winston shook his head.

'Where can he have got to?'

'Well, m' dear, the only ones to come out of that building in the last half hour were a couple of workmen. They jumped off that platform thing down the side there. Gave us a bit of a shock they did. They went off in a mucky old white van parked opposite.'

'That'd be the one what nearly ran me down as I was walking up here,' said Winston pulling a face. 'Going like the clappers they were. Had to jump half way up the hedge to avoid being hit.'

All the evidence indicated Barry must still be in the building, but Fiona decided it served no good purpose to have the rest of the party milling around making wild speculations. Much as she wanted to stay until Barry had been found, it would be more sensible to take everyone back to the hotel.

On the coach, Fiona took out her clipboard. She ticked off every name and then double-checked. She'd lost enough people for one day. As the coach drew up outside the hotel, Fiona's first inclination was to disappear straight up to her room with a calming cup of tea, but there were things to be done.

She helped the last of the passengers off the coach and wondered if she should contact Elspeth. No point in spreading alarm too soon. Still deep in thought as she entered the hotel, it was a moment or two before she registered someone waiting by the reception desk.

'Mr Montgomery-Jones! I'm so sorry, with all that's been going on, I'd completely forgotten you were coming.'

Fiona told him all that had happened. He wasn't the avuncular type who would pat her on the arm and tell her not to worry but, at the end of her somewhat rambling account, he said, 'In all probability, there will turn out to be a simple explanation.'

She shook her head in frustration. 'But no one saw Barry leave. Kathleen and Brendan were outside all the time. He couldn't have got past them unnoticed. And there is no other way out. I asked one of the staff,' she said defiantly.

'If you are suggesting he is still inside, why did the search party not find him?'

'I've been thinking about that. They assumed he'd wandered off and got lost. They weren't looking behind every barrel and in all the nooks and crannies. That place is a maze. He might have been affected by the same bug that made the others ill and could be lying unconscious somewhere out of sight. I said as much to the man in charge but whether he took me seriously is another matter.'

He stared at her thoughtfully. 'If it would put your mind at rest, I will make a call straightaway and arrange for someone to go over there and assist. In the mean time perhaps we should go somewhere a little less public and you can tell me all you know about the phone call he received outside the wine cellar.'

Her first instinct was to tell him she had other things to worry about than a misdial, but logically there was nothing else she could do at the moment. As they drank tea in a corner of the bar lounge, she told him the little she knew.

'Could it be related to his disappearance?' It was a silly question but she couldn't stop herself asking. 'Do you think he might be hiding deliberately?'

Had she really said that out loud? It was a thought she'd been trying to push away for the last half hour. Ever since they'd got back on the coach.

'Is there any reason why he might choose not be found?' Why did he have to answer every question with one of his own?

'Do you suspect him of Graham's murder?' She tried not to make it sound like an accusation.

'That is not for me to speculate, Mrs Mason. Do you?'

'I really don't know what to think any more.' She sipped her tea feeling helpless.

As they walked together to the hotel entrance, another thought struck her. 'I've been trying to decide if I ought to ring Elspeth. I don't want to worry her unnecessarily and in any case it's hardly the sort of news to give over the phone.'

'I suggest we wait until a more thorough search has been conducted. If he still has not been found, I will arrange for one of my people to go over and let her know personally.'

Thank goodness, she thought, one less thing to have to worry about.

Fiona stood under the shower for much longer than she'd intended letting the pounding of the water on the back of her neck and shoulders ease away some of the tension. Did Barry's absence incriminate him further? He did have a motive of sorts plus the opportunity and, other than Vivien, there didn't appear to be anyone else who had.

It must be almost impossible to stab someone like that without getting covered in blood. Barry's room had been given the fine toothcomb treatment but what about the others? The police certainly hadn't been into her room, at least not in the morning while she was there. Montgomery-Jones had said the search had been thorough so perhaps the investigations had been done in the afternoon while the Super Sun party was out. Which meant the murderer must have taken the blood-stained clothing out of the hotel and dumped it somewhere.

A dim memory stirred in the back of her mind. She turned off the taps and stood deep in thought until the goose bumps on her arms made her realize how cold she had become. It wasn't proof. She was probably reading too much into a perfectly innocent action. She would need a lot more evidence before she started throwing accusations around.

Twenty-Six

Despite all the delays, Fiona was still one of the first down to dinner. The only other person in the dining room was Brendan sitting on the end of the banquette at his table.

'Kathleen not with you?'

'She's gone to the bar to get us some drinks to have with our meal. That's why we're down early, but after my little upset this afternoon she insisted I come straight in here and sit down.'

'Quite right,' Fiona said with a smile. 'Though you are looking much better now.'

'I'm fine. Kathleen does tend to fuss so. Any news about Barry? As if his poor wife hasn't got enough to worry about.'

'Quite.'

'Have the police arrested her sister? The rumour is the two of them were having an argument and she stabbed him.' He gave a long sigh. 'And who could blame the poor lady. She's had a lot to put up with.'

'Really?'

Brendan leant forward looking at his hands. 'Her husband was not a nice man. Charmin' of course but ... Still one mustn't speak ill of the dead.'

'Had you met Graham Spellman before this trip?'

He looked up at her suddenly, realizing he'd said too much. 'Oh no. No. Just the gossip.'

Fiona slid onto the bench opposite still holding his gaze. 'But you knew your daughter had worked for him.'

Brendan's eyes widened in surprise and his jaw dropped.

'Who told you?'

Fiona shook her head. 'No one. I guessed. Barry happened to mention he could never forgive Graham for what happened to his secretary but he had no idea Bernadette was your daughter.'

'Please don't say anything to Kathleen. She still thinks Bernadette's death was an accidental overdose and she knows nothin' about the abortion. It would break her heart. When we were young, they still wouldn't bury suicides in holy ground.'

'So how did you find out?'

'I discovered her diary when I was sorting out her effects. I should never have read it, I suppose. I felt guilty poking into it but I wondered if there were appointments and such like I ought to cancel. She didn't actually name the father, just the initial G, but there was enough to piece the whole sordid business together.' He wiped a hand over his eyes. 'She was so excited; he was going to take her on holiday. Always fancied the Rhine Valley, he told her. He was going to tell his wife it was a business trip. Bernadette had been on the internet and downloaded all this stuff about castles and the little towns like Rudesheim and Boppard. They were all in her bedside drawer. All well thumbed. It was obvious how much it all meant to her.' His voice began to break.

Fiona put a hand on his and gave a reassuring squeeze.

'So that's why you came here.'

He nodded. Then, his voice barely more than a whisper, he said, 'It was a pilgrimage like, for her. I promised her I'd light a candle in her memory at every place we stopped.'

'It can't have been easy for you.'

He sat up suddenly, brushing the tears from his cheeks. 'The last thing I expected to find that bastard here as well.'

'You recognized him?' Fiona was astonished.

'Good God, no! T'was only when we were all talking at dinner that first evening and Graham mentioned the name of the company he and Barry worked for I put two and two together,' he continued. 'I've not been able to get it out of mind ever since. It's been a burden. I couldn't even talk to Kathleen about't. When I heard the man had had a heart attack my first thought was – serve him bloody right. And even when it came out he'd been murdered, all I could think was I hope the bastard suffered like he'd made my little angel suffer.' He stifled a sob. 'What kinda Christian does that make me? But I can't forgive him. He's responsible for the death of my beautiful baby that never did no harm to a livin' soul.'

Fiona sat silently as Brendan lay slumped over the table, his head buried in his arms. Eventually the gently heaving shoulders relaxed.

'Did you never face him with it?'

Brendan looked up. 'No. I thought about it. But what would've been the point? If I were twenty years younger I might have punched his lights out.' He gave a bitter laugh. 'Oh Fiona, you don't know what a relief it is to talk to someone about't. I don't know whether I've been comin' or goin' ever since.'

'Is that why you forgot your sweater the other day?'

'In that café, do you mean? Kathleen was really cross with me.' He managed a weak smile. 'T'was a new one. She bought for m' birthday a month or so back. She made me ask the young lady on reception to find the telephone number of the place. Lucky for me they'd found it and now they're keeping it for us till tomorrow when we can call in and collect it.'

'That's wonderful.' Fiona gave him a beaming smile and a sense of relief swept through her. If he thought her reaction was somewhat over the top, he didn't show it. He couldn't be making up that story and if the sweater had been covered in blood, surely someone in the café would have mentioned it to the police by now.

Others were now arriving. Fiona rose to her feet and put a hand on his shoulder as Kathleen came up the steps, a glass in each hand.

'Sorry I've bin so long, m' darlin'. I got talking. You know what I'm like.'

Had Fiona seen the small army of men who had descended

upon the Fischer Wine Cellar with all their paraphernalia, she wouldn't have been concerned her request for a more detailed search had been taken lightly.

Even with the powerful searchlights, it looked as though the men's efforts were proving fruitless. James Fitzwilliam stood anxiously waiting for the last team to come back to the storehouse, the only room with something approximating to decent lighting large enough for their needs. He took out his mobile and began to fiddle with it.

'Take that worried look off your face. The Commander isn't going to blame you. It's not our fault the man's done a runner.'

James gave Laura a grimace. 'Let's face it; we're not going to get a pat on the back. We were supposed to be keeping tabs on them all.'

'Yes. But, as you said yourself, we could hardly barge in with them. It was a private tasting after all. What more could we have done? We do know he didn't come down to the main road we would have spotted him. The whole of the time we were in that café, no one came down the path and the only person who went up was the coach driver. Unless Glover was hiding in the back of that white van, he couldn't have come past us.'

'Perhaps he spotted us earlier and made his way across the hillside.'

The last group of men came through from the passageway. The man in the lead shook his head. 'No joy, I'm afraid.'

James sighed and turned to Laura. 'Here, you take the car keys. The Commander thought you'd be the best person to tell his wife Glover's missing in case someone needs to stay with her. I'd better let him know.' He frowned. 'Signal's not too good in here.'

James was about go through the door to the adjacent dispatch bay when the disgruntled proprietor strode over demanding his attention.

'The van has been waiting outside for nearly an hour. We will miss the day's delivery if we do not go soon.'

211

'Yes, I'm sorry we had to hold you up.' He dithered for a moment but there was no good reason to delay the man any further. 'Go ahead and load up.'

Needing no further encouragement, the man hefted one of the stacked crates and walked towards the opening. As James followed in his wake, a thought suddenly struck him. 'Herr Fischer. I thought the delivery had already gone?'

'No. The van is waiting. You can see it.' The proprietor cocked his head to the pristine vehicle backed up to the far end of the delivery bay. James could just make out the red lettering above the large bunch of grapes logo along its side.

'But there was another earlier, wasn't there?'

'No.' The man sounded surprised. 'Only one on a Saturday.'

'But there was a white van parked out there earlier in the afternoon. I saw it leaving.'

The moustachioed man shrugged his broad shoulders.

Hurriedly, James punched the Commander's number into his mobile.

'Fitzwilliam. Good news I hope.'

'No, sir. It looks as though Glover got away in the back of an old van parked outside. Either he sneaked in when no one was looking or it was all arranged earlier because the owner assured me it had no connection with the wine cellar.'

'According to Mrs Mason, the coach driver was almost run down by a van.'

'Sounds like the one we saw. It was going like the clappers when it passed us. Two men in the front. Dark, swarthy chaps. Neither of them could have been Glover. He must have been hiding in the back.'

'Hiding or had he being taken against his will?'

'Kidnapped do you mean?' James couldn't keep the surprise out of his voice.

'It is a possibility. Either way we need to trace the van. Did you by any chance take the number?'

'No, sir. There didn't appear to be any reason to do so at the time.'

'No matter. The coach driver may have done. Has Miss

212

Philips informed Mrs Glover of her husband's disappearance yet?'

'No, sir. Laura's still here. We waited to see if the search produced anything before she left.'

'Perhaps we should delay no longer. Keep me informed of any developments.'

There was little room in the tiny hotel office by the time extra chairs were brought and all five of them sat down.

'I apologize for keeping you all from your coffee but I know you appreciate the urgency. As Mrs Mason has no doubt explained, we are trying to ascertain exactly what happened to Mr Glover, Barry. We have already established no one saw him after the unfortunate incident with those who were taken ill.' Montgomery-Jones raised a questioning eyebrow at Fiona.

'That's right. I asked everyone when we first realized he was missing and no one saw him leave the room. I asked again when we all got back on the coach before we left.'

'So there is no one who can account for his movements thereafter.'

'He certainly didn't come out of the front door,' Kathleen assured him. 'The only person we saw was Ernest when he came looking for Barry.'

'So I understand. But there is a side entrance.'

'Not what you'd call an entrance exactly. It's a good three feet off the ground.'

'But it is possible Mr Glover might have used that route to leave the building.'

'We'd have seen him.' Brendan was emphatic.

'Exactly,' confirmed his wife with emphasis. 'We saw the two delivery men jump down, clear as day.'

'Were these men loading their van?'

'No, no. They just crossed over to the parking space and got straight in. In a great hurry they were.'

'Did you get a good look at them?'

'I wasn't paying much attention to be honest. What about you, darlin'?' Brendan turned to his wife.

'One poked his head out the opening earlier. I can remember thinking he looked surprised to us sitting there. I thought he was going to shout at us. That's why we moved round to the front of the building.'

'How long was this before they left?'

'Not long. Four or five minutes, I suppose.' Kathleen glanced at Brendan who nodded his agreement.

'But you are certain neither man was Mr Glover.'

'Oh no. A bit scruffy-looking they were. In jeans and T-shirts. Barry is always smartly dressed, wearing a proper shirt he was. I do remember that.'

'They were much shorter anyway,' Brendan added. 'Not much taller than me.'

'That's right,' agreed his wife. 'Barry's almost six foot.'

'And they got straight into the van and drove off?' confirmed Montgomery-Jones.

'Exactly. If you're thinking Barry could've sneaked into the back of the van earlier, I can tell you, we would've seen him.' Kathleen was adamant.

'Can you tell me about the van? Did you happen to notice anything in particular about it?'

Both Kathleen and Brendan shook their heads.

'And you, Mr Taylor. Is there anything else which comes to mind about the van or the men in it?'

'Apart from the dangerous way it was being driven, no. I was too busy jumpin' out the way.'

'Thank you. That has been most helpful. I am grateful to all three of you and I will not detain you further.' Montgomery-Jones rose to his feet and shook hands with the Irish couple and the big West Indian towering behind them.

Fiona held open the door as they all shuffled out of the confined space. She went to follow them but Montgomery-Jones asked, 'How are the people who were taken ill?'

'They're all back to normal, more or less. None of them needed a doctor. It seems, although Holly felt very nauseous, she wasn't actually sick. Len is much better and Edith, who was the worst affected, actually came down to dinner although she only had soup and a couple of mouthfuls of mousse.'

'I see.'

'If there is any news about Barry would you let me know?'

'Straight away.' He smiled. 'Before I go, would it be possible for you to give me a quick plan of where everyone was sitting during the tasting?'

'I'll try,' Fiona said doubtfully.

She was tempted to ask why but she knew she would only get an evasive answer. Once she sat down and began to jot down names, it proved less difficult than she'd thought.

'And everyone remained seated throughout?'

'Except for Kathleen and Brendan. They went out after the first few tastings. And then there was Ernest and Viktor. They sat at the head of the table and helped to hand out the glasses but they didn't leave the room. People started getting up when Edith rushed out to the toilet.'

'I see.' He sat staring at the plan for a few moments and then said, 'Will you go through exactly what happened after that point?'

'It was all a bit confused. And it was so dim in there, it's difficult to know.'

'Just tell me everything you remember, no matter how seemingly irrelevant.'

Only after Montgomery-Jones left did it occur to Fiona to wonder why he'd wanted such detail. There had to be a reason, though for the moment she couldn't work out what it was.

Twenty-Seven

Montgomery-Jones unlocked the door but before he could climb into his car, his mobile rang.

'We've found him, sir.'

'Thank God for that! Where?'

'In the wine cellar. It looks as though he's been knocked unconscious or possibly drugged then bundled into an empty barrel. One of the winery staff was in the storeroom and heard the groans as Glover came to. He's not making a lot of sense yet, I'm afraid.'

'Good man. I am on my way.'

Any questions had to wait until the doctor, a terse British ex-military medic, had completed his examination.

'He's hallucinating at the moment which suggests something like Ketamine. Not difficult to get hold off these days. It's sold on the black market as a recreational drug. There are two sets of needle marks; one on his right buttock and the other on his upper arm. Could be he was given a jab to put him in a dissociated state and then a second dose sufficient to knock him out. He's coming round now. Vital signs rapidly returning to normal, respiration and heart rate have calmed down so I see no need to hospitalize him. Luckily, Ketamine doesn't produce any long lasting effects. He's already making a good recovery and, apart from a mild hangover, by the morning he should be back to normal.'

'How soon will he be fit for questioning?'

'I doubt you'll get much sense out of him for some time. At the moment, he doesn't even know his name let alone how he got in that state. He has several small bruises and abrasions, probably from when they dumped him in the barrel, plus a severe bruise on his right hip, which will probably give him hell when the anaesthetizing effects wear off. Probably best to keep an eye on him for a bit. Keep him well wrapped up. Any change, give me a call.'

'Is he sufficiently recovered to be moved back to his hotel?' asked Montgomery-Jones.

'He could well puke up any minute and movement will probably compound the nausea. But on the other hand, bed is probably the best place for him.'

'I think Herr Fischer will be pleased to see the back of us,' James Fitzwilliam said to no one in particular.

'Indeed. I will inform him we are leaving.' Montgomery-Jones rose to his feet and turned to James. 'You can put him in the back of my car. But you can find a bucket and *you* will be sitting next to him on the journey back. First you should give Miss Phillips a call. I am sure Mrs Glover will be relieved to know her husband has been found.' Montgomery-Jones took out his pocket watch and clicked open the case. 'However, that reminds me, I did promise to inform Mrs Mason so, if you men will take Glover to my car, I will be with you shortly.'

He handed his keys to James and walked towards the door.

It had been a difficult evening. Her suggestion Barry had probably gone to be with Elspeth and Vivien had failed to quell the constant questions, especially as he'd told no one he was leaving. When the call from Montgomery-Jones came through, she'd had to leave the noisy lounge bar to take it, but decided it might be best to stop more speculation by letting them all know Barry had been found and all was well.

Fiona waited outside the hotel for their arrival. She wrapped her arms around herself, unsure if her goosebumps were due were due to the chill of the evening air or a growing sense of foreboding. For some reason she could not explain, her initial relief at the news of Barry's discovery had given way to a marked state of apprehension. She watched the burgundy

Mercedes draw up to the entrance.

A thickset man with closely cropped hair and hardly any neck, incongruously dressed in a dark double-breasted suit and black tie, extricated himself from the front passenger seat. He opened the rear door and proceeded to heave Barry out of the back seat and onto the pavement as the casually dressed, youngish man pushed and shoved from inside the car. Supported on either side, Barry was half lifted, half dragged inside. Anyone watching would have thought Barry was drunk. He seemed to have no idea of where he was or what was happening. Had the situation not been so serious, the spectacle would have been comical.

'Would you mind getting the key to his room?' the younger man asked Fiona.

There was something vaguely familiar about him but there were other more important things to occupy her. She hurried to the reception desk as the trio shuffled along the narrow corridor towards the lift.

Fiona unlocked the door and stood back. They carried Barry inside and dropped him clumsily on the bed, arms akimbo, where he lay staring up at the ceiling with a vacant stare, his lips parted in a cherubic smile. The effort had exhausted the young man who now sat slumped forward on the end of the bed. Even the one who looked like a nightclub bouncer perched wearily on the corner of the low chest of drawers. Fiona lifted Barry's legs into a more comfortable position.

For several minutes the room was filled with the sound of heavy breathing punctuated by an odd humming and the occasional 'wheee' from Barry as he languidly waved one hand in the air like a conductor's baton.

They heard approaching footsteps in the corridor followed by a sharp rap on the door. Without waiting for answer, Montgomery-Jones came in and surveyed the scene. The bouncer jerked to attention.

Much as she wanted to ask what had happened, Fiona knew it was time for her exit too. These people had things to discuss and her presence would not be welcome. She moved towards

218

the door.

Montgomery-Jones smiled. 'Mrs Mason. Assuming you do not have rush off to see to your other passengers, I would like you to stay. We may need your help with Mr Glover.'

The bouncer stepped forward. 'If you don't need me any more, I'll get back, sir?'

'Indeed. Thank you for your assistance, Hamilton.'

Once the door closed, Montgomery-Jones said, 'I take it you two know each other?'

The young man smiled. 'By sight, but we haven't been introduced.' He pushed himself up from the bed and held out a hand. 'James Fitzwilliam.'

She remembered where she'd seen him before. 'Aren't you staying here in the hotel? I've seen you with the girl with dark hair.'

'That's right.' He had a pleasant, if not particularly memorable face, and the hazel eyes looked kindly as he grinned at her engagingly. That explained why he and his supposed girlfriend appeared to be visiting the same places as the Super Sun group so often.

A tuneless humming came from the bed.

All three of them turned to look at Barry waving both arms in the air occasionally reaching out with a hand as if trying to catch hold of something.

'Fly away, whee. Fly awaaay.' His voice fell with an elongated gentle sigh.

'Do you know what happened?' Fiona asked.

It was James who explained how and where Barry had been found. 'All we could get out of Glover was, "Buzz buzz bit me." The doctor seemed to think he'd been drugged, but when and who by we've yet to discover.'

'Do you know what with?'

'The doc was fairly certain it was something called ketamine.'

'At least there shouldn't be any long term effects, thank goodness.' James looked at her in surprise. 'I was a nurse. We used it to anaesthetize older patients.'

'On top of the wine the doc thought it might take a bit longer than usual for him to come round. The bang on his head when they upended him into the barrel couldn't have helped either.'

Fiona nodded. 'It wasn't just wine. He'd been drinking pretty heavily after lunch. Would you mind helping me to pull the duvet out from under him? He needs to be kept warm.'

Together they eased Barry into a more comfortable position and Fiona tried to tuck the covers around his shoulders. Not an easy task as Barry continued to wave his arms around smiling inanely at some private vision.

'It would help with the hallucinations if wasn't so bright in here.'

Montgomery-Jones switched off the main light, walked over to the small table in the corner, and pulled out one of the two upright chairs. Much to Fiona's surprise, he removed the charcoal grey jacket revealing its sky blue silk lining and arranged it carefully over the back of the chair. She had never seen him in shirtsleeves before and felt vaguely disconcerted.

He must have seen the look registered on her face because a faint smile twitched at the corners of his mouth and he said, 'I suspect this is going to be a very long night for some of us.'

Fiona sat in the armchair by the bed keeping a watchful eye on her patient while the two men sat at the table talking quietly. Although she tried not to listen, it was impossible not to overhear odd snatches.

'The men in the white van. Surely they must be involved, sir?'

'It is a possibility.'

'Perhaps Glover went out to meet them,' James suggested. 'Didn't he get a phone call just before the tasting trying to arrange something of the sort?'

Fiona felt compelled to leap to Barry's defence. 'Barry said it was a wrong number and why mention it at all if he was trying to keep it secret?'

Both men turned to look at her. So much for keeping a low profile. She half expected Montgomery-Jones to ask her to leave, or at best give her one of those looks of his.

Instead, he said, 'Mr Glover remarked on his caller's strong accent. Was it German do you know?'

'He just said it was foreign.' She frowned. 'Do you think it was the same person who tried to call Graham?'

'There is that possibility.'

'Do they…'

'Go on,' he prompted.

'I was wondering…' Too late to hold back now. 'Do they speak Turkish in Turkmenistan?'

There was a long silence. Montgomery-Jones voice lost a fraction of its usual cool detachment. 'Why do you ask?'

'It's probably nothing. I was talking with Barry after lunch. He was feeling pretty down blaming Graham for all the world's ills. Not only for Elspeth deserting him, but for all the bad feeling at work over this contract with some Asian country. He'd had a lot to drink and it was only a throw away statement but he said something along the lines of who in their right mind would want to do business with Kirgizstan. I wasn't really paying that much attention but it could have been Turkmenistan, Kazakhstan or any other of those Central Republics.'

A marked tension filled the room. The two men clearly knew something she didn't.

Montgomery-Jones got to feet and extracted his mobile from his pocket. 'Excuse me for a moment.'

As the door closed behind him, James gave Fiona an embarrassed smile. As if to break the silence he asked, 'If Barry Glover didn't go looking for the two men in the van, perhaps they tried to talk to him.'

'But why for goodness sake?'

He shrugged his shoulders.

'I'm certain no one came into the tasting hall,' she said, resentful that he was still intent on implying Barry was up to no good. 'It wasn't exactly well lit in there, but we would have noticed a couple of strangers.'

'Even when things became more chaotic?' James was nothing if not persistent.

'But those two couldn't have known what was going to happen. It's just too big a coincidence.' Fiona frowned. 'Unless you're suggesting they deliberated engineered that bout of food poisoning.'

'That might be a little difficult to accomplish without the co-operation of someone already in the room.'

'One of the two waiters slipped something into the wine do you mean? It couldn't have been the vintner-master because he didn't go anywhere near any of the bottles.'

'The waiters or perhaps one of the other passengers.'

Fiona felt a sudden chill. She'd known that was the inevitable conclusion all along. That was why Montgomery-Jones had asked her earlier to draw up a plan of who'd been sitting where. She just hadn't wanted to admit it to herself.

'Could it have been Glover?' It was obvious James did not want to give up on his earlier idea of Barry's prearranged meeting.

'Definitely not,' Fiona snapped. 'He sat on the other side of the table and further down from the three who were taken ill.'

Montgomery-Jones came back into the room and Fiona took the opportunity to move across to Barry. Not that he needed her ministrations, but James's questions had irritated her and she need to do something to stop herself coming out with something she'd regret later.

'Elspeth?' Barry looked at her with unfocussed eyes as she took his hand.

'It's Fiona, Barry. How are you feeling?'

'Where's Elspeth?'

'I expect she'll be here soon,' she lied. It would hardy help the situation to remind him his wife had walked out on him. 'Why don't you rest for a bit?'

He closed his eyes and Fiona turned to stare at the other two, daring them to suggest he was fit to be questioned. Whatever they might think, surely Barry was a victim not a perpetrator.

The sudden jarring ring of a mobile phone broke the silence.

Twenty-Eight

The unexpected noise made all three of them start.

'Montgomery-Jones.' Fiona watched as he listened intently to the caller. 'I see. He is refusing to say anything at all? ... I see. That is interesting. ... Thank you for informing me so promptly. I will send someone straight away. Would you be kind enough to give me the address of the hospital?'

Montgomery-Jones extracted his gold pen from his pocket and wrote it down on the small complimentary hotel notepad lying on the table then handed it to James.

'It would appear our friends in the white van managed to crash into an oncoming car taking a corner too fast. The driver was unhurt and ran away but the passenger was not so lucky. He is in hospital at Geisenheim. It would seem he is not badly injured but he is refusing to talk. He is pleading diplomatic immunity. Get over there and find out what is going on. Get the local police to push him hard. Even if it turns out he does have a diplomatic passport, he will still have to answer questions relating to the traffic accident.'

'Yes, sir.' At the door, James hesitated. 'But Laura has the car. She's gone to tell Mrs Glover about her husband.'

Montgomery-Jones got to his feet, took out the keys from his jacket pocket and threw them to James.

'Take mine. It is in the parking area at the top of the hill.'

Once James left, Montgomery-Jones took out Fiona's rough sketch of the seating plan, laid it on the table and studied it in silence. It was probably time for her to leave. She'd been ne-

223

glecting her party for most of the evening and if any of them needed her, they would have no idea of where she was. She glanced at her watch. It was getting late and by now, the older couples would already be on their way to bed. She was still reluctant to leave Barry to be cross-questioned. It wasn't that she didn't trust Montgomery-Jones exactly, but he was a forceful man with a job to do and, even at his best, his aristocratic bearing could be intimidating.

'You know these people better than most, do you have any suspicions about any of them?' he asked her unexpectedly, his eyes still on the paper in front of him.

'Suspicions? Do you mean who might have tampered with the wine? I can't think of a reason for anyone to do that to the Websters or Holly.' She frowned. 'Unless it was as a diversion to get Barry out of the room and why would any of my party want to do that? He seems to get on with most people.'

'Did he appear to be concerned about anything in particular today? You mentioned he had been drinking at lunchtime, was that usual?'

'No, but ...' she hesitated. 'It's only my opinion, but I think things have been a little difficult with his wife these last few days,' she admitted reluctantly.

'I see.' He looked at her but it was impossible to tell what he was thinking.

'Why would anyone want to abduct Barry? Do you think he saw or heard something to do with Graham's murder?' she asked.

Montgomery-Jones gave a non-committal shrug.

Stupid idea, she told herself. If that had been the case, they could just as easily have killed him as drugged him. She shook her head in frustration. Perhaps now was the time to tell Montgomery-Jones about Brendan.

'I don't suspect him at all. He'd already left the tasting room so I can't see how he could have put anything in the wine but ...'

He listened to her faltering explanation of the connection between Brendan and Graham Spellman and the saga with the lost sweater, his face expressionless.

'As you say, I cannot see how that is relevant to this situation and at this stage I see no good purpose in questioning him further.'

Fiona let out a long sigh of relief.

'What about the others? I respect your wish to be discrete, but is there anyone else in the party who has aroused your suspicions?'

'I don't know of any reason why they might want to aid and abet Barry's abduction or to have any grounds for wanting to kill Graham. On the face of it, they seem pleasant, ordinary people. One or two can be quite difficult in their different ways, but that's a different matter altogether.'

'Will you give me your impressions of each of them? What about,' he glanced down at the paper on the table, 'Devesh Najaran? What can you tell me about him?'

'A real gentleman. He and Anita are being cold-shouldered by most of the others. Because of the furore at Frankfurt airport, Sidney Pettit is convinced he's a Muslim terrorist straight from Pakistan and that antipathy is spreading. As far as I know, they have had no previous connection with Barry or Graham. They have always lived in the East Midlands, nowhere near Maidenhead. He and Ernest Blake went looking for Barry after he'd gone missing, but Devesh never went near the three who were taken ill or touched any of the wine. He never left the bench throughout the wine tasting. I can vouch for that because he sat almost opposite me.'

'And Ernest Blake?'

Half way through telling him all she knew about the sprightly elderly man with a keen sense of history who kept much to himself, they heard the sound of footsteps running down the corridor. The door burst open and a haggard-looking Elspeth stood staring at the figure on the bed oblivious of anyone else in the room. She rushed over and began stroking her husband's brow.

'Barry, my darling. How are you?'

Barry was still groggy, but he clearly recognized her voice

and managed a weak smile whispering, 'Pumpkin. You've come back.'

At long last the combined effects of the drug, the drink and the bang on the head were beginning to wear off.

Moments later, a petite, rather plain girl arrived in the doorway, looking decidedly apprehensive. 'She insisted on coming straight away, sir.'

'Naturally. I anticipated she would.'

The girl looked relieved but obviously still felt the need to justify herself. 'I did try to ring James to tell him we were on our way but his phone's switched off.'

'In all likelihood, the hospital requested he do so. He is following up another lead.'

Now Barry had his wife to care for him, Fiona was free to leave. 'If you need me, I'll be in my room.'

'Mrs Mason, thank you for everything you have done this evening. We will talk in the morning.'

Fiona reached the end of the corridor when she heard someone call her name.

'Mrs Mason. Do you mind if we have a chat? I'm Laura Phillips, James's girlfriend. I work at Vauxhall Cross.'

'I'm sorry?' What was the girl on about?

'Headquarters.'

'I'm sorry, Laura. I'm still none the wiser.'

'I'm only a humble researcher, a glorified secretary really, but the Commander sent me with James to help act as a cover. James was sent out here to act as liaison but when Spelman was murdered we were drawn into shadowing your party.' The words came out in a nervous rush. 'I just wanted to ask you what's been going on. I didn't like to ask the Commander, he can be a bit terrifying. Has Barry been arrested? Is it all over?'

'Should you be telling me all this?'

'But you've worked with the Commander before and already know all about James. But you're right of course; we ought to go somewhere private.'

Fiona stayed in Laura's room for some time. The girl obviously felt isolated and out of her depth and needed a sympathetic listener. Once she began talking, it was almost impossible to stop her. The assignment had proved far less exciting than she'd anticipated, especially as James's total preoccupation with his newfound role meant he had little time for her. The romantic, fully paid holiday she'd imagined was not working out at all as she'd hoped.

'I thought we'd at least have a chance to look round the area together but James spends most of the time over at the station or with the Germans and it's not much fun on my own. When we do go out playing tourists together, all we do is sit outside cafés keeping a watch on anyone making contact with your lot,' she said with some bitterness. 'To be honest it's all pretty boring especially when I've no idea what's going on or what we're supposed to be looking for. Even James tells me only the bare minimum as though I can't be trusted.'

'So you don't know what's happening to Vivien?'

'She still doesn't want to come back to this hotel and you can see her point. The Commander suggested I go and sit with her to keep her company when James is at meetings, but I don't think she wants me there particularly. Though sitting cooped up in a hotel room all day isn't helping. I suggested we went out to do a bit of sightseeing to take her mind off things and get some fresh air but she said she wasn't in the mood. Last time, I did get her to come out for a coffee. I think the walk did her good but she's still pretty low.'

'Have you any idea when she'll be allowed to come home?'

'None at all. I do know the Commander wants the case wrapped up fast. He's pressing the local police to either charge her or let her return to England. All I know is he and James discussed it and the BND are involved.'

'BND?'

'The Bundesnachrichtendienst. The German Intelligence Agency.'

Not till the small hours did Fiona finally climb into bed but her mind was still far too active for sleep. Laura's babblings had confirmed several of Fiona's suspicions and helped slot one or two other things into place that had been puzzling her, but that still left major questions unanswered. Who had bundled Barry out of the wine tasting and for what conceivable reason. And why dump him in a barrel minutes later?

If they'd wanted information, it made no sense to pump him with ketamine. He'd be in no state to answer questions. Had the plan to abduct Barry been thwarted when his captors spotted Kathleen and Brendan sitting outside? But what did Barry know? Was it something to do with the mystery documents? There were enough people, including whoever broke into Graham Spelman's room and Montgomery-Jones, who appeared anxious to get their hands on them. Those documents seem to lie at the heart of everything and it was odds on they had something to do with this dodgy contract Graham had been trying to negotiate.

Had James had been right all along and Barry's abduction merely a ruse to make him appear innocent? It was possible that Barry had acquired Graham's documents and arranged to meet the two men to hand them over. Barry's explanation about the call on his mobile could have been to put her off the scent. The food poisoning incident could have been mere chance and nothing to do with the handover. It had merely provided a convenient opportunity for Barry to slip out. But why all the rigmarole with the ketamine? A convenient alibi so no one would suspect him? But surly he wouldn't have needed one. He could have slipped back in at any time in all the commotion and no one the wiser.

Had the white van been there when the Super Sun Party arrived? She didn't remember seeing it as they sat waiting on the wall but then why should she. Brendan and Kathleen were outside by the time the others were taken ill so if the men were already inside by then who had let them in? The oversized wooden door had no handle so without a key someone must have opened it up for them. Three or four people had taken the opportunity to visit the washrooms before the tasting started but she was fairly certain Barry wasn't one of them because she'd been waiting for a chance to mention her call to Montgomery-Jones and would have noticed.

The only other way in was the loading bay. The two men could have climbed up earlier. Those doors may have been shut when the men had first arrived but, as Fiona had noticed when she'd looked for something for Kathleen to sit on, they'd not been locked. They would certainly have needed to be inside for some time in order to find their way through the maze of passageways.

Fiona sighed. All she had was a pile of questions and answers seemed pretty thin on the ground.

And she hadn't looked at her notes for the next day! Still, if she remembered rightly, that shouldn't be too much of a problem. There wasn't a lot for her to do apart from making hot drinks for her passengers on the journey. The morning's guided tour of one of the castles meant Fiona could tag on the end of the queue and let someone else do all the work. The afternoon was free for everyone to do some last minute shopping before they went home. Assuming they would be allowed to leave the area of course. If all this business wasn't sorted out tomorrow, heaven knows what might happen. Where would they stay for a start?

Day 8 Sunday

This morning we visit Burg Marksburg, the only hill castle on the Rhine which has never been destroyed thanks to its strong defences built in the Middle Ages. Beginning with the construction of the keep in the 12th century, the castle grew throughout succeeding centuries. Occupied for over 700 years, in more peaceful times it was used as a state prison.

After lunch, we return to the beautiful riverside town of Rudesheim where you can spend time exploring the quaint Drosselgrasse and perhaps enjoy a glass of local wine in one of the many small bars as you listen to traditional Rhineland music. You may care to explore the many fascinating little shops to see the exquisite carved wooden dolls and do some last minute shopping. You may even be tempted to take home a few bottles of wine.

Super Sun Executive Travel

Twenty-Nine

Next morning, Fiona was in and out of the shower in half her usual time. Apart from wanting to check Barry had recovered from his ordeal, she was curious to know what had happened with the occupants of the white van and how they fitted into the picture. Though finding out the current state of play might prove a little tricky. Montgomery-Jones may have been considerably more communicative last night but the chances of getting anything out of him were about as high Sidney and Devesh becoming best buddies. She could try asking Laura; but the girl was unlikely to know anything even if she were prepared to pass it on.

A frantic knocking at her door interrupted her musings.

Without all the jewellery and minus the customary green lidded, kohl rimmed eyes; it took a moment or two for Fiona to recognize the woman. Whether it was the lack of make-up or her obvious distress, Hilary looked ten years older.

'Whatever's wrong?'

Fiona put an arm around the agitated woman and led her to the bed.

'It's Viktor. He's missing. He never came up last night.' The rest of the story came out in a rush. 'I was tired after dinner, not like me at all, and around ten I'd had enough. I told Viktor to stay and enjoy the music; he's an even bigger night owl than me; never in bed before midnight. I must have dropped off straight away and it wasn't till this morning I realized he hadn't come up.'

'Perhaps he woke early and decided to go down to breakfast without disturbing you. Have you checked the dining room?'

'No,' she admitted reluctantly. 'I just threw on some clothes and came straight here.'

'I'm sure that's what's happened. Let's go down and see, shall we?'

'But his bed hasn't been slept in.'

Fiona squeezed her hand. 'It's easy enough to flick the duvet back into place.'

The only person in the dining room was Winston and, according to the waitress, no one else from the Super Sun party had yet put in an appearance.

'You stay here with Winston while I check at reception.'

According to the balding, middle-aged man at the desk, no one had left the building since he'd unlocked the two side doors. The only other way out was through the staff entrance straight into the kitchen where he would have been seen. By now, even Fiona was beginning to worry. Surely, this wasn't another abduction? She pulled out her phone and rang Montgomery-Jones's number.

When she had explained the situation, he asked where she was.

'I'm in reception. Hilary is still in the dining room. I'm just on my way back to her. I could put her on the phone if you'd like to talk to her.'

'That will not be necessary. I would prefer to speak with her directly.'

Before she could make any comment, he'd rung off. How long were the two of them going to have to hang around? People would be coming down to breakfast soon and the last thing Hilary needed right now was the rest of the party fussing around her asking all sorts of awkward questions.

Back in the dining room, Winston had taken Hilary to one of the more secluded small tables tucked into a corner behind the trellis screen well away from the other hotel guests who were beginning to arrive. Fiona pulled out a chair and sat down opposite Hilary.

'It's still a little early to contact the police but I have rung ...'

'No! I don't want the police involved.'

Fiona barely had time to reassure Hilary when Montgomery-Jones appeared in the doorway. He was still dressed in the same pinstripe suit and sober, striped club tie he'd been wearing the previous night and he never wore the same suit two days running. He must have been here all night.

'Mrs Mason, Mr Taylor.' He held out a hand to Hilary. 'Mrs Kasar? Allow me to introduce myself, Peter Montgomery-Jones. I understand you are anxious about your husband.' He took the remaining chair at the table.

He asked her to repeat what she'd told Fiona. Apart from confirming Viktor was missing and she hadn't seen him since the previous evening, Hilary seemed unwilling to say a great deal. She answered each of his questions with the minimum of words and it took some time for him to tease out the details.

'So you are uncertain as to whether your husband returned to your room after you retired last night?' Hilary nodded. 'And you can think of no possible reason for his departure? There was no friction between the two of you?'

'No. Nothing like that,' she mumbled

'What about his clothes and the rest of his possessions? Have you checked they're still there?'

'Nothing's gone.'

'Did he have his passport with him?'

Fiona intervened, 'The police asked me to collect them. They're in the hotel safe.'

'I see.'

Montgomery-Jones took out his small notebook and un-clipped his pen from an inside pocket. Hilary physically cow-ered and what little colour she'd had, drained from her face.

'Would you give me your husband's full name? And I think you had better spell it for me.' He gave her an encouraging smile but Hilary still looked wary, although she visibly re-laxed when he'd finished writing and returned the book and pen to his pocket.

233

'It might help if you gave me a few background details. Anything which might give us a better picture so we can help find him for you.'

'What sort of thing?'

'For a start, what nationality is your husband?'

'He's from Azerbaijan.'

'How long has he been resident in Britain?'

'A couple of months. He came over when we got married.'

Montgomery-Jones maintained the gentle smile. 'Did you meet while you were over in the Caucuses?'

Hilary looked totally confused. 'We met through an internet-dating agency.'

'He has never gone off on his own like this before?'

'No never.'

'And you can think of no reason why he might choose to leave the hotel without informing you?'

Hilary shook her head. 'He's probably gone out for a cigarette. He usually does after breakfast most mornings. That must be it. He knows I don't like him smoking in the bedroom.'

'Let us hope that is the case.' He moved his chair back a little. 'You mentioned the last time you saw him he was with Mr and Mrs Lambert in the lounge, the next logical step for me might be to speak to them, 'If you would like to stay here with Mr Taylor and finish your coffee and perhaps get yourself some breakfast, I will return shortly. Mrs Mason, would you mind coming with me?'

Hilary looked as though she wanted to protest but Montgomery-Jones was already walking to the door. Fiona followed him out into the main corridor trying to catch up with his long-legged strides as he headed for reception. One of the other hotel guests was at the desk making enquiries about train times so they hung back.

'You know the lady better than I,' Montgomery-Jones said quietly, 'but how would you describe Mrs Kasar's state of mind?'

'I'd say she was terrified.'

234

'My assessment exactly. Can you think of any explanation or are you about to accuse me of intimidating the woman?' The grey eyes twinkled.

'No. She was like that before you arrived. They're an unlikely couple. I know they say opposites attract but I don't think I've ever met two people with quite so little in common. She's a sociable body always laughing with the others but he's very reserved and intense and I don't think that's just down to the language problem.'

Fiona stood lost in her own thoughts.

'It is still a little early to start worrying unduly.' Montgomery-Jones's comment brought Fiona back from her reverie.

Fiona shook her head. 'Something Hilary said that puzzled me. If he's been living in Britain for so short a time, would Viktor be eligible for a British passport? I remember it particularly because foreign passports can slow things down when we go through controls. People get tetchy if they have to wait around.'

'There may be an explanation; an English mother or some such, but I grant you, it is somewhat unexpected.' It was a relief to know she wasn't wasting his time. 'Perhaps it might be worth taking a look into it.'

'Do you want to see if Viktor's is still in the safe?'

'It might be a good idea.'

Viktor's passport was with all the others. If he'd done a bunk he'd have no way of getting out of the country, but if someone had succeeded in abducting him what could possibly be the reason?

'Before we speak to Mr and Mrs Lambert, there are a couple of phone calls I should make, if you would not mind waiting.' Montgomery-Jones raised a questioning eyebrow.

'Of course not.'

'Perhaps you would be kind enough to ring through and ask if they will speak to us.'

'Certainly.'

To Fiona's relief, Ian answered her call so she was spared the daunting task of fielding Rita's inevitable questions. Not surprisingly, Montgomery-Jones had not returned by the time she'd finished. People were still coming down to breakfast so Fiona perched herself on the top step of the small flight up to reception out of everyone's way, at least till someone wanted to get to the desk.

Fiona looked up at the large wall clock. At this rate, she would be lucky to get any breakfast before it was time to board the coach. She didn't mind missing out on the food but a cup of tea first thing was one of life's essentials. Oh well, it looked as though she would have to make do with the instant variety she served on the coach during their journeys. The powdered stuff masquerading as tea was undrinkable as far as she was concerned, but the hot chocolate was passable.

She sat lost in thought until she looked up to see Montgomery-Jones towering over her.

'You look pensive.'

'I wonder,' Fiona hesitated, 'Viktor went missing around the same time as Barry after the tasting. Not for long admittedly, but Devesh had to go looking for him. It occurred to me, while Viktor was in the cellars he might have seen something that might explain what happened to Barry. I don't mean the actual abduction because he would have said last night, but something suspicious.'

Montgomery-Jones did not look convinced. 'Such as?'

'I don't know. Someone in the wrong place perhaps. Down in the cellars or coming out of the cellars or talking to a stranger. Viktor may not have realized its significance at the time, but once the full story comes out, he might put two and two together.'

'Are you suggesting someone has abducted Mr Kasar?'

'It was just an idea. The Lamberts are happy to see us now up in their room if that's alright?'

'Excellent.'

Thirty

As they climbed the stairs to the second floor, Fiona had another question. 'Have you seen Barry this morning? Do you know how he is?'

'Not since last night, but he seemed none the worse from his ordeal when I left. He has a sore head and a few bruises from when he was manhandled but there appear to be no ill effects from the drug. I expect he is still sleeping. It was late by the time we finished talking.'

I bet it was, Fiona thought glaring at him. 'Does he know what happened?'

'Not in any detail.'

'So what does he remember?' Fiona persisted. When all she got was one of his disdainful glances, she snapped. 'I can always ask him of course.'

Montgomery-Jones raised an eyebrow and said reluctantly, 'He recalls getting up from his bench in the tasting room and feeling a sharp stab in the backside. Things became a little hazy after that but someone, he has no idea who, helped him out into the corridor. Apart from a few disjointed recollections about a couple of strangers marching him to what we believe must have been the delivery area and a fierce argument between them, he remembers nothing until he was back here.'

They had reached Room 7.

'Perhaps I should warn you, Rita Lambert is the group gossip. I doubt she knows the meaning of the word discretion.'

Fiona introduced Montgomery-Jones and explained he wanted to ask a few questions.

'Has something else dreadful happened?'

Before Rita could give full reign to the histrionic display she so obviously relished, Montgomery-Jones cut her short.

'We are merely attempting to clarify certain events that occurred last night and it would be helpful to know who was present in the hotel lounge later in the evening.'

Rita was clearly impressed by the obvious importance of her aristocratic visitor and to add gravitas to all her answers immediately refined her estuary accent although her stilted attempts at a more sophisticated and formal vocabulary made even her husband cringe.

After a diatribe on the behaviour of some of the younger members of the party during the evening, Rita continued, 'Hilary complained of being tired and decided to retire early. She told Viktor not to spoil his evening and he stayed to talk with us. It's not easy to converse with Viktor. He's Russian, well from one of those former Russian countries that became independent after the break-up. Not that I have anything against foreigners you understand, but his comprehension of English does leave a great deal to be desired. Of course we all try to make him feel welcome and part of our happy little band.' She finished with a simpering smile.

Like you do Devesh and Anita! Fiona thought bitterly of how Rita had taken to pointedly ignoring the Indian couple over the last few days.

'Did Mr Kasar leave the bar before you?'

Neither of them could give the exact time Viktor left but agreed it was well before the end of the evening's entertainment.

'Normally the pair of them stay and have a nightcap at the bar after the music's over and the band packs up for the evening. I expect he went to see how his wife was doing,' Rita suggested.

'Went for a smoke more like.'

Rita looked none too pleased at her husband's muttered contradiction. 'Thinking back, Viktor did appear to be even moodier than usual, I wonder if there might be some marital difficulty, purely temporary I'm sure,' she simpered.

'That has been extremely helpful, Mrs Lambert.' Montgomery-Jones rose to his feet.

Now her curiosity had been wetted, Rita was reluctant to let them go without an explanation. 'Has something happened to Viktor? You haven't told us why you want to know …'

'Thank you both so much for your time.' Montgomery-Jones' manner was enough to quell even Rita's questions.

Once outside the room, Montgomery-Jones turned to Fiona and in a rare display of irritation said, 'Does that woman ever stop talking?'

Fiona chuckled. 'I did warn you.'

'Hmm.' He gave her a sidelong look. 'Next time, it might be more opportune to do so before we knock at the door.'

She stifled a giggle. The situation was far from humorous. 'It remains to be seen just what kind of story she makes of all that. And how long she manages to keep it to herself; especially when Hilary and Victor fail to turn up for the morning trip.'

Winston was waiting for them just inside the dining-room door.

'The lady's gone back up to her room. I said you were both coming back but I couldn't exactly stop her.'

'We do appreciate that. Thank you for your help, Mr Taylor.'

'I'd better get off.' Winston took a few steps down the corridor then turned back. 'Fiona, sweetheart. I know you're busy trying to sort this mess out but, young lady, you haven't had any breakfast yet.' He waged an admonishing finger. 'Look, I can see to everyone when we get to the castle so if you want to stay here and sort things out just give me a buzz.'

Winston could always be relied upon not to milk a crisis.

'Thanks, Winston. But that really won't be necessary. I can't do much here except get in everyone's way.'

He placed a hand on her shoulder. Dwarfed by the two men head and shoulders above her close on either side, she suddenly appreciated what a strange tableau the three of them must make.

Montgomery-Jones took Fiona by the arm and instead of following Winston into the main part of the hotel steered her back into the dining room. 'Mr Taylor is quite correct. I think breakfast is the next thing on the agenda for you, Mrs Mason, while I go and talk to Mrs Kasar.'

'Forgive me, I don't wish to sound impertinent, but I think she might open up a little more freely with me there. She knows me and if she really is frightened of something she's less likely to confide in a stranger.'

He smiled and said, 'Very tactfully put, but I have to agree her failure to wait does indicate her unwillingness to talk to me.'

'We don't need to ask her room number. I know it already. Her room is next to mine. Shall we go?'

'No. On reflection, I think it best if I let you handle this on your own.'

'Me?'

'As you have so rightly pointed out, I am probably not the best placed to illicit exactly what is troubling her, and my presence may only serve to exacerbate the situation.'

'But what do you want me to ask her?'

'Simply get her to talk. You have the knack of getting people to open up. If anyone can get her to say what is distressing her, that person is you.'

'I'll do my best,' she said doubtfully.

'Although you might like to ask if her husband's jacket is missing,' he added as she turned to leave.

Fiona knocked tentatively at the door. She wasn't surprised when there was no answer.

'Hilary. It's Fiona. May I come in? I'm on my own.'

Fiona heard footsteps and the sound of a key being turned in the lock. The door opened only a crack.

'Any news?'

'Not yet I'm afraid. Are you alright? I was worried about you when you disappeared.'

'That man isn't with you?' Hilary opened the door a fraction wider and peered down the corridor.

'Mr Montgomery-Jones? No; he's still downstairs.'

Hilary may have decided to forgo breakfast, but her husband's absence had not been enough to stop her slapping on the war paint and arming herself with her customary profusion of bangles, necklaces, rings on every finger and earrings dangling to her shoulders.

She must have noticed Fiona's stare and said quickly, 'Feel naked until I've done my eyes and put some lippy on. That's why I came up.'

Fiona glanced around. Unlike her own, No 25 was a twin bedded room and, as Hilary had told her earlier, the nearest bed looked as though it hadn't been slept in, but there were a pair of sunglasses and a man's oval hairbrush on the bedside table. One of Viktor's sweaters hung over the back of the chair.

'He's a bit scary that chap. Is he a policeman?'

'Oh no. But don't ask me what he does exactly. I met him when I was leading a tour in Holland a couple of months ago. He helped when one of the party went missing so I thought he might be able to help now.' Hilary looked less than convinced. Best to move on quickly. 'Are you going to join us on the trip today?'

What a tactless question! Why hadn't she given it a moment's thought before jumping in so quickly?

'I don't think so.' Hilary's voice was wistful. No trace of outrage at the suggestion. 'By now, I suppose they all know what's happened. If you spoke to Rita it'll be all round the hotel.'

'No. All she knows is we were asking questions about what happened in the bar last night.'

'I suppose there's no point hanging around here all day,' she said wistfully.

'Exactly. Look, if anyone asks where he is, we'll simply tell them he wasn't up to coming with us today. You don't need to lie, just make it sound as though he's not too well or something. You're an actress, you'll think of something. If he does turn up, Mr Montgomery-Jones will ring straight away.' Hilary visibly brightened. 'So have you thought of anything else that might help find Viktor? Did he have his wallet with him in the lounge last night?'

'I'm not sure. Because of his English, I always pay for the drinks.'

'So is it here now?'

Hilary opened up the wardrobe and began searching through the pockets of his jacket. With all of the chaos of the previous evening, Fiona couldn't remember what Viktor had been wearing. Apart from a few shirts, there was nothing else of his in there.

'Is that the only jacket he brought or was he wearing a different one last night?'

'I suppose it must have been. He didn't bring much.'

Fiona knew Viktor had an anorak, a bottle green one, which he always wore when the weather was bad. There was no sign of it in the wardrobe and there was nothing hanging on the back of the door. Unless for some strange reason it was in the bathroom, it had gone. One thing was certain; Viktor would never have come down to dinner wearing it.

'What about the rest of his clothes. Is anything else missing?'

Hilary looked nonplussed then shrugged her shoulders.

'What about his trousers? Doesn't he keep those in the wardrobe?'

'He only brought a couple of pairs and, now you come to mention it, he hasn't worn his jeans since the start of the holiday. As I said, he travelled light. He only brought that small grip.' She indicated a canvas holdall little bigger than a flight bag sitting on the top shelf above the rail. 'He only brought one pair of shoes and there're not here. Still,' she managed a weak smile, 'makes up for all my stuff, doesn't it?'

Her over-large, hard-shell case stood in the corner.

Thirty-One

Montgomery-Jones waited for her in the small recess area off the corridor. It wasn't the best place to hold a private exchange nor, Fiona thought, was it a good idea to whet the appetite of any of the Super Sun party who might happen to pass by. Best to keep it short.

'...And I don't know if it's relevant but I'm fairly certain he was wearing a dark sage green short sleeved shirt on the journey over and that wasn't there either. Of course he might have put all his dirty clothes back in his holdall or a drawer. It wasn't my place to search.'

'Interesting. Thank you, Mrs Mason. That is very helpful.'

Would he be prepared to return the favour? No point in subterfuge. 'Did the injured van passenger have anything to do with what happened to Barry? Do you know why they did it?'

Montgomery-Jones was already on his feet but he turned and looked down at her. After a long pause he said, 'The man has been interviewed but he is still somewhat reticent about explaining himself. We can only hope when he is faced with being charged with grievous bodily harm and the attempted abduction of a British citizen, he may prove a trifle more cooperative.'

Trying to keep any hint of irony from her voice, she said. 'I am sure you will be very persuasive.'

He raised both eyebrows in a mock affront, shook his head then gave a reluctant smile.

She watched him disappear round the corner then hurried

back to her own room. Time to put her things together and get down to the coach. So much for reading through her notes on the castle. Not that it really mattered. Once they got there, there would be an official castle guide to show them round and any introductory information she might give them on the journey, she could read straight from the sheet. Though, when she had a spare moment once they were on the coach, it might be a good idea to read what the guidebook had to say. Given the kind of day she was having, odds on some bright spark would start to ask all sorts of questions about the place she couldn't answer.

On her way to the stairs, Fiona passed the Glovers' room. She wondered how Barry felt this morning. She looked around to double check no one was about then pressed her ear to the door. The last thing she wanted to do was disturb them if they were still sleeping.

She wasn't certain, but she thought she could detect the gentle murmur of voices and when she heard a definite laugh, she tapped lightly on the door.

'Just a minute,' came the call.

The door opened a crack and Elspeth peeped round.

'I hope I didn't wake you.'

'Oh no, Fiona.'

'I just wanted to ask how you both were this morning. Everyone was worried and although I spread the word Barry was back safe and sound, I know they're going to badger me with questions.'

'He's much better this morning, aren't you, love?' She glanced over her shoulder. 'Almost back to his old self. Still a bit tired so we are going to have an easy day.'

'I'm fine. A few bruises and bit of a bump on the head, but you can tell them all I'm fighting fit,' came a chirpy voice from inside. He certainly sounded strong enough.

'Excellent news. I won't keep you. Have a good day both of you.'

'And you,' they chorused.

Things were definitely looking up. Not only were both Barry and Elspeth back in the fold, but marital harmony had been restored.

Having missed breakfast, there'd been no opportunity to check up on the Websters and Holly this morning. Although the girls usually skipped breakfast in any case.

Barry's return to the hotel had prevented her from anything more than a cursory few words with Edith and Len before dinner last night.

Fiona was pleased to see the elderly couple already waiting in the small pull-in by the church for the coach to arrive.

'How are you both this morning? I hope you've got your appetites back.'

'Tip top, thank you, my dear. I said to Daphne earlier, we were ravenous when we came down to breakfast and made absolute gluttons of ourselves.' Edith's broad smile put Fiona's fears to rest.

'Cereal, scrambled egg on toast plus a mountain of toast and jam afterwards. The works.' Len added.

'And it's not as though we'll be going hungry at lunch time with a lovely lunch lined up. It's just so hard to resist with all that delicious food laid out in front of you,' Edith said with a grimace.

'That's what holidays are all about. I'm so pleased to hear you're both completely recovered.'

Other people were jostling for Fiona's attention eager for news about Barry. She needed to work out a plausible story to account for all of yesterday's goings on or they would pester her with questions for the rest of the morning not to mention imagining all sorts of even worse scenarios.

As soon as she'd counted them all onto the coach and they were sitting down, Fiona made her announcement. 'For those of you who didn't hear, Barry is back with us safe and sound. It seems he was in the cellars after all. He took a wrong turn and ended up back in that maze of corridors. He must have tripped and knocked himself unconscious so he didn't hear the search party calling out for him. Elspeth is also back with us but the two of them are going to have a quiet day today and we'll see them both at dinner.' Fiona had long since given up the effort of trying to twist the truth to give a false impression. Now she was lying like a trooper.

One advantage of the focus of interest on Barry was no one had commented on Viktor's non-appearance. He and Hilary always sat right at the back of the coach so most people probably hadn't noticed. No doubt, someone would eventually cotton on, but it was up to Hilary what story she decided to tell.

'As you know from your tour booklets, today we're off to Marksburg Castle which will make a truly memorable finale to our stay in the area. It really is a fantastic place, one of Germany's must see castles, and I know you're going to love it. So settle back everyone and relax.'

Now was her chance for a quick word with Holly. The girl certainly looked bright enough.

'It was nothing really,' Holly protested.

'She's been way worse, believe me,' laughed Cressida, not unkindly. 'You should see her when she really gets hammered on a proper night out.'

Holly gave a sheepish grin. 'We both cut back a bit on the booze last night.'

With a smile, Fiona flipped down her own seat in the stairwell and strapped herself in. Another problem solved.

Montgomery-Jones barely had time to reach his hotel room before the call came through.

'The police tracked the number of the white van to a hire company but we had to wait until they opened up this morning for details. It was taken out two days ago and we do have a name. The woman who handled all the paperwork was a bit suspicious. The chap's German was pretty limited. Not a problem in itself, they get a fair number of tourists hiring cars obviously, but he couldn't give any explanation of why he wanted a van without any markings on the side. Being the wife of the owner, she asked to see his passport to check it tallied with the driving licence and then make a copy of them both. While she was in the backroom she also rang the hotel in Wiesbaden he'd given as his temporary address.'

'Resourceful lady.'

'The passport and licence are inevitably forgeries but we've sent someone over to the hotel. There's only a one in a hundred chance the driver of the van will return there, but we may learn something useful.'

'Excellent work, Fitzwilliam. However, I think it is time you got back to your hotel and got your head down. It has been a long night.'

'Yes, sir.' The relief in his voice was all too evident. 'Thank you, sir.'

It wasn't easy to concentrate on her notes. Try as she might, she found it hard not to think about Viktor. Why would he leave? Her suggestion earlier he might have been kidnapped seemed overly dramatic in retrospect. It was difficult to ignore a feeling somewhere deep in her subconscious that she had the answer or at least a clue. Snatches of some half-remembered inconsistency kept nagging away. Was it something she'd seen or perhaps heard that didn't quite add up? Some small trifle that had puzzled her at the time but she'd dismissed. She was trying too hard. No amount of wondering would give her the answers so she might as well concentrate on the job in hand and hope it would surface when she least expected it.

For the third time she started to read through the history of the castle's seven hundred year occupation starting with the Counts of Eppstein right up to its present function as the headquarters of the German Castles Association.

The road curved around the tight inner meander, north of Boppard. Soon the castle would be coming into view. Fiona picked up the microphone.

'As we round the next bend, look out for the castle up on the skyline. It has an unusually tall, slender keep rising up out of the ramparts and, unlike all the grim, dark ruins we've been passing, Marksburg is a light, creamy white colour.'

Crowning the near precipitous, densely wooded hill, encircled at its foot by the little town of Braubach, no one could deny the setting was as impressive as the attractively turreted castle itself.

'We don't have to walk up there do we?' From the apprehensive looks on several faces, Holly was not the only one feeling anxious.

'You don't expect me to drive this thing up there do you?'

Fiona couldn't help laughing as she saw the girl's jaw drop. 'Don't worry. Winston is teasing you. There's a perfectly good road up to the car park on the other side of the hill and it's no more than a five minute walk from there to the first gate.'

'Thank goodness for that!'

'Once we get off the coach, I'd like you all to make your way through the Drawbridge Gate to the courtyard while I collect the tickets and then we'll go and meet our guide. The tours are usually in German so we're lucky to have one in English today.'

Like everyone else, as their tour progressed Fiona was impressed with everything there was to see. So much so, she was able to forget, or at least push right to the back of her mind, all the chaotic events of the last few days. Hilary had teemed up with Gloria who, with her garrulous sociability, would keep her from dwelling on what might have happened to her husband. There was something to interest everyone from the extensive display of armoury and weapons and the torture chamber to the Great Banqueting Hall and the magnificent bedchamber with its enormous matrimonial four-poster hung with opulent red velvet hangings.

'I hope you've laid on a mediaeval banquet complete with the roast ox and suckling pig, Fiona,' Ian joked when their tour was over. 'Plus the pretty serving wenches and the odd minstrel or two, of course.'

'I'm afraid you'll have to make do with a light lunch on the restaurant terrace, but I can promise you a magnificent view of the river down in the valley.'

Once she'd waved them all goodbye in Rudesheim, Fiona climbed back onto the coach.

'Sure you don't fancy a wander around the shops? It's the last chance you're gonna get.'

'Thanks Winston but I'd rather get back to our hotel. I've several things to sort out not to mention making a start on my packing. Besides, Sunday's my day for ringing the boys. It will be a good time to catch them. The UK is an hour behind us so Martin will have just finished lunch and over in Canada the family won't have set off on whatever they've got planned for the day.'

She wasn't in the mood for playing carefree tourist. Viktor hadn't phoned Hilary in the course of the morning. Not that she seemed bothered by it. Heaven knows what would be happening tomorrow. How could they head for home with one passenger still missing never mind leaving Vivien to the mercies of the German police? Perhaps there would be some news when they reached Hotel Pinger.

Marthe looked up as Fiona reached the reception desk.

'Good afternoon, Mrs Mason. What can I do for you?'

'Do you happen to know if Mr and Mrs Glover are still in the hotel?'

'I have not seen them come back. They ordered a taxi mid-morning. I think they were going to spend the day with Mrs Spelman.'

'Of course. Have there been any messages for me?' Marthe shook her head. 'No news of Mr Kasar?'

'Not that I know of. You might like to ask the tall gentleman who always wears a suit.'

'Mr Montgomery-Jones? Is he still here?'

'He came back about twenty minutes ago and went up to Room 8 with the young couple.'

There was absolutely no way she was going to knock on that particular door. Not that she wouldn't dearly love to be a

249

fly on the wall. If she had all the available pieces, it might help sort her own jumbled thoughts into some kind of order. However, any rapport she'd built up with the inscrutable Peter Montgomery-Jones would be lost forever if she attempted to muscle in.

Fiona sat on the bed propped up against the pillows attempting to complete some of the seemingly endless paperwork lying all around her. What was this mania the whole world appeared to have with tick boxes? Every area of life required a dozen forms in triplicate at each stage of the process before anything could get done. On top of all the essential customs and immigration paperwork, Super Sun had added its own wodge of forms. A detailed account of each day's activities including the weather, timings at the various stops and any problems as well as reports on the hotels and the food including the daily menu! Too many self-important managers who needed to make everyone else jump through hoops to justify their existence.

She checked everyone's passport details to fill in one of the return forms. Now she had another problem. She stared at the passport in her hand. Viktor Kasar. As yet, there was no way she could add his name to the list of passengers on the form needed when they reached Calais. So what should she do with the passport? She could hardly take it back with her but leaving it in the hotel safe was hardly a practical option either.

She leant over the side of the bed and rescued her bag from the floor. It was as good an excuse to ring Montgomery-Jones as any.

'Mrs Mason?'

'I am sorry to disturb you but I need your advice.' Fiona explained her dilemma.

'Do you have the passport with you?'

'Yes. I have them all.'

There was a short pause. 'Would you like me to take responsibility for it?'

'Please.'

'What time do you expect to be back at the hotel?'

'I'm here already. The programme includes a free afternoon in Rudesheim but I came back with Winston.'

'I see. In that case would you mind bringing it to Room 8 on the second floor?'

'Now?'

'If that is convenient.'

Fiona slipped the mobile back into her bag with a smile. It didn't mean he would answer any of her questions of course but at least she had a good excuse to gatecrash the discussions and at least put them to him. Slipping back into her shoes, she fluffed her hair back into shape and checked herself in the mirror.

Thirty-Two

Laura answered her knock. It crossed Fiona's mind the girl might just take the passport and close the door but, before she could say anything, Laura smiled and stood back to let her in.

'Please don't get up on my account,' Fiona protested as the two men made to stand.

She felt very self-conscious as she walked over to the small table and handed it over.

'How is Mrs Kasar? I trust she is not too distressed?' Montgomery-Jones asked.

'Not all.' Fiona grimaced. 'After all the histrionics first thing she seems in excellent spirits. I don't understand the woman, though to be fair she did complain of a bad headache. Even that disappeared when we reached the castle.'

James chuckled. 'No doubt be the effect of the Mickey Fin he slipped into her drink last night to cover his get away.'

'I take it there's been no news of Viktor?'

'Not yet,' replied Montgomery-Jones.

She itched to ask what the background reports he'd sent for earlier had come up with, but she knew he would never divulge such information. As he returned his gaze to the laptop, she said nonchalantly, 'There was something else.'

Montgomery-Jones looked up again.

'My geography of that part of the world is a trifle hazy but Samarkand isn't in Azerbaijan is it?'

The polite smiles on the faces of both men instantly disappeared. After what seemed a long time, but was probably only a matter of seconds, Montgomery-Jones replied calmly, 'No, it is not. Why?'

'The other day when we were talking over lunch, Hilary mentioned Viktor had worked there.' There was a marked silence in the room. She had gone too far to stop now. 'Yet this morning she told us he came from Azerbaijan. As I told you earlier, Barry mentioned Graham had been negotiating a contract with a Central Asian country. I just wondered if there could be a connection.'

'Samarkand is in Uzbekistan.'

She could not hide the grin of satisfaction. 'Isn't that the place where the chap who was blown up in Frankfurt last week came from?'

He looked at her for a moment, shook his head then gave a boyish chuckle. 'Not a great deal escapes you, does it, Mrs Mason?' He waved her to the vacant chair. 'Laura my dear, do you think you could rustle up some tea for the four of us?'

'Certainly, sir.'

It seemed the hotel did not provide room service but would provide a tray of tea if someone was prepared to fetch it.

'Let me go. It could be heavy.' James leapt to his feet.

'I'll come with you and open the doors.' Laura clearly felt the need to do something useful.

Once the young couple had left, Fiona decided to take advantage of Montgomery-Jones's good humour. 'I've been wondering if Viktor's disappearance and Graham's murder, the attack on Barry and the men in the white van could all be pieces in the same jigsaw.'

'Why would you think that?'

'They do all have one significant connection. My Super Sun Party. Whoever engineered the food poising incident had to have been in that hall at the time just before Barry was dosed with ketamine. Those two events must be connected.'

'Assuming Glover is to be believed.'

'You think he's lying? The whole attempted abduction business was staged to make him look innocent. Is that what you're telling me?' Fiona was on the edge of her chair and could feel her temperature rising.

'No. That is not what I am saying. However, it cannot be ruled out.'

'Do you think he murdered Graham too?'

'Spelman's death may or may not be connected to the other incidents. May I remind you, the police still have a suspect and Mrs Spelman was not present at the wine tasting?'

'But it couldn't have been Barry who broke into Graham's room and ransacked the place on Friday. He was on the coach with the rest of us at the time. And it couldn't have been Viktor either. No one from the Super Sun Party was in the hotel, apart from Brendan.'

'True.'

'But there had to be a reason for someone to break into that room. And we still don't know what the intruder was looking for.' She looked at him expectantly but he wasn't forthcoming. 'Though you must have a pretty good idea.'

Montgomery-Jones clearly did but if Fiona hoped he'd confide in her, she was to be disappointed.

'You were going through Graham's papers for a long time when you searched his room. It was obvious you were looking for something specific.'

His eyes narrowed but he said nothing.

'So if it wasn't in his room, what happened to it?'

'That is what we want to know.'

'At one point, I did consider Spelman might actually be working for you. On a mission to ferret out factions that might pose a threat to the stability of the region or possibly our own national security. But I dismissed that idea pretty quickly. The facts don't fit.'

He stifled a smile. 'True.'

'I can't help wondering if it might be something to do with the contract which provoked so much friction with his business partner. Perhaps Graham had decided to go ahead with it anyway. But it couldn't have been any run-of-the-mill commercial project or why would you be interested? That wasn't a question by the way. Just thinking out loud. I know you can't tell me.'

'Umm.' It was obvious he knew what she was up to but he looked more amused than annoyed.

'But I'm sure you must know exactly what that contract was for.'

'Are you now?'

'Assuming he brought the plans for that project with him, presumably your interest is in stopping those designs from falling into the wrong hands.'

'You are making a great many assumptions.' He gave her a warning look but she was not prepared to stop now.

'From that brochure Graham gave me, I know his company manufactured thermal imaging equipment. Obviously I know very little about such things, but isn't it just possible the technology could be used in some kind of weapons system. What if Graham was trying to sell the designs to the Uzbek forces or perhaps some revolutionary group . . .'

'Mrs Mason!' He visibly tensed and the grey eyes narrowed. He asked sharply, 'Has Glover told you this?'

'No, of course not.'

'Then I urge you, Mrs Mason, under no circumstances do you mention this fanciful idea to him or anyone else.'

She had obviously hit a nerve. The tension in the room was broken by the return of James and Laura with the tea.

The hiatus caused by the removal of the laptop and other bits and pieces on the small table onto the bed to make room for the oversized tray gave Fiona the opportunity to think. She was so lost in her own thoughts it wasn't until Laura repeated her question she realized it had been addressed to her.

'I'm so sorry. I was miles away.'

'I only asked if you'd like a biscuit.'

Fiona shook her head and turned to Montgomery-Jones. 'You are going to be even angrier with me.'

Thirty-Three

Montgomery-Jones raised an eyebrow. 'Why should I be angry with you?'

'For not telling you before. I think I know where those designs are?'

'I beg your pardon!' The normally impassive countenance turned to one of wide-eyed astonishment.

'I've only just realized,' Fiona went on quickly. 'They never were on paper were they? That's why you asked me if Graham had brought a laptop and later you wanted to know if there was anything else in the envelope Graham gave me. You were looking for a computer disk.'

'He gave it to you?'

'Hardly! I would have told you. I think he hid a memory stick on the coach. I found it in the first aid box one morning. I assumed it was for storing photos but when I asked if anyone had lost one, no one claimed it. I assumed it had been found on a previous trip and put there for temporary safe keeping and forgotten.'

'Have you any reason to suspect Spelman put it there?'

'I may have got this all wrong of course, but when we were on our way from Cologne, I needed a bandage for Hilary's ankle and Graham said he'd put the First Aid box back up on the parcel shelf for me. As far as I know, he was the only other person to handle the box. Though why he thought it necessary to hide it there, I can't imagine. If it was valuable, how come he let it out of his sight?'

Montgomery-Jones shook his head and looked as puzzled as

she felt. 'He must have had a reason why he did not want it found on him.'

'He did receive a phone call earlier on when we were in Cologne that seemed to upset him. He kept looking around but I never gave it much thought at the time.'

'And where is the stick now?'

'Still in the box on the coach.'

'Do you know where the coach is at the moment?'

'I presume it's in its normal parking place up the hill somewhere. Would you like me to phone Winston?'

Winston was already at the coach performing his daily task of washing down the windows and cleaning out.

'I really am sorry,' she said after James had left to retrieve it. 'I should have realized sooner.'

'You have nothing with which to reproach yourself, Mrs Mason. As I recall, I did tell you not to play detective.'

At least he didn't hold it against her. 'Because you spent so much time studying his papers, it didn't occur to me you might be looking for something else.'

'People do not usually take a whole folder of papers on holiday. I wondered why Spelman had chosen to do so. They were all concerned with wine production and lists of local growers but, as far as I could tell, they were all perfectly genuine.'

'He was trying to break into a new market. He said he wanted to talk to people about how his company could be of service.'

By the time James had returned, the tea tray had been moved onto the bed and the laptop sat on the table.

It was probably time for Fiona to go, she'd made her somewhat belated contribution, but she needed to know if it really was what Montgomery-Jones and his team had been so anxious about. As the two men sat huddled together pouring over the small screen, Fiona and Laura removed themselves to sit on the bed talking quietly.

'Yes!' came a sudden cry.

Fiona turned to see James punching the air in his elation. Even Montgomery-Jones sat back with a smile of satisfaction.

'Thank you, Mrs Mason. You have removed a considerable burden from the department's shoulders.'

'I do appreciate this proves nothing,' she replied tentatively, 'But will you at least concede Graham's murderer could well have been whoever was so keen to get their hands on those designs, and Vivien is not the only suspect.'

Montgomery-Jones gave a slow smile, the grey eyes twinkling. 'I always have, Mrs Mason. From the very beginning.'

Before anything further could be said, his mobile began to ring. They watched as he listened intently but nothing could be deduced from the inscrutable expression.

When the call ended, he said, 'Interesting. German security forces have picked up a man answering the description of our Mr Kasar.' There was a tantalising pause. 'He arrived at the hotel of our friends in the white van asking to be put through to their room.'

It took a moment or two for the consequences of this announcement to sink in.

Fiona spoke first. 'I shall be leaving with Winston for Rudesheim in a quarter of an hour, would you like me to tell Hilary her husband's been found or do you want to talk to her first.'

'I will need to speak to her in the near future but I need to be in Wiesbaden as soon as possible before Kasar is interviewed. If as you say she appears to be not overly concerned; for the time being it might be best if you said nothing.'

'If she's involved in all this business with Viktor, there's always the possibility she will have made her getaway already.'

He gave her a knowing smile. 'I doubt that.'

'Of course.' Fiona stared back at Montgomery-Jones. 'I should have realized. Your team have had her under observation all day.'

Fiona tried to remember if she'd seen Viktor on the morning of Graham's murder but to no avail. He only ever had coffee and the odd slice of toast then went for a smoke whilst Hilary sampled the full works – cereal, yogurt, cheeses, meats and occasionally the hot dish. Besides which, Hilary liked to natter with the others at the table.

Despite what she'd been told, Fiona was on tenterhooks as she waited by the coach at their designated pickup spot. Even when she saw Hilary laden with shopping bags strolling towards her alongside a similarly burdened Gloria, she still felt a little on edge.

Back at the hotel, everyone hurried to their rooms to sort out their packing before dinner. Fiona hesitated at Hilary's door as she passed wondering if she should knock or not.

'Hi there. Do come in, Fiona.'

'I was just wondering how you are.'

'Oh, you know. Bearing up.' She looked as though she was doing much more than that.

'There's been no word from Viktor?'

'Not a dickybird. Just having a little pick me up. Would you like one?' Hilary indicated the open half bottle of gin on the small table. 'Hang on, I'll get another glass.'

Before Fiona could refuse, she'd disappeared into the bathroom for the second glass tumbler.

'Here we are.'

Hilary was far from drunk but the booze was making her garrulous. She did not appear to be drowning her sorrows as much as celebrating the fact she was shot of the man. She handed the glass to Fiona then swept the clothes laid out on the bed ready for packing to one side and the pair of them sat down.

'Thought I'd make a start,' she said indicating the half-filled suitcase on the far bed. 'Not quite sure what to do about Viktor's things though. He'd be cross if I touched anything of his so I'll have to leave them in the wardrobe and hope he's back by the time we leave tomorrow. Assuming he's coming back.'

'Do you think he planned on disappearing?'

'God only knows. No use asking me.'

259

Hilary must have noticed Fiona's frown. 'To tell you the honest truth, I wouldn't shed any tears if I never saw the miserable old sod again.'

'So this is by way of a celebration is it?' Fiona raised her glass and grinned conspiratorially.

'Something like that. I was in a bit of a panic first thing when I thought the bugger had run off without paying me but, credit where it's due, he must have put the money in my bag when I was asleep.'

'Paying you?'

'Umm. Did I say that? Slip of the tongue.' She raised her glass with a laugh. 'Blame it on this stuff. I meant leaving me any money.'

Dare she risk it? If she put the woman on her guard, Montgomery-Jones would never forgive her. 'So this was just another acting job was it?'

Hilary's bellow of laughter echoed around the room. 'Clever girl! When you get to my age, spending half your life travelling from one crummy provincial theatre to another and staying in second rate digs begins to pall somewhat, and the occasional voice-overs aren't enough to pay the booze bill. Bizarre as it was, this was just too good an offer to turn down, a couple of thousand quid cash, half upfront and the rest when we got back. Not to mention a free holiday thrown in, as well as all my spending money.'

'So you're not married at all?'

'Nope. Hilary De Silver, that's me.'

'Have you any idea what Viktor was up to? Why the charade? What was it for?'

'Ask me another, sunshine. I neither know nor care. Part of the deal. No questions asked. It would suit me down to the ground if he's gone for good. Today's been the best yet without him casting a shadow over everything.'

They both giggled like schoolgirls.

'Do you mind if I use your bathroom?'

It was the only ruse Fiona could think of for getting rid of the gin.

Hilary brandished the bottle when she returned. 'Like a top up?'

'Not for me, thank you. I really ought to be getting back to my room. I've still got to pack before dinner,' Fiona lied.

Half an hour later, Montgomery-Jones entered the interview room wearing a self-satisfied smile. Though he had been watching the proceedings from behind the one-way window, he'd taken no part in the interrogation so far.

The man behind the desk, who'd been calling himself Viktor Kasar, looked up and stared at the imposing figure as he walked over to take the chair vacated by the nearest German officer. Only when Montgomery-Jones placed the passport on the table, did Kasar's eyes show a flicker of emotion.

'I understand you are refusing to answer questions on the grounds you claim immunity as a member of the Diplomatic Service of the Republic of Uzbekistan. On behalf of Her Majesty's Government, I am here to clarify any confusion because according to this,' he tapped the passport with his right index finger, 'you are Viktor Kasar born in Baku, Azerbaijan and a naturalized British citizen.'

Kasar's jaw tightened but he continued to say nothing.

'That is also what your fellow Super Sun passengers on the Romantic Rhine Tour with whom you left the United Kingdom a week ago appear to believe. Although Ms De Silver with whom you were travelling states she was paid a considerable amount of money by an intermediary to act as your wife throughout the trip.'

Kasar spat something unintelligible and made a sudden lunge across the table sweeping the passport to the floor with his arm. The German officer rocked back in his chair, but Montgomery-Jones remained motionless without a flicker on his impassive countenance.

That evening, the Super Sun party divided into two camps; those who retired early, either to complete their packing or to get a good night's sleep before the long drive home, and those

261

determined to make the most of their last opportunity to live it up until the small hours in the bar.

Fiona would dearly have loved to have been one of the former but decided it might be as well to keep an eye on the more exuberant members of the party if she didn't want them inflicting the consequences of massive hangovers on everyone else on the full day's journey back to England. Even the normally circumspect Joe and Celia Ennis appeared to be keeping pace with Ian Lambert who, Fiona noticed, had developed the habit of propping up the bar the last few evenings no doubt in an attempt to distance himself from his garrulous wife intent on ferreting out the latest gossip. Gloria and Hilary seemed to have some sort of competition as to who could knock back the most but both were hardened drinkers and could hold their booze with the best of them.

It was a relief when the shutters came down on the bar, the lights dimmed, and everyone started to make their way to the lift or the stairs.

Fiona had a nagging feeling there was something else she'd meant to do. She'd spoken to Barry and Elspeth at dinner so that wasn't it. Oh well, if it was that important she'd remember it in the morning.

Day 9 Monday

Sadly, today we must bid farewell to Germany and the wonderful Rhine Valley. At the Eurotunnel terminal in Calais, it will be time for us to wish bon voyage to all our fellow passengers and transfer to the feeder coach for the last leg of the journey home.

Super Sun Executive Travel

Thirty-Four

Cases had to be out in the corridor by seven so there was no chance of a lie-in for anyone. Fiona heard the rumble of the collection trolley a good ten minutes ahead of time and fervently hoped no one on the top corridor had left it to the last minute.

A gentle tap on the door made her heart sink. Not another problem.

Her eyes widened in surprise to discover Montgomery-Jones standing there, but before she could say anything, he got in first.

'Mrs Mason, I have brought you a visitor.'

He stood back.

'Vivien!' Fiona flung her arms around the smiling woman before ushering them both inside.

'The police have returned my passport and I'm free to travel back with the rest of you, if that's alright.'

'What wonderful news! Do Elspeth and Barry know?'

'Not yet. I didn't know myself until half past one this morning and they must both be down at breakfast at the moment. I would have phoned them first thing, but in order to get here before you all left, Mr Montgomery-Jones had to pick me up at the crack of dawn and so I decided to surprise them. Not that I slept much after that phone call, I can tell you. It's such a relief.'

Ten minutes later, after Vivien and her family had been re-united, Fiona and Montgomery-Jones had the chance talk.

'Does this mean Graham's killer has been found? Was it Viktor?'

'It is dubious it will ever be possible to prove it as the man is refusing to say anything, but the German police are now in no doubt he was responsible. As you surmised, the missing clothes indicate he disposed of his blood stained clothing. The best hope would be traces of spatter on his shoes but it will be several days before we get the results of any tests.'

'But if he was the one buying the designs why come all this way when it would have been so much easier to do the deal in England?'

Although he did not answer, for once she detected no glint of warning in the steady eyes that looked down at her.

'Sorry. I know I mustn't ask.' She frowned. 'But that doesn't stop me wondering.'

His lips twitched into a teasing smile. 'His objective was to prevent the exchange going ahead.'

'I don't understand.'

'Now you are pushing.'

The puzzled frown on her forehead deepened. 'So if Graham had arranged to sell the designs to a rival faction, is this anything to do with the man blown up in Frankfurt? He was from Uzbekistan. And presumably all those strange phone calls to the hotel for Graham were from the same group.'

'That would seem logical.'

'And the break-in. That was them too?'

'That is a distinct possibility.'

A deep furrow creased her brow. 'Graham must have suspected someone was out to wreck the deal which is why he hid the designs. Viktor could have gone to search for them and, finding Graham alone in the room, demanded he hand them over. There was an argument and Viktor grabbed the nearest thing to hand – the paperknife.'

Montgomery-Jones's face remained impassive. He obviously knew something he wasn't telling her.

'Have you any idea,' she snapped at him, 'just how frustrating it is to be so involved in something like this and have

265

to walk away never knowing the full story.'

The deadpan expression softened to a smile. 'We do not know exactly what happened. For what it is worth, my belief is he had every intention of killing Spelman. Even if he obtained the designs or prevented their delivery, there was nothing to stop Spelman from reproducing them. They were his designs after all.'

'And the argument between Graham and his wife provided him with an ideal opportunity for pinning the blame on Vivien.'

'That does sound a logical explanation. If Kasar happened to be passing and overheard them, he might well have seized the moment.'

She thought for a moment. 'And it must have been Viktor who searched my room thinking Graham had passed the designs over to me that first evening. He'd know which one was mine because his was next door. He could easily have picked up my key that day in all the confusion with the other girl on reception.'

'I cannot come up with a better explanation.'

Fiona sighed. 'And I suppose he was one who stole my bag when he found nothing in my room.'

'I am afraid that does not help our efforts to retrieve it for you. My German colleague searched his room but it was not there. I asked Kasar what he had done with it but he was singularly uncooperative even when I explained the reason why.'

She shook her head. 'It doesn't matter any more. I've learnt to accept it's gone.' Before she started feeling sorry for herself again, she hurried on, 'If Viktor and his white van colleagues were prepared go to such lengths, taking out both Graham and his contact not to mention trying to kidnap Barry, those designs must be dynamite. I can see why you were so eager to find them.'

'I could not possibly say, Mrs Mason.' The twitch of his lips and the gentle tone in his voice told her the predictable comment was no admonition. 'I wish you a pleasant journey back to England.'

266

'Thank you.'

'And, Mrs Mason, do try to steer clear of trouble in the future.'

She could not suppress the girlish bubble of laughter. 'I will endeavour to do so, Mr Montgomery-Jones. I assure you, I have quite sufficient excitement in my life without courting more trouble.'

'I am very glad to hear it.'

She walked with him to the door and, when he turned towards her, she held out her hand.

He looked down at it with an amused smile then took her hand and pulled her towards him. She felt his lips gently brush her cheek.

'Take care.' It was barely a whisper.

With that, he was gone.

Was it all over at last? Fiona hurried down to breakfast in something of a daze. Only a handful of Super Sun folk were left in the dining room, just Sidney fussing about his pills, the two girls and Rita and Ian sitting up in their section plus a couple of others at the breakfast bar. Everyone else had been and gone.

'Have you seen this morning's news, Fiona?' Edith was at her elbow.

'No. I haven't had time.'

'They've caught all those dreadful terrorists. Rounded up the whole gang, so they say. One of the waitresses told us it's in all the papers. They weren't from Pakistan at all. Uzbek rebels apparently.'

'That is good news. I expect everyone will be relieved.'

After a hurried cup of tea and a roll, Fiona escaped before she was delayed by anyone else intent on chatting away the precious last minutes. Winston would be loading the cases but he wouldn't know there'd be one more now Vivien had returned.

'All taken care of, sweetheart. Your chap told me on his way out and her brother-in-law brought it down five minutes ago.'

'Why does everyone refer to Mr Montgomery-Jones as though he was somehow something to do with me?' She did her best to keep the irritation out of her voice. 'Still, I suppose I'd better get on or it will be me keeping everyone waiting.'

Back in her room, Fiona cleaned her teeth, zipped up her toilet bag and slipped it into her hand luggage. She had completed all the paperwork the previous afternoon so, apart from a final check nothing was left behind, that was it. Except for supplying everyone with teas and coffees and changing the DVD on the journey, her duties for this tour were almost at an end.

She glanced at her watch. After all that rushing about, there was still a good half an hour to go. The nagging feeling that she'd had last night still lurked at the back of her mind. There was something else she'd meant to do.

Suddenly it came to her. The boys! She hadn't rung Adam or Martin. It would still be the middle of the night over in Canada but she might catch Martin before he left for work.

'Hi, Mum. How's tricks?'

'I'm so sorry I didn't get round to ringing you yesterday, darling. Things were a bit chaotic.'

'No problems, I hope.'

'Oh no,' she lied wondering what he'd say if she told him the truth. 'Last day before we go home and I got caught up in things that's all.'

'You might like to give Adam a buzz later though.'

'Oh?'

'Don't sound so alarmed. He rang me when he didn't get a call. You always ring on a Sunday and he's convinced you're not talking to him because of what he said on Thursday. He knows he went over the top. I told him he was a selfish prat and, for once, big brother was quite penitent. He said Kristy gave him a real ear bashing. Serve him right.'

'Oh dear. I was a bit abrupt but that was because I was in a meeting. I said I'd ring him back when I was free but I forgot. I'll give him a ring when we stop for lunch.'

'Fine. So how was the holiday?'